DISNEP

A DARK ASCENSION NOVEL

The Wishless Ones

To every child
who was raised to be a villain,
but decided otherwise

Published by Disney Press, an imprint of Buena Vista Books, Inc.
No part of this book may be reproduced or transmitted in any
form or by any means, electronic or mechanical, including
photocopying, recording, or by any information storage and
retrieval system, without written permission from the publisher.
For information address Disney Press, 1200 Grand Central Avenue,
Glendale, California 91201.

Printed in the United States of America
First Hardcover Edition, January 2025
1 3 5 7 9 10 8 6 4 2
FAC-004510-24298
Library of Congress Control Number: 2024933631
ISBN 978-1-368-07861-0

Designed by Soyoung Kim

Visit disneybooks.com

SUSTAINABLE
FORESTRY
INITIATIVE

Certified Sourcing

www.forests.org
SFI-01681

Logo Applies to Text Stock Only

DISNEY

A DARK ASCENSION NOVEL

The Wishless Ones

#1 *New York Times* best-selling author

HAFSAH FAIZAL

DISNEP PRESS

LOS ANGELES · NEW YORK

1

– Before –

JAFAR

There were days when Jafar thought his wishes would destroy him. He might have been only eight years of age, but he knew in his heart of hearts that he was destined for more.

And yet today, he was zigzagging through the bustling bazaar, a sack of fresh vegetables clutched in one hand, his little brother's fist sticky in the other. Shouts from angry merchants nipped at their heels because they hadn't brought a single coin in their tattered pockets. But this was their routine: sneaking from the house at the cusp of dawn, darting through the stalls, snatching what they could when the merchants looked elsewhere.

Rohan was sobbing and falling behind. Jafar sighed. He had to do all the work, and it was starting to annoy him as he turned a sharp right and squeezed between two massive carts, doubling back to pull Rohan into the shadows with him. And now there was sand in his sandals. While Rohan was trying hard not to cry out of fear, Jafar was trying hard not to cry out of frustration.

Being the eldest son of parents who were poor in more ways than one gave a child little time to *be* a child.

"Are we going to be safe?" Rohan asked, his tears drenching the small leather pouch he had been tasked with carrying.

They were chased every other day. This was nothing new.

Rohan was just weak. He was six years of age and behaved like a baby, but he was also Jafar's brother, and Jafar would do anything for him.

"Of course we are," Jafar said, pulling him tight against his side and kissing his forehead just as Mama would do to ease him. He tapped the pouch in Rohan's hands. "I'll keep us safe, but *you* need to keep this safe for Mama, understand?"

Rohan looked down at the pouch and nodded, successfully distracted.

From the gap between the worn wood of the carts where they hid, Jafar watched with bated breath as the merchants ran past their hiding spot. He waited until the sand settled in the lonely street. Far above, a falcon cried as its shadow swooped over him. In the distance, someone strummed a sitar, children laughed with their father, and a camel protested against its owner.

"Now let's get you home, eh?" Jafar asked, rising with caution. Rohan nodded solemnly, picking up the neatly wrapped, painfully sweet malban that had slipped from the pouch to the dusty ground.

The walk back home was quiet, the streets outside of the bazaar still shaking off the dregs of last night's slumber. A rare sandstorm had just swept through, and villagers were either scrambling for provisions or huddling in their homes and counting blessings.

Jafar and Rohan's parents were doing neither of those things.

He heard the yelling before he even reached the house, but Rohan was oblivious, throwing open the door before Jafar could stop him. Sound ceased with the creaking hinges. Jafar should have been used to it by now, but his parents' fighting still sparked his nerves like lightning in one of the few thunderstorms he'd witnessed. He looked from Mama to Baba and, unsure of what to do, set the vegetables on the table between them.

"This is what I mean," Baba spat. "He is a thieving street rat yet struts around like a peacock."

Jafar said nothing, though he took a step forward to put his brother behind him.

"And now we will have something to fill our bellies,"

Mama said, before a series of horrible coughs racked through her. Concern flashed across Baba's face, there and gone. It should have relieved Jafar that Baba loved Mama, even when they fought, but Jafar couldn't deny the truth of what that meant: Baba didn't like *him*. His eldest child, his son who was doing more for their family than he was himself. And as much as Baba loved Mama, it sometimes appeared as though Mama loved her boys more.

She pulled Jafar close while Rohan slipped under her other arm, and Baba stormed past the curtain to his room.

Rohan swallowed. Jafar bit the inside of his already raw cheek.

Mama looked between the two of them, a thousand and one emotions swimming in her eyes the color of smothered embers. Her skin was a little duller than it had been yesterday, her hair thinner. She finally settled her expression in a pained smile and picked up a pot, the hem of her gown flaring with her spry movements. "Did I ever tell you the story of the golden scarab?"

So began a new tale, Mama's usual method for distracting her boys from the world and its troubles. Jafar had found comfort in the stories, once. But they did nothing to change their reality, only made it go away for a while, and Jafar didn't think he was a little boy anymore.

And he might have stolen the food they would eat

tonight, and had eaten every night for the past however long, but it was still more than his father had done.

Jafar was worth more than the disgust curling Baba's lips. If only he could make Baba see that. If only he could control Baba the way Baba tried to control everything.

"It is said that an ancient enchanter created the golden scarab as a compass," Mama said, slicing through his angry thoughts.

"A bug?" Rohan asked, making a face. "That's not a compass."

"It was made to find something that didn't want to be found," Mama said, "and so, its creation required years and years of studying, scouring accounts on history, lore, and"—she leaned closer to Jafar, sensing his disinterest—"alchemy."

Jafar felt the hairs on the back of his neck rise at the word *alchemy*. Alchemy, Mama had once told him, was the study of something as close to magic as reality allowed. And because Jafar wasn't fond of his reality, it fascinated him.

"Did he study alchemy in the House of Wisdom?" Jafar asked.

"Oh, but, Jafar, all great men do," Mama replied with a smile. "He was, however, unaware of the powerful treasure the scarab could lead its owner toward, of the genie that could grant his master three wishes. When he learned of the potential power, which no one person should ever possess, he split the scarab in two and hid each half far, far away from the other."

Rohan gasped. Jafar's gaze had strayed to the curtain at the end of the hall that led to Baba's bedroom.

"And then what happened, Mama?" Rohan asked. He was still full of wonder, still rife with the awe that only a younger child could keep alive.

"The two halves remain divided, and for whoever gathers both pieces and joins them together once more, a great reward awaits. Do you see, Jafar?" Mama asked, slicing an eggplant into neat circles.

"What?" Jafar asked, only to indulge her. He gathered the slices in a bowl before pulling out her basket of spices.

Mama smiled. "My little helper. They are two halves of a whole—"

"Like me and Jafar!" Rohan exclaimed.

Mama laughed. "Indeed. Good catch, my daffodil. Together, you are both as powerful as the golden scarab. You can do anything and stand up to anyone, remain strong against adversity."

"And summon a genie?" Rohan asked. "I already know what I'd wish for." He was looking at the small pile of sweets on the counter.

Mama's laugh grew. "Yes, even summon a genie who will grant wishes beyond your wildest dreams."

Jafar wished he could dream. Jafar wished he could control the world around him. He wished he had clung to his mother's stories more. Appreciated the distractions for what they were: little morsels of escape from the reality of life in this village. He wished he had better shown her how much he loved her.

Because it wasn't even three days later when her body was cold and the sands were smoothed over her grave.

2

– Current Day –

ROHAN

It had been eleven years since Rohan had learned of the genie in a lamp, and he was still enamored with the tale. Perhaps because its telling was soon punctuated by a pivotal time in his life. Or because it seemed almost implausible, which made him wish for it even more.

When Mama had told Jafar and him the story, Rohan had known exactly what he would wish for: money that didn't need to be returned, food that didn't need to be stolen, a house that wasn't crumbling at every turn.

He also remembered distinctly what Jafar had wanted even if he had never voiced it aloud. Rohan had seen it in the way Jafar's gaze had darkened and strayed to Baba's room at the back of the hall. Rohan shuddered at the memory now, barely moving out of the way when a maid hurried past.

He hadn't needed a genie after all.

Now, they had coins in abundance, food stocked by servants, a house that was several times the size of their old hovel, clothes no longer stiff with patches. Rohan regarded it all with a deep, troubled sense of guilt. He remembered wanting that lamp so deeply, so desperately, that when his wishes came true after Mama's death, it almost felt as though he'd traded her for them.

And now, their house was so large that the emptiness was almost tangible—even if it was masked by the servants bustling down the halls, scribes rushing out the door, and a parrot's squawk rising above the hubbub. No piece of Mama remained, not her few treasured necklaces, not her old shawl that always hung on the back of the chair, not even her books.

If Rohan *did* have a genie, he would use one wish to bring his mother back, one to make his father a better man, and the last to eradicate the shadow in his brother's eyes.

When Mama had told them the story of the golden scarab, she had really been telling Rohan to watch over Jafar, to keep the family together. Which was why, though Rohan was aware there would be no wishes left for him, he would be content—because he'd be *doing* the wishing, and that made him feel, in a way, almost as powerful as Baba.

He crossed the hall to the dining room, where the low

table was laden with food: pots of labne surrounded by colorful platters of roasted vegetables, like beets and carrots and eggplants beside more eggplants, all seasoned to perfection and bright with garnishes from crunchy nuts to tangy sumac. At the table's center was a roasted leg of lamb, glistening and fragrant, while steam rose from a fresh stack of blistered flatbread.

Jafar was already there. He was a wisp of shadow, towering above the food with clothes as dark as his hair. His jaw was sharp enough to cut, his nose long and slender. Jafar had always looked effortlessly handsome, striking and commanding, a contrast to Rohan, who could look in the mirror and still be confused by what stared back.

When Rohan's greeting went unanswered, he followed Jafar's gaze to the four different dishes of eggplant, and he knew his brother was no longer here in this room, waiting for their father to sit before a feast fit for a noble. No, in his mind, he was back in their decrepit kitchen from a decade before, gathering eggplant in a bowl, helping Mama season it, tracking everything they didn't have and everything he wanted to give them.

Against the backdrop of their father's approaching footfalls, the two of them sat down, Rohan on his knees, Jafar with his legs crossed. The rug beneath them was a vibrant crimson, with a multitude of colors woven to tell a story of beauty.

"Relax," Jafar said softly.

Rohan's brow furrowed. "I am."

"You're sitting like you might have to flee," Jafar said, quickly matching Rohan's silence as Baba sat on a cushion across from them. The gold edging on their father's ebony-dark cloak caught the sunlight slanting through the window. His attar was heavy with black musk and saffron, his lips pressed thin. He leaned into the light, and shadows crowded in the fine lines of his brow and around his mouth.

"Did I not tell the cook I was tired of lamb?" Baba asked.

Rohan tensed. Only their father could look at something so lusciously alluring and complain. Rohan slid a glance at Jafar, always worried that the latest words out of their father's mouth would make him finally snap. His father wasn't like them; he didn't remember how difficult it had once been, how scarce food used to be. And Rohan couldn't blame him for choosing to block out reminders of the loss of his wife.

"Barkat *is* getting older," Jafar said about the cook, and Rohan exhaled in relief at both his brother's choice of words and his calm tone. "He either didn't hear or forgot."

Baba grunted in reply, tearing into the lamb with a piece of flatbread. It wasn't clear whether *Baba* hadn't heard or had forgotten how to be civil, but Rohan was too famished to care. He snatched up his own flatbread, warm and still dusted in gritty grains, and dug in.

"Either way, his cooking is as delicious as ever," Rohan

remarked as flavor burst across his tongue. He loved sumac; the tang and the texture. He'd add it to everything if he could.

Jafar, conversely, barely touched the food. He poured himself water, then tilted his glass to and fro in a ray of afternoon light, deep in thought. Some days, Rohan thought Jafar ate less than the parrot the two of them had gifted Baba months ago, the thing that did nothing but mimic anyone and anything all day long.

"Have you"—Jafar's voice caught for the barest instant, imperceptible to anyone but Rohan—"heard from any messengers today?"

Baba finished chewing, and then put more food in his mouth, letting Jafar's question hang in the air between them for no reason at all. Jafar pretended not to care. Rohan wished they could have a nice meal for once.

"About?" Baba asked, a notch colder, no doubt anticipating that Jafar would ask about his newest trade route or his latest agreement with yet another tribe. Once Mama died, Baba had thrown himself into his business, pushing himself to great lengths to become the merchant he was today.

Jafar had a great deal of opinionated input about every aspect of it, some of which Rohan had overheard and thought made very good sense, but Baba was, well, Baba. He was one of those people who believed wisdom only came with age, and thought being older was synonymous with being an elder.

In short, he wasn't fond of Jafar's ideas.

"My scholarship," Jafar said at last, with a cautious glance at Baba.

Fortunately, it seemed Jafar wasn't interested in discussing business—and having a fight—today.

But Baba wasn't paying him any attention, still chewing away while eyeing the spread around them with far more interest than an ordinary lunch warranted.

He finally swallowed, his mouth dipping into a slight frown: the barest display of concern. "I don't believe so."

The concern was gone in an instant, leaving one to wonder if Baba had ever cared to begin with. And when Rohan looked at Jafar, he paused. Perhaps it was the glare of the sun through the window making it hard to see, but Rohan thought he saw that same darkness in his brother again. A darkness that made Jafar look cold, distant, almost evil.

That expression was partly the reason why Rohan had his own qualms about Jafar's scholarship, but he felt for his brother just then. It was maddening to witness a fractured relationship that could so easily sing with perfection—for Jafar never asked for much, nor had Mama. Rohan *himself* never asked for much.

"I see," Jafar said, disappointment wrapped in the terse delivery of the words.

Baba was set in his ways, and slowly, Jafar was cementing

his own. Rohan would simply do what he could before it was too late.

"I must say this lamb is perfectly"—Rohan began cheerily but faltered when Jafar set his glass down with a resounding thud—"tender."

"Baba?" Jafar said. Rohan recognized that tone and braced himself. "Isn't your meeting about that new deal happening today?"

The words were bait, and Rohan swallowed, knowing Baba could not resist.

"It is," Baba replied, oozing with pride. "I'll be securing a new trade route and a new line of coin by the next moon."

"It's between you and the son of the Bani Jari chief, isn't it?" Jafar asked, a level calm settling over his voice. The Bani Jari tribe, Rohan racked his brain to remember, was as unforgiving and relentless as the desert heat.

"The son?" Baba scoffed. "Why, were you hoping to school me in the fact the son is immovable and hates every part of this? I know. Just as I know that the father is too senile and too tired to do anything but agree with our terms. It's especially helpful, as the proposal can only be touched by the chief and me and is soon to be signed for posterity."

"I never school you, Baba," Jafar said softly. A stranger might have mistaken his tone for chagrin, but Rohan knew better. It was a sardonic sort of gentle. Almost pitiful.

Baba knew better, too. His nostrils flared, his right eye twitched.

Jafar's strength lived and breathed in his brain, which was evident in the way he'd helped route trade lines, how he'd suggested a strategy cleverer than brute force during a skirmish, how he'd formulated a method to keep perishable goods cool for longer periods of time by hanging damp reeds. Baba's business could never have grown to what it was without Jafar, and Baba's sin was that he never once appreciated Jafar's insight.

Jafar didn't give Baba time to explode. "I read the proposal, Baba. I've never seen anything more inclined to fail."

Baba recoiled as if Jafar had slapped him.

"It's riddled with holes, the largest of which is the fact that the chief of the Bani Jari and his son share the same name, so the moment the elder dies, the son will renege on your deal and you'll be left to pick up the pieces.

"Your men should have seen that," Jafar continued, "because now you won't be securing anything. I wouldn't be surprised to learn that the son took matters into his own hands and buried his father already." Jafar leaned back and tossed a cube of halloumi into his mouth, unfazed by Baba's temper quickly shifting from its usual simmer well nigh to boiling. "You'll have to be more careful, Baba. Sons can be deadly sometimes."

Rohan didn't think commenting on the lamb would do any good just then.

A line pulsed in Baba's jaw, and it was unclear if he had bitten down into a bone or if the sound was the grinding of his teeth. And then he rose and settled his problems the way he did best: with violence.

3

JAFAR

The sun had barely shifted after lunch when Jafar was thrown into the broom closet under the stairs, his face stinging with the shape of an angry palm. He wasn't surprised his moment of calm with Baba had lasted so short a while.

He was, however, surprised by how fresh and new his anger felt each time Baba unleashed his own. It had been a slow and gradual burgeoning, for in the beginning, he would feel only relief that *he* was the target of Baba's wrath, and not Rohan. Men like Baba sometimes had the tendency to enact their ire on everything in their vicinity.

But lately, Jafar's anger was much like his father's: raw and inundating, a thrashing thing that rested dormant until

17

he was thrown in here, the door locked from the outside as if he were a rabid animal, not a voice of reason Baba was too proud to hear.

Jafar sighed, leaning back against the cool wall. He understood that common sense was hard to come by, but did he have to be punished for having some?

He should have known the day would be terrible when he had seen his most loathed of dishes, but he'd been so focused on his scholarship. Eggplant was the tastiest of the vegetables, and it was his mother's favorite. When he was young and spent his dawns running through the bazaar, angry merchants on his heels and Rohan's small hand in his, he was almost always carrying an eggplant or three. For Mama.

Once Mama died, his appreciation for food died, too. He ate only to sustain himself. Not to taste, not to savor.

He blamed that on Baba, who had always despised him. Really, the only thing that had changed since Mama died was how *subtle* Baba had become with his distaste until it culminated in violence.

The broom closet was small and unfurnished, not even a broom closet anymore. *A Jafar closet,* he thought. The only light slipped in from the crack beneath the door. He never felt like opening the dusty curtains in front of the closet's tiny window and getting the grime on his hands. Jafar pressed his ear against the door, listening to the house carrying on as if nothing were amiss—not that his insolence was anything out of the ordinary. He held back a groan when a squawk rose above the bustle.

Even that wretched parrot had more of a voice than Jafar.

He regretted every second of its existence in their house. Every second since he had told Rohan that *actually, yes, a parrot would most certainly make an excellent gift for our father*.

At the time, Jafar had been as excited as Rohan in the bazaar, though not for the same reason. Rohan had been thrilled to present their father with something so unique; Jafar could hardly wait for it to grate on their father's nerves.

He was still waiting.

While Baba's men gathered around for their meetings, wearing lavish ankle-length thobes and snooty expressions, the parrot sat on a pedestal, squawking every so often yet irritating no one aside from Jafar. Hearing everything. Sometimes repeating the things he heard in, eerily, the exact same voice. Baba tolerated that bird more than he tolerated Jafar. He probably even loved it more than he loved Jafar. He certainly never tried to control it.

"It doesn't matter," Jafar told himself, as if saying the words out loud would help.

Once his scholarship was approved, he would leave. More important, he would find an appreciation for his intellect, rather than scorn.

He knew he was worthy of apprenticing at the House of Wisdom. It was in the grand kingdom of Maghriz, ruled by a sultana with a doted-on prince, protected by an army and sprawling with cities. Maghriz was everything their little town in the middle of nowhere was not. The trip there was no small journey, either; he'd have to cross half the desert and a fairly large inlet. It would take days.

And it would be worth it.

The House of Wisdom accepted no more than seven novices per year. Each was tasked with gathering and recording history and facts and conjuring up ways of improving the future by using the past. Their compensation? A lifetime of knowledge at their fingertips. Every detail on the known world was housed within the walls of the House of Wisdom.

Jafar longed to walk through the shelves, to gulp down every word that he could. Mama would have wanted that for him. He knew that many details in her stories were outlandish lies, exaggerations to make the tales more exciting, but no story existed without a shred of truth. When she spoke of genies and golden scarabs, powerful gemstones and flying carpets, she also spoke of history, of magic.

Of alchemy. The thing that made it all attainable.

Rohan liked to accuse Jafar of not believing in Mama's stories, but that couldn't have been further from the truth. It wasn't that he didn't believe in genies and golden scarabs; he simply preferred other stories. Like the one Mama had told them about a pair of ruby-red gemstones that granted the power of possession to the one who possessed them. Anytime he spoke to Baba now, he liked to imagine Baba's eyes glowing the same red that rubies did.

Jafar stared at the closed door trapping him inside like a genie waiting to be unleashed. He supposed he liked the idea of being in control far more than he liked the idea of a powerful genie who might be in control of him. It wasn't as though he were greedy or desperate.

Control, Jafar had learned from his lifetime under Baba, was important. That and, well, Jafar didn't trust anyone as much as he trusted himself. Rohan wouldn't understand.

If he was being honest, there was another reason he was waiting on pins and needles for his scholarship's approval. To apply, one had to prove they were worthy by providing either insight into the importance of recording knowledge and history or an invention that could improve life.

Jafar's application was a compilation of ways he'd attempted to improve Baba's business, including the hanging of damp reeds to prolong the life of perishable goods in transit and the installation of a looking glass in a transport rider's line of sight so that they could see anyone approaching from behind. Baba might not have cared for Jafar's innovations, but he would care if he knew Jafar had told others of them.

You think to tell the world about the little that you've done? Baba would likely say, not realizing the answer to his question was there in his belittling words and disparaging tone. *You look to them for approval and love?*

Oh, to be accepted! Jafar would finally receive validation for every slap he had received over the past however many years.

Another squawk jarred him from his thoughts, followed by the sound of men laughing boisterously at something Baba said. It was the grating kind of laugh that should only be reciprocated with a punch in the jaw. Jafar wasn't much for physical altercations—overcoming someone with brute force required no real skill—but that didn't mean he couldn't wish for it. He forced his breathing to calm. Forced the steadily increasing anger in his veins to stop. He was a candle of rage and his wick was burning quick.

A square of parchment slipped under the door, zigzagging in the darkness, and then there was a quiet shuffling outside. Despite himself, Jafar smiled.

"You are aware that it's too dark in this closet to read, right?" he asked.

The shuffling stopped.

A voice came from the other side. "Yes."

Jafar couldn't hold back a laugh.

"I came to check on you," Rohan said, his protest muffled by the door.

Rohan always visited Jafar when he was locked in here. The room was secluded, connected to the rest of the house by a small windowless hall. But as much as Jafar appreciated Rohan, his brother was his brother. Rohan saw the best in everyone, and in a very flawed way, too. He might not say it aloud, but he blamed Jafar for this predicament. *Baba only got angry because you were disrespecting him,* Rohan would likely say if he had more of a backbone—which was true, of course, but a little support would have been nice.

"Baba's going to lose that deal," Jafar said, wanting to redeem himself for whatever reason.

"Or Baba will eventually take your advice," Rohan replied, because he didn't know how pride worked.

Jafar rolled his eyes and said nothing. They were only two years apart, but there were moments when it felt like lifetimes. Rohan was still a child in so many ways that Jafar almost felt that it would be wrong to make him see reason and mar whatever view he had of his own father. Jafar didn't want to steal that innocence away; he wanted to protect it.

He *had* to protect it. He'd sworn an oath to Mama long ago.

"Someone's coming," Rohan said in a rush. "I have to go. But I—I'll talk to Baba."

For Rohan, "talking" to their father meant half begging him to let Jafar out.

But it was only a door. If Jafar cared enough, he could

break it—or, truer to himself, tinker with the lock or the hinges so that it only appeared locked.

That would mean caring enough.

He had come to enjoy his moments alone in the dark. It gave him time to think, space to let his anger bloom and take shape. He had done nothing wrong to deserve this, which raised the question: What good was there in *being* good? What did it matter how he behaved if he was going to suffer either way? It wasn't as if either of his parents had ever even reprimanded him for stealing. They had all but directly encouraged it: Mama with her praise for keeping them fed and Baba with his clearly bruised ego.

Perhaps he should give his father a real reason to punish him.

"Your scholarship," Jafar reminded himself. That was what he was waiting for, what all this patience was for. It was bound to arrive any day now. He could feel it.

He paused as he felt something else, too: a presence, lingering on the other side of the door. He held his breath and pressed his ear against the wood, unsure whether it was Rohan coming to tell him he had failed or one of Baba's men coming to let him out. *Neither,* Jafar thought. Whoever was on the other side of this door was unfamiliar to Jafar.

"You're not leaving, you know."

Jafar froze at the smarmy, almost smug voice. Everything

about its nasal tone seemed designed to vex him, but trepidation crept into his veins at the words.

"And who are you?" Jafar asked.

"Eh." This time the voice came from far lower down than it first had. Closer to the floor, as if whoever it was had crouched. "I guess you could call me a friend. I'm tired of watching your baba fail. You were right about the bandits, by the way."

Jafar held back a groan. The bandits had been the cause of a fight two days earlier, when one of Baba's advisors had suggested taking an easier route and Jafar had known it was too good to be true. The road might have been nice and paved, but it was winding, which meant it was full of prime spots for an ambush.

In truth, he had no reason to believe the voice, but it wasn't as if he had anything better to do.

"All right, *friend*," Jafar simpered. "What kind of leaving are you referring to?"

A strange choking sounded from the other side, almost like Baba's parrot whenever someone fed him a cracker he clearly loathed.

At last, his "friend" cleared his throat and said in a mock whisper, "You know what I'm talking about."

Jafar ignored the sinking feeling in his gut.

"And how do you know this?" he asked.

In answer, another slip of parchment came through the gap. It was creased in half, like a pocket holding something within. Jafar bent over and picked it up.

He bit back a sigh. He was going to have to touch those dank curtains, wasn't he?

Right before he could, there was a whoosh of air, and a weak beam of light slipped beneath the door. A candle, Jafar surmised. It wasn't much, and Jafar refused to thank his "friend" for it before he knelt toward the crack and carefully unfolded the parchment. It was full of scraps, ripped shreds of another parchment.

Jafar rubbed one of them between his fingers. It was rich, far smoother than even the premium papyrus Baba used to make his missives appear more important. He leaned closer to the light, trying to make out what was written on the scraps.

"What is this?" Jafar asked. He made out words: *pleased*, *welcome*, and his name in bold script where a nib had gone over the letters twice.

And then his blood went cold.

It was his scholarship.

He didn't see the inky black of the room anymore—he saw red. He felt it, too, like a brand over his heart, burning and searing and angry.

It had arrived. His scholarship had finally arrived. He had been accepted into the House of Wisdom, one of the most prestigious institutes in their world, and he couldn't even celebrate. He couldn't—he didn't know what to think. *This* was the outcome? This was his reward?

"Your silence is scaring me," said the stranger, the statement punctuated by a weird squawk-like sound that was likely a chortle at Jafar's expense.

What if this wasn't real? What if whoever was on the other side of this door was playing him for a fool or trying to provoke him into doing something to Baba? Jafar didn't even know what he would do. He'd never been this angry. He'd never felt so helpless, so unattuned with his own emotions.

"Is this some sort of joke?" Jafar finally asked, surprised by the hoarseness that grated from his throat.

He didn't like that this stranger had a hold over him. He was trapped in here, unable to see the face of the one who had delivered such horrible news, unable to read his body language or his expressions.

"I found it on your father's mess of a desk," came the reply.

How did this stranger even *get* to Baba's desk? Baba was a merchant on the rise. His circle might not be the smartest, but he kept them close. They were loyal—to a fault. They wouldn't defy Baba even when it was clear from the glimmer in their eyes that they agreed with Jafar.

Which crossed all their names off the list of Jafar's possible suspects.

"Baba would never do this to me."

If only Rohan were here. He was the one person on Jafar's side, the one person who could help him right now.

"The proof is in your hands, Jafar." The snooty response was followed by a sigh. "If it makes you feel any better, your baba *was* torn until your brother swayed him over to a solid no."

"Rohan?"

"Unless you have another brother I don't know about."

Jafar ground his teeth against the reply he wanted to lash right back with. Baba's ripping the scholarship to shreds was more believable than Rohan's having a hand in it. Jafar folded the scraps back into the makeshift folder, growing more and more suspicious by the second.

"I think you should leave," Jafar managed to say. He was reeling, spiraling. He *wanted* the stranger to be lying; he wanted the scraps in his hands to be a cruel joke.

He heard another whoosh outside the door—a sweep of the stranger's robes as he left, but it sounded different through the roaring in Jafar's ears. So much like the wind cutting beneath a bird's feathers that Jafar was reminded of Baba's parrot. Oh, the secrets that bird would be able to tell if he could truly speak. If anyone knew what had happened to the scholarship, it would be him, perched where he was by Baba's desk.

"So what are you thinking?"

Jafar startled at the voice. He hadn't heard the stranger's

returning footsteps on the other side of the door, and Jafar knew the tiny hall outside this room like the back of his hand.

"I can see Baba doing this, but not Rohan," Jafar replied.

Jafar imagined the stranger shrugging. "The truth still remains."

"And I'm supposedly meant to believe you care for me? At least Rohan is trying to get me out," Jafar said. "Rubbing my misfortune in my face while I'm unable to do a thing about it doesn't precisely make you a friend."

It made him a bully, and Jafar knew from experience that bullies, in general, were simply—

A click halted his thoughts. It sounded like the lock.

The door swung open.

Jafar looked into the hall, but his savior was nowhere to be seen. The hall was empty, only a little less dark than the broom closet he'd been locked inside.

"As if you needed help getting out of there."

It was the stranger's smarmy voice, only it was coming from—*below?* Jafar looked down and blinked at what he saw, certain the effects of being repeatedly locked inside a cramped broom closet had finally gotten to him. He blinked again.

It really was the bird. His nemesis. Baba's wretched parrot.

"Y-you," Jafar sputtered.

"You're welcome," the parrot replied, tossing the key he had clutched between two yellow talons to the corner and landing on the marble tiles.

Jafar could only stare as the clattering subsided. "You can talk."

It *was* talking, wasn't it?

"It can talk," Jafar breathed to himself.

"I'm a he, and you're kinda stating the obvious there, pal," the parrot deadpanned. "Thought you were the smart one."

Which was precisely why a talking parrot was so dumbfounding a concept.

"So what are we going to do about that?" The parrot jerked his head at the parchment folder.

Jafar blinked down at his hand. Right. The scholarship.

But he couldn't stop staring. The parrot's movements were so oddly human, it was fascinating to watch. As if he were a human shoved into the body of a parrot.

He squawked. "You're staring. The longer you take, the deeper a hole your father digs for himself."

He was right about that, but Jafar didn't care about the hole Baba was digging for himself—only the one he was digging for Jafar. He clutched the torn scholarship and realized something else just then: the parrot wasn't like Rohan. He wasn't trying to paint Baba in a better light, or make Jafar see something that wasn't there. Talking to the parrot didn't feel as though Jafar were trying to navigate some labyrinth.

It appeared the parrot saw the world much as Jafar did. He fluffed his feathers, causing the shreds of the scholarship to scatter. Jafar hurried to gather up as many as he could.

"Do you have a name?" he asked.

The parrot sighed. "This better not be the start of an interrogation. My name's Iago."

The name didn't sound as though it originated from any local tongue. It was unusual, but so was a talking parrot.

"Well, Iago, my *friend*," Jafar said, straightening up to his full height, "it's time we got to the bottom of this."

4

ROHAN

Rohan knew that Baba was a creature of habit. Before relenting, he typically waited a few hours until he was certain Jafar was too defeated to start up another argument. Jafar, on the other hand, might give the illusion of defeat, but Rohan didn't think Jafar ever truly felt it. He appeared, more often, to simply stop caring; at that point, he would stop engaging, too.

Still, Rohan had left the broom closet determined to try, for his brother's sake. Baba's office wasn't far from the broom closet in which Jafar was locked. It was in the center of the house, a large and spacious room that quickly shrank when

Baba's men were there, voices loud and pride louder. Now, it was empty, save for Baba, seated on one of the many majlis cushions that created an intimate nook for his business discussions. His headdress was on the pillow beside him, a dark crimson coil bedazzled with a golden tendril at its center, and his dark brows were furrowed.

Rohan kept his footsteps light. "Baba, can you please let Jafar out? He didn't intend to be rude."

Baba heaved a weary sigh and looked up from his work. Sometimes, he gave the impression that he didn't think Rohan was all that bright. "I know you think your brother is smart, but he's in there for his own good. Brilliance means nothing without respect."

Rohan didn't think that was necessarily true.

"He has good ideas," Baba continued, reading his mind, "but his heart isn't always in the right place. Intention goes a long way, far more than actions ever do."

Baba filed away several sheaves of papyrus notes into a wooden box and looked up when Rohan didn't respond.

"You know this. You've said so yourself," Baba said.

Rohan lowered his gaze. He didn't always "say so himself" as much as find himself in positions where he couldn't disagree with Baba. It happened just last week, when Baba was grumbling about Jafar's scholarship, which Baba knew would arrive soon. It had surprised Rohan, because he hadn't thought Baba paid enough attention to Jafar to have been keeping track of the days and thinking about the scholarship a week ago. Enough to be contemplating whether or not his son should attend the House of Wisdom.

It will be a win, yes, but he'll leave us, Baba had said, and Rohan thought it a strange reason when Baba rarely cared for Jafar's presence.

Baba's stare had made Rohan squirm. He felt as though his head was being split open, his thoughts sifted through with unwelcome fingers. He started to say, *I do not—*

And it will change him, Baba had interrupted, still watching him.

It would, Rohan had agreed.

For the worse, Baba added. *No?*

Jafar had already changed greatly with Mama's death—and not in a way Rohan admired. Would attending the House of Wisdom cause that darkness in Jafar's gaze to grow? Rohan didn't know.

And so, he had voiced no protest. That was days ago.

Perhaps Baba was so harsh with Jafar because he saw himself in him.

But slapping Jafar and throwing him in a closet over and over again didn't help. It simply enraged both of them while Rohan watched helplessly.

If only Mama were here. She could gather up the torn

ends of their family and sew them back to perfection again. Rohan clasped one of his hands in the other, imagining it was Mama's, guiding him, grounding him.

He would have done anything to get her back. Given anything to not feel so alone. *Anything.* Even if the cost was their fancy mansion and Baba's business.

Pull yourself together, came Jafar's voice in his head. Jafar, who could easily wrap up his feelings and tuck them into a well-worded gibe. Rohan often wondered if there was something *missing* in Jafar. How else could he be so cavalier and uncaring?

Baba said nothing else, and Rohan waited until beads of sweat began trickling down his own back. Even this—the act of standing idly, saying nothing, simply *breathing*—felt like defiance.

He opened his mouth.

"Is that all?" Baba asked, but he might as well have said what he meant: *Leave.*

Rohan swallowed his sigh and ventured back to the tiny hall near Jafar's household prison, pausing when he thought he heard the rushed sound of a door quickly pulling closed. There was no other door in this hall except the one to the broom closet.

And what was that smell suddenly assaulting his senses? He tried to place it before something fluttered to the floor, catching his eye in the shadowed space. A scrap of parchment. He picked it up and turned toward the light. Jafar's name was on it, next to the word *welcome*.

Jafar's scholarship.

Rohan's breath caught as he recognized the parchment. He had seen it in Baba's hand earlier that morning, but he hadn't known it was Jafar's scholarship. And that meant . . . *no*. That meant Baba had lied when Jafar asked.

Rohan rubbed the parchment between his fingers, refusing to believe it, trying to ignore the voice in his head that was insisting over and over again: Baba had ripped it to shreds.

Despite it all, a smile stole across Rohan's face. Jafar had done it! He really had done it. That dream Jafar had hoped to achieve since Mama had told the tale and lit his eyes with something like magic — he'd made it a reality.

Truth be told, Rohan hadn't fully considered that Jafar might be accepted into the House of Wisdom, but he'd never imagined in a thousand and one years that Baba would do *this*. Tear Jafar's dream to shreds. Rohan swayed, his head feeling light and untethered as guilt swarmed through him like locusts. He remembered, again, his silence when Baba had asked him if it would change Jafar for the worse. Had that silence ultimately swayed Baba's indecision? Was this Rohan's fault?

A loud *thunk!* snapped him out of his thoughts, and he turned the scrap over in his hands, eyeing the shadows.

Why was it here of all places? He heard another sound, like a rustle. No, a crackle. He sniffed the air, brow creasing. The smell was getting stronger. Strong enough for him to decipher what it was:

"Fire?" he asked no one in particular. Something was very likely burning on a stove, but the kitchens were on the opposite end of the house, too far away for him to smell it here. Movement caught his eye from the side of the corridor near Baba's meeting room, like a figure stepping in front of the light.

Rohan turned. Not a figure—smoke.

Spilling into the assembly room, billowing toward the hall, crawling to him.

A meal burning in the kitchens didn't produce that much smoke. *Nothing* small and contained produced that much smoke.

"Fire," Rohan repeated, stumbling back. This wasn't what he'd meant when he thought he would give up anything— Baba's mansion included—to have Mama back.

The only way out was through that smoke, and when he heard a loud crack followed by a series of bone-chilling crackles, Rohan knew: flames raged just on the other side.

He reached for the walls to steady himself.

"Fire!" someone shouted in alarm. Several of the household staff echoed the call; others screamed, making him realize the gravity of the situation. They couldn't contain the fire. This was the desert; it would take them far too long to collect water.

They could die here.

He didn't know if Baba was safe. If the maids and his advisors and scribes and— Jafar! He was trapped in a broom closet, where he would suffocate to death. Rohan needed to find the key. He needed Mama's genie, Mama's direction. She would know what to do. Jafar would know what to do.

Think, Rohan, he told himself. He needed to get the key from Baba, but that required wading through the smoke. He wouldn't be able to see more than a foot ahead of him. He might even stumble on the fire. *You can do this.*

Rohan gulped down clean air and took a step into the quickly darkening hall.

Smoke billowed closer, and he gasped, allowing it to siphon down his throat. It made him woozy, almost drunk. Or perhaps that was panic. He coughed, and his vision crossed and blurred. He tried to laugh at how weak he was, falling apart from a little smoke. He was spiraling, breathing so hard that his head felt light. Then he felt a gust of air. Blinked and saw dim light. He even thought he heard his name. Mama?

She lurched him back into the present, as if she were reaching through her grave to pull him from the abyss.

Jafar! Rohan had to save him. He whirled toward the broom closet and stopped in his tracks. The door was open.

Something red was bouncing up and down inside the room, hovering, almost like it was flying.

Rohan didn't have time to figure out what it was or how the door had been opened. All he cared about was that Jafar was there and safe. Rohan yelled, "The house—it's—it's on fire."

A chilling thought tore through Rohan: this was his fault. He had been so ready to give up their sprawling house and Baba's business to see Mama again that he'd wished without a genie again, and now another of his parents would pay the price. He needed to stop thinking about Mama right now. They had to save Baba, and Jafar could— Rohan paused. What was Jafar doing? He wasn't trying to save anyone. He was pulling Rohan into the room and closing the door behind them.

"I know," Jafar said.

"You know?" Rohan repeated, trying to blink away the blurriness, to clear the fuzz that was blanketing his mind and crowding his mouth. He was imagining things. Surely that red thing wasn't fluttering to the ground and shoving something beneath the door. Securing them inside. With soured features, Jafar left Rohan trembling and threw open the curtains to the tiny window on the opposite wall—the one that led out onto the street—then shoved a robe-wrapped fist through the glass.

"We need to go back," Rohan said weakly, relief flooding him as the cracks in the glass began to spread. "For Baba."

Jafar didn't blink, didn't even flinch. He pulled back for one final punch, and the glass shattered completely. He didn't look the slightest bit apologetic or upset, or perhaps the smoke was making Rohan imagine things, because surely his brother wouldn't say:

"No, we don't."

5

JAFAR

Under a merciless sun, Jafar led his younger brother and Iago deeper into the shadows as villagers hurried past, sand stirring in their wake. People rushed with buckets of water, voices crashing one into the next, panic rising as thick as the smoke billowing to the skies. No one noticed as the three of them huddled in the remains of an old shack.

Jafar had never been so happy to leave that broom closet. His prison. His sanctuary.

Baba's manor was on fire. Devastated. Jafar hadn't known stone could crumble so quickly, but there was enough that was combustible within to send the entire thing crashing down on everything Jafar knew. It only served Baba right for having rid the house of everything Mama had once touched.

"Are we the only ones who escaped?" Jafar asked Iago. He still couldn't quite believe he was conversing with a talking parrot.

The parrot looked grave as he settled on the jutting stone nearest him. "I nearly singed a wing out there."

"You—you talk?" Rohan sputtered, swiping at his eyes.

"Not this again," Iago moaned.

"Answer the question," Jafar snapped.

Iago narrowed his eyes at Jafar, clearly irked by the command, but he finally relented. "Yes, I talk."

Jafar dragged a hand down his face. "*My* question, Iago."

"Yes, Jafar." Iago sounded bored. "I didn't see any other survivors."

Jafar slumped back against the wall, unsure if it was in relief or exhaustion. He couldn't bring himself to care about the rough stone snagging at his robes. *No other survivors.* They were all dead. The maids and servants and kitchen staff. Baba. The house, shredded like the remains of the awarded scholarship, much of which was still in his pocket.

He could not summon tears nor sorrow. The fire had scrubbed at his insides, leaving him raw, untethered in a way. Numb. Relieved to be unharmed. Guilty to be alive. He envied Rohan and his emotions.

"Do you think it was Barkat?" Rohan asked, staring into the distance. "Baba went and yelled at him after we finished our food."

"Vengeful cooks have more subtle ways of getting back at people," Iago said, and when neither Jafar nor Rohan asked him to elaborate, he did so anyway. "You know, like poison. No? Guess I have to do all the talking around here."

Iago couldn't understand their silence, and how monumental a moment this was.

Jafar had been waiting for his scholarship for more reasons than one. Acceptance into the House of Wisdom would have been a way to squeeze distance between himself and his father. That desire for space was what eventually led to him feeling some sort of twisted enjoyment whenever he was locked in that broom closet, wasn't it?

An entire realm separated him and Baba now.

Armed men marched past their dilapidated hideout. The village's governing caliph was just, and his guards were always quick to respond. If they were here, both Baba's supposed cohorts and enemies might not be far behind.

The village of Ghurub was small and insignificant, lost in the crossroads between several kingdoms, but that was where an advantage was to be had. And their father, despite his numerous decisions gone wrong, had known it. He had been establishing trade routes and carving out a place for Ghurub on the map of the world. He had stepped on toes and created one too many foes—even his own allies respected him about as much as soldiers respected a heartless general.

Jafar wasn't about to face them.

Rohan sniffled. "Baba—"

"Shh," Jafar hissed.

But Rohan didn't care about the platoon of guards. He didn't even care for the snot running down his face. He never had. Jafar understood that he was hurting and grieving, but he really could have been more presentable.

"He could be hurt, Jafar. He could be—"

"Dead?" Jafar asked flatly, and Rohan flinched.

"He's probably nice and crispy," Iago added.

Jafar shot him a look.

"What?" Iago asked. "I thought we didn't like him. I certainly didn't." He shuddered and lifted a wing in a way that was very much like a man waving an arm in dismissal. "All those stale crackers."

But the words made Rohan look more appalled than sad, which Jafar considered a triumph. It meant he wasn't spiraling.

The flames soon died down. Embers shone like diamonds in the rough, taunting him. Everything that he was had been reduced to a pile of ash and crumbled stone.

No one could have survived that fire. If not for the broom closet, neither Jafar nor Rohan would have survived, either. Jafar could already hear the cries of alarm and hushed whispers from the rubble where they hid now, paces from the remains of their house. Like a feather slowly drifting to the ground, the truth settled in him with finality.

Their father, one of the city's most prosperous merchants, was dead.

". . . the sons died, too? What a shame," a guard was saying, shaking his head as he passed. Jafar watched from a hole in the wall, breath held. "Came from nothing and back to nothing they go."

Rohan straightened. Iago perked up, too. "We're not—"

Jafar slapped a hand over his brother's mouth and yanked the parrot back with a hand around his scrawny neck.

"What's gotten into you?" Iago asked, as if he knew Jafar. Then again, he *did*. Jafar was the one who knew nothing about this relationship.

"What is wrong with you?" Rohan echoed, slowly teetering toward hysterics. "Why are we even hiding? You're acting like *we* killed him! You're acting like the man that's—that you say is *dead* isn't our father! Our blood!"

Jafar bit back a snort, because if what Iago had said about the scholarship was true, *Rohan* had acted like Jafar wasn't his blood. They weren't too different. Iago opened his mouth, and Jafar knew he was thinking the same. He silenced him with a look.

Because Rohan was still his brother.

"I'm sorry," Jafar said, and he truly was. He wiped away

Rohan's tears with the edge of his sleeve and bent closer to him. "I know that he was our father. I know that he was all we had. But when a powerful man like that winds up dead, his enemies come looking, and I won't risk our getting hurt. I will always put you first."

He could tell Rohan was trying not to cry again, and Jafar wanted to shake him. Rohan was seventeen years old, not four.

"He has a point, you know," Iago said, crossing his wings. Jafar was starting to like having the parrot on his side.

"There's nothing left for us here, Rohan," Jafar continued. He tried dusting off his clothes, but it was futile. The sand and dust in this little hovel had sat undisturbed long enough to be eager for something new upon which to cling. "Nothing. Not Mama or Baba, not our belongings, not our home."

Nor did they have anyone else. They were at that age when no one wanted anything to do with them, oftentimes not even their father.

"Baba's business," Rohan said, grasping at straws for whatever reason. "We can't just throw away all his work."

The ground beneath their sandals rumbled, sand and little pebbles shaking loose with the distant thunder of hooves. Horses. "Hear that? Everyone who wants a piece of Baba's fortune—*our* fortune—is already on the way. You know as well as I do that they won't give us what we're owed by right."

Rohan stood on weak legs to face Jafar in the meager light. His brow was creased. "So that's it? We're giving up?"

"Yeah, what's the plan here?" Iago asked.

Jafar wrapped a checkered keffiyeh around his neck and the bottom half of his face before doing the same for his brother. The sands were calm, but he didn't want to take a chance at being recognized. He stepped into the open, pulling Rohan behind him, and the dry heat assaulted them as readily as the sun.

Jafar guided Rohan away from the plumes of smoke still huffing into the sky. "Iago, stay close. No, that doesn't mean sit on my shoulder."

Iago remained on his shoulder, talons digging into his robes and settling just on his skin. Jafar let him be. He had more pressing concerns, like remaining unseen.

"Ah, he wants me to pry," Rohan said to no one in particular, but if he was exasperated by Jafar, it meant he was distracted from everything else, and that was yet another victory. "What are we going to do, then?"

The scholarship weighed heavily in Jafar's pocket. But his chance at admission might yet exist, even if it hung by a thread, and with Baba gone, Jafar had never felt so hopeful. And cautious, as Iago's words about Rohan still rang loud.

Jafar looked to the skies and the sands dusting the blue with gold and grit. The heat of the early afternoon sun across his robes was not unlike a mother's embrace. Presumably. He remembered less and less of his mother as the years went on.

"Remember the last story Mama ever told us?" Jafar said finally, knowing it was his brother's favorite.

"The golden scarab and the genie in a lamp, yes," Rohan said, though he looked a little guilty when he said it, for reasons Jafar couldn't place.

Jafar would have liked to say that he still wanted to apprentice in the House of Wisdom—that, instead of seeking out the scarab or the lamp, he wanted to find those enchanted rubies from a whole other story for reasons Rohan couldn't understand.

A falcon swooped through the air with a cry, its limber form silhouetted against the light, and as Iago dug his talons deeper into Jafar's shoulder in fear, Rohan looked up at it with a soft expression. He would take it as a good sign.

Jafar smiled. "That's the one. We're going to get our three wishes."

6

ROHAN

Rohan was the one who had killed Baba, and Jafar could never know. It wasn't Barkat exacting vengeance or a neglectful kitchen hand who let the fire grow high enough to catch a curtain, it wasn't a glass left in the wrong ray of the desert sunlight, it was Rohan.

Jafar wanted to find the genie lamp and utilize those promised wishes as they were meant to be used. Unlike Rohan, who hadn't used a genie to make his wish, just a handful of bitter, angst-ridden thoughts. He peered through the hole at the remains of their house, and he knew, deep, deep inside of him, that Mama had not returned. And instead of trading Baba's riches for Mama's return, he'd lost Baba, too.

The weight of that threatened to crush him.

Rohan had killed Baba, which made him certain now more than ever that he had also killed Mama, and if Jafar and the parrot hadn't saved him, he would have died, too, in a moment of his own making.

Jafar pulled him from the old shack, and as they darted from the shadows of one enclave and alley to the next, Rohan snuck a glance at him, certain his brother could hear his thoughts. Sweat was dripping down his back, dampening the keffiyeh wrapped around his nose and mouth. They crossed one street and then another, that bright red parrot on Jafar's shoulder. *Talking* parrot. There was so much happening at once that Rohan didn't think he'd fully grasped his current situation. His looming future.

Baba was *dead*.

For as long as Rohan could remember, he had been Jafar's shadow. And for as long as he could remember, he had been more than content to *remain* his brother's shadow. Even now, as he trudged along after Jafar, his heart sinking like his footfalls in the sand, he was grateful he wasn't alone. Grateful his brother didn't know the truth.

"Too bad we've had some good rain lately, or this one would have been a hero with all the water leaking out of his eyeballs," Iago snarked from atop Jafar's shoulder as Rohan swiped the tears from his face.

He hadn't thought the parrot would be cruel when he and

Jafar had purchased him in the bazaar. Then again, Rohan hadn't thought the bird could speak, either.

By the time Rohan realized where they were going, Jafar was looking both ways before wedging his dagger behind the latch of the door. It snapped open, and the three of them stepped into one of their father's storerooms not far from their house.

"Why are we here?" Rohan asked. His throat closed when the scent of Baba's attar welcomed him. *I'm sorry, Baba.* He, too, had never been close to Baba, but their relationship had still been special in its own way. They shared secrets and conversations Jafar might never know about. Baba sought him out at times, even afforded vulnerability—a rare moment when he'd allowed himself to shed tears about Mama.

Focus. Jafar had a plan in mind. The genie lamp. If Mama's stories were true, the lamp could do anything. Not only would Rohan bring Mama back, not only would Rohan right this horrible wrong by returning Baba to the world of the living, but he could wish for Baba to be a better man. Mama would appreciate that, too.

He would rewrite their entire lives for the better, and best of all: he would be responsible for their happiness.

It wasn't often that Rohan was in accord with Jafar's plans, but this time, he was.

Jafar wiped imaginary dirt off the blade and slipped it back in its sheath. Rohan was surprised there had been enough time for Jafar to grab his dagger as they were escaping from the house. It wasn't as if he'd been forewarned of the catastrophe. "We might as well make use of something that's ours by right."

Rohan flinched at the heartless words and couldn't stop the ice from slipping into his own. "He's dead, Jafar. He might not have always been good—"

"Never, Rohan," Jafar whispered, and for whatever reason, he looked betrayed when he said it. "He was never good to me."

His voice was laced with pain, a cold and bitter kind of sorrow that Rohan felt in his bones.

"You can still be the better person," Rohan countered. "You can still choose to respect the dead."

Jafar looked away. "You're right. I'm sorry. He was my father before all else."

His tone and demeanor had changed so thoroughly, Rohan had to look away, too. He hadn't expected Jafar to respond like *that*. He'd braced for a dismissal, perhaps, or even some chagrin, not full-out regret. It was almost hard to believe.

"It's all right," Rohan forced himself to say with a feeble smile for Jafar's sake. Jafar was trying, and so should he. "No one—no one really teaches us how to get through the death of a parent, let alone both. But why the sudden interest in the genie lamp?"

There were only certain stories of Mama's that Jafar had ever paid attention to, and Rohan hadn't thought the genie was one of them. Jafar rarely seemed to dream or indulge in fantasies like Rohan.

Jafar gave him a look. "To make our wishes, of course. We just lost everything. Don't you have anything you want?"

"I—I do," Rohan stammered. "Of course I do. I just— I guess I never thought you believed in the lamp."

Rohan watched Jafar snatch one of the maps from the basket in the corner and unroll it across the main table. As the silence dragged on, Rohan felt a twinge of distrust.

"You didn't tell me what you want," Jafar said at last.

Rohan didn't know how to say what he wanted. "It's like you said. We lost everything. I know Baba was never good to you, but we can get him back."

"You would use a genie wish to get Baba back?" Jafar asked, and Rohan was relieved he sounded more curious than angry.

"I would use another to make him a better man. And then the last to bring Mama back."

"You'd be all out of wishes then," Iago pointed out, tilting his red head.

Rohan was well aware of that. "We'd be the wishless ones, but we'd also be happy because we'd have everything we could ever want or need."

He looked at Jafar while he said the words, trying to see

past the cool mask of his features. Did Jafar agree with him? Did he want the genie for the same reasons? He might not miss Baba, but Jafar certainly missed Mama.

Jafar spread his hand across the map, tamping down the curling edges.

"For Mama," he said, meeting neither Rohan's nor Iago's eyes.

"Anyway, how do you plan on finding one tiny lamp in an endless desert?" Iago asked, peering down at the papyrus. "You've got Agrabah, Maghriz, Hulum."

"You can read, too?" Jafar asked, incredulous.

"I can fly, Jafar. Are you really surprised I can do all those other things?" Iago replied.

"Because you're a parrot!" Rohan exclaimed.

"And?"

Rohan sputtered, "And parrots can't talk or read, or move their feathers about like they're—they're human fingers."

Jafar paused, scrutinizing Iago as if for the first time. "Why are you like that, anyway?" He held up a finger, stopping Iago's protest before it began. "If you didn't want to be questioned, you shouldn't have spoken."

"Why, I oughta leave you two here in the dust," Iago huffed, and when neither brother budged, he sighed, his chest deflating. "I don't know. Everything in me feels wrong, like I don't fit in my body, but I've been a parrot for as long as I can remember. Which isn't very long, by the way. I remember the bazaar and the shopkeeper feeding me stale crackers, then you two bought me, and here I am. If I try to recall anything from before the bazaar, the memories turn hazy and give me a headache. Happy now?"

It didn't make Rohan happy as much as feel he could understand Iago in a way. He never felt like he belonged, either.

"For now," Jafar said, and Rohan thought he could have been nicer, but Iago didn't seem to care.

He dismissed Jafar with a flap of his wing and shifted his focus back to the map.

"We're not looking for the lamp," Jafar said. "We need to find the two halves of the golden scarab that will lead us to it—*and* make sure such a thing exists."

"I thought your mother said that it does," Iago said.

"Are you saying you don't trust Mama?" Rohan asked, looking at Jafar in the light slanting through the narrow window.

"I trusted Mama," Jafar said. "Which is why I trust that what she told us was a story." He studied the borders and routes. "Let's see here. Hulum has more weapons and mercenaries than it does books or people to read them. Agrabah is a trade center known to possess enchanted objects, but going bazaar hunting will be like looking for a needle in a haystack. We want to go to Maghriz so we can learn about the lamp and the scarab halves and, most of all, verify that it's all true."

"Why can that only happen in Maghriz?" Rohan asked. The name was familiar, but he couldn't place it. He was too overwhelmed by everything that had happened and was still happening.

"It's where we'll find the House of Wisdom," Jafar said.

Rohan froze. Of course. He knew all about Maghriz and the House of Wisdom. Jafar spoke about it endlessly.

Jafar's scholarship.

The words sprang to Rohan's tongue: *Your letter came today. You were accepted, but—* but what? How could he tell Jafar that Baba didn't want him to attend, and so their father had ripped Jafar's one prestigious ticket into shreds? And that Rohan might have had a hand in it all?

Baba was dead now. The scholarship burned to ashes. Gone, just like everything else in their life. And the last thing Rohan wanted was to sour Jafar's last image of Baba even further.

Rohan was vaguely aware that his guilt was getting in the way of his awareness, but he couldn't fight it. Still, if Jafar was planning to reach the House of Wisdom's gates and speak of a pending scholarship, that could be infinitely worse. They wouldn't hesitate to tell him that he had indeed been accepted. Jafar was smart enough to piece together the rest.

Iago squawked. "Too bad you don't have that scholar—"

Wretched bird! Rohan hurried to speak over him.

"But the House of Wisdom is near the palace, filled with guards—" Rohan started.

"There are plenty of—" said Jafar at the same time.

They stared at each other, and in the silence, the sounds of people going about their days echoed from outside. Only their lives had changed. Rohan had gone and killed his father, and the rest of the world kept moving.

"You first," Jafar said.

Iago looked between the two of them with far more attitude than a parrot should possess.

"It's impossible," Rohan said. "The House of Wisdom is in the capital city, near the Maghrizi palace. Think about how tight security might be."

"Spoken like a true coward," Iago pronounced.

Rohan gritted his teeth. He was beginning to regret buying the parrot. "What's in it for you, anyway? You're just lucky Jafar decided to trust your ugly hide and save your life."

Jafar looked taken aback at Rohan's outburst but still shifted an expectant gaze toward Iago.

"You too?" Iago asked, hurt flashing in his eyes. "I told you guys. I want to know why I'm like this as much as you two bozos. The House of Wisdom is my best bet."

Jafar pursed his lips, pleased with the response. He glanced at Rohan. "Nothing is ever impossible," Jafar assured him. "I overheard during one of Baba's meetings that Maghriz is on the brink of war. Something, something, treaty, alliance. They won't be too concerned about us."

Rohan wanted to argue, but he needed to be less afraid. He needed the lamp. Possibly more than Jafar did. Rohan couldn't live with himself knowing what he'd done.

It wasn't some fluke that had killed Baba. Rohan was used to making wishes in times of desperation, and it always resulted in fate laughing in his face. Which was another reason he needed the lamp: so his wishes would come true without any extra casualties.

Jafar folded up the map and tucked it away, straightening his shoulders and then his robes of crimson and black as if they weren't singed and covered in soot.

"Stop being so glum," he said. "When have I ever steered us wrong?"

Rohan hid a smile. Jafar had been there for him, always and always. He had filled the shoes of a parent when their mother had died and their father no longer had love to give. He had protected Rohan even when it was to his own detriment.

Perhaps that was why Rohan had agreed with Baba about the scholarship.

"Never," Rohan said.

7

JAFAR

By the time the three of them finished discussing their plans—or debating, because Iago had much to say and Rohan liked none of it—darkness was easing into the sky, and Jafar deemed it safest to spend the night in the storeroom. The desert cold was working its way through the many crevices and gaps in the stonework, but it would have to do.

"But it's so dusty," Iago whined.

"Sleep in midair, then," Rohan said.

"The more I get to know you, the more certain I am that you have no brain," Iago retorted.

"Enough, both of you," Jafar cut in. He wasn't exactly

thrilled to be lying on a musty blanket in this dusty old storeroom, either.

He sighed and closed his eyes. He didn't want to track down the scarab halves or the genie. He didn't want to bring his parents back—Baba was better dead, and Mama . . . well, Mama had been gone far too long. Jafar didn't think she'd like the man he'd become.

She hadn't been here to stop it.

Besides, Jafar didn't know if a genie could *bring* someone back to life. Surely even wishes came with limits. They were already limited numerically. Jafar exhaled long and slow. None of that mattered. He didn't care for the lamp. What mattered was that Rohan did—deeply.

And that is where the problem lies, no?

Jafar turned on his side, his back to the wall. Across the room, in another corner by a row of rickety shelves, Rohan lay facing the other wall, still and unmoving. He wasn't crying, as Jafar had expected, though Iago's presence might have had something to do with it. He bit back a sigh.

At first, Jafar hadn't known why he'd lied to Rohan about the lamp.

Jafar had been only two when his brother was born, and Rohan was so tightly woven into the fabric of his being that there were times when Jafar felt he would cease to exist without him. With Mama dead, Rohan became Jafar's tail, his twin. When Jafar ate, Rohan ate. When Jafar slept, Rohan slept. When Jafar went outside to play with the other boys, Rohan came with him. When Baba beat Jafar, Rohan winced as though he shared the pain.

The only time they were apart was when Jafar was locked away. Though Rohan would visit him from the other side of the door, he couldn't see how Jafar coped. Jafar bottled up his hurt, letting it ferment into something darker, biting his tongue as he was beaten again, and again, and again.

As much as Rohan liked to believe he'd built a better relationship with Baba than Jafar did, it was really only *because* Jafar's relationship with Baba had been so sour and strained. Men like Baba needed someone to villainize, if only to convince themselves that they had good hearts. It was as if Baba had a bottle of anger that needed depleting every day, and if he hadn't hated Jafar as much as he did, half of that would have sloshed over to Rohan instead.

So hearing those words from Iago when he'd spoken ominously from the other side of the door, *your brother swayed him over*, hurt far more than Jafar had originally realized. Did that mean Rohan agreed with Baba's assessment of Jafar, or was there another reason? Jafar didn't trust Iago any more than he trusted the rain, but something nagged in the back of his skull, giving him pause, and so he had lied. It was the safest route at the moment.

If all went well, he'd never have to tell Rohan the truth: he wanted that pair of enchanted rubies his mother had spoken of, more realistic than a golden scarab and more attainable than a genie. More capable of getting them what they needed, even if that meant leaving their parents in their graves.

After Mama had ensnared him with the story all those years ago, Jafar had tried to learn all that he could about the rubies—especially the actual history surrounding them. Truth and facts. According to one of the tattered books he'd found in Mama's room, the earliest known account of the rubies was about a distraught sheikh ousted from his rightful throne.

An old woman gifted the man the rubies, and despite his initial hesitance, he eventually came to a point where he had nothing left to lose. He used the rubies to influence and control, trapping those around him under his spell. He could persuade someone to bring him food, someone to paint their walls in garish hues—or even in the blood of their enemies. Still, controlling another was not an easy task. There was work involved, unlike rubbing a lamp and prattling off a wish. That alone had caught Jafar's interest. Knowing the rubies required work was yet another reason why Jafar trusted the rubies more than he trusted in a genie.

But as with all things, the rubies had their limits, too, and it was almost a game of cunning and strategy, for the sheikh had to carefully select whom he persuaded in order to make his way back to the top.

The top, in this case, was the kingdom of Maghriz that everyone salivated over today. What Jafar had always loved most about the story was that the sheikh ended up claiming a throne that wasn't even his own.

And he did it all himself.

If Jafar had those rubies in hand, he would be just as strategic, just as cunning, and everything else would fall into place: appreciation for who he was and his capabilities. And then, to placate Rohan, perhaps he'd utilize the rubies to find the scarab and genie, too.

Regardless, he was free now, and when he finally drifted off to sleep, he did so with a smile on his face.

As the early morning sun brightened the dusty skies, Jafar and Rohan crouched behind a ledge overlooking the lower village. Half of Ghurub sat on a low hill, the rest just beneath it. From here, he could see the last of the smoke rising from the remains of their house. Behind them, the caliph of Ghurub's mansion stood even more magnificent because of the rise it had been built upon.

"He could be ratting us out in there," Rohan said, glancing back at the mansion.

The *he* in question was Iago, and though Jafar wouldn't admit it, he'd considered it, too.

Fortunately, Iago saved him from having to respond by swooping toward them with a swoosh. He flew like a drunk man walked, and nearly rammed into a date palm on his way. Jafar sighed. Of all the allies he could have had.

Then again, Iago's ability to fly was starting to prove useful already. Jafar needed a way to keep the caliph distracted for a while, and Iago was making that job easier by scoping out the place for them.

"Well?" Jafar asked, watching a maid enter the mansion through the back doors.

"The caliph is still asleep," Iago said.

Thanks to Baba's business, they'd visited the caliph's mansion several times over the past few years. They knew the layout, the staff, his pet—and most importantly, the caliph's plans to join a fully packed caravan leaving later that day. Jafar and Rohan needed his and his servant's seats, and Jafar had devised the perfect way to finagle it.

"And his beloved tiger?" Jafar asked.

"Locked in his cage. He hasn't been fed yet, it looks like," Iago replied. "I saw them cutting up chunks of meat."

Jafar tossed the last of the almond-stuffed dates he'd found in the storeroom into his mouth. "Perfect."

"Are we sure this is a good idea?" Rohan asked, biting into a slice of oversweet halvah that didn't qualify as breakfast. "There has to be a better way to go about this."

"Oh, live a little," Iago snapped.

Jafar held back a laugh. He rarely spoke his mind to Rohan—his first instinct, typically, was to placate his brother, not tell him exactly what he really felt. Iago had no such qualms; Jafar could get used to this. "We need to get to the House of Wisdom for our genie lamp, don't we?"

Something dark passed over Rohan's face, too quick for Jafar to decipher. "Yes."

Jafar waited a beat for Rohan's thoughts to catch up to him.

"It's just that . . ." Rohan went on, "you know how we had so few chances to do the right thing, because Baba always decided otherwise? He's gone now. We could start fresh. Do the right and honest thing from here on out."

"I think he might have inhaled too much of that smoke," Iago said in the silence. "How do you expect to do that? By begging?"

Iago was right. There wasn't another way to get on that caravan, or to get to Maghriz short of traversing the sands on their own, but Rohan's words transported Jafar back to the bazaar from their childhood, filching food not because he wanted to fill his own belly but because he knew it would bring a smile to Mama's face. Stealing wasn't right or honest, but when her eyes would glitter with joy, it felt a little like both.

"We haven't begun our fresh start yet, have we?" Jafar asked.

Rohan's brow furrowed. "I . . . suppose not."

"Exactly. Now, we can't do this unless we're all fully committed, so no more doubt, understand? We *know* the caliph is leaving today. And aside from loitering near the caravan and abducting someone right then and there to take their place, we don't have any other way of sneaking aboard. I would say taking the caliph's place is the more 'right' thing to do in this instance, as opposed to taking the seat of someone who might not be traveling for leisure."

Jafar nodded toward the caliph's mansion. "Here's the plan. Iago will go in and unlatch the tiger's cage—"

"Are you kidding me?" Iago asked. "I unlatch that cage and the monster will eat me. Tigers are faster than parrots."

"He has a point," Rohan said.

Jafar sighed. Since when did Rohan care what happened to Iago? "Fine. Iago, you'll have to knock on the front door and blabber—"

"Imitate." Iago corrected him.

"What?" Jafar asked. He was growing tired of the interruptions.

"I'll imitate the caliph," Iago said. "I can fly out of sight and imitate his voice, and the staff will be as confuddled as you need them to be."

"I need them distracted," Jafar replied, "not confuddled."

"Thank you, Iago," Iago snarked in an exact imitation of Jafar's voice.

"If that's how you plan on imitating the caliph, you're going to fail," Jafar lied, quickly schooling his features before Iago could see his surprise. He'd heard Iago's imitations while the bird was perched by Baba's desk, but he'd never heard it done *this* well. "No imitating."

Iago threw up his wings with a snarl.

"While Iago does *as I've told him to*," Jafar continued, "I'll slip in through the side door and let the tiger out."

"He's hungry," Rohan pointed out. "What if he attacks you?"

"It's a latch. I just need to hook a string in and pull at it from a distance."

Jafar climbed over the ledge before either of them could question him and gestured for the parrot to follow. "Rohan, stay put. Iago, let's go."

"No," Rohan said, and both Iago and Jafar turned to look at him.

"No?" Jafar asked, lifting an eyebrow.

"I'm coming with you," Rohan said.

Jafar hesitated before nodding. This was what he had wanted, no? For Rohan to come out of his shell. For him to soldier on and stand on his own. But Rohan's desire to be less coddled always appeared with force and confidence, as if it was always there, as if he used his courage as a weapon whenever he saw fit.

The caliph's house was wide and welcoming, creamy stone bright against the golden dunes. Pops of color painted each of the windows where the curtains swayed in merriment.

"Poor caliph," Rohan said as they neared the house.

"Poor tiger," Iago said.

"It's the caliph's own fault for having a beast as a pet," Jafar said. "Tigers belong outside in the wild, not cooped up like a house cat—or parrot. If I were an animal, I'd be a serpent. No point being a feral cat like that if someone can put me on a leash. Plus, I'd be fast and small *and* deadly."

"I'd want to be nimble, too. Maybe not deadly, though," Rohan said.

Jafar cast him a glance. Once, he might have pegged Rohan for a harmless, guileless animal, but now Jafar wondered if Rohan was more cunning than not. "A rat, then."

Rohan pulled a face, not realizing Jafar was being partially serious. "I like my baths, thank you."

Jafar laughed as they reached the little grove of date palms near the caliph's house. He stepped into the shade, toying with the spool of yarn in his pocket that he'd foraged from Baba's storeroom.

"This is where we part ways," he told Iago. "Count to twenty and knock on the door." Then he glanced at Rohan and pursed his lips. He couldn't stop being an older brother, being a protector. "And you, stay here so you can keep an eye on us both."

Jafar saw Iago readying to poke fun at Rohan, and Jafar was prepared to feed him to the tiger.

Iago must have seen the look on Jafar's face, because all he said was "How will I know when to leave?"

"You'll know," Jafar said, and before Rohan could protest, he disappeared into the trees.

8

ROHAN

ohan tamped down his relief as best he could when Jafar told him to stand guard instead of following him to the tiger's cage. He leaned back against one of the date palms, and when the leaves rustled with an errant desert breeze, he thought they were speaking to him.

Gaze to the oasis, Rohan.

Jafar said the phrase to him often, when panic was scrambling up Rohan's throat and threatening to drown him. The words calmed him, slowly bringing him back to the present.

As the studded front door swung open, he saw Iago's red plumage disappear from view and a maid's head poke out.

Seconds later, from the side of the house, he heard the telltale screech of the tiger's cage swinging open. He hadn't thought he'd be able to hear the sound all the way here and wondered if he should be fearing for his life just now.

He peered through the trees, catching a glimpse inside one of the windows to a lavishly furnished majlis. The plush, legless sofa beckoned with jewel-toned cushions, and after a night of sleeping on the stone floor of a storeroom, he was almost willing to leap through the window and curl up on it.

No. Jafar was risking his life for them, for something Rohan wanted. And quickly—when Jafar had a goal in mind, he moved without hesitation and with precision. Still, despite all of Jafar's reasoning, these trickster ways bothered Rohan. He didn't want Jafar following in Baba's footsteps, behaving in accordance with the conniving merchants abundant across the desert.

He caught a glimpse of someone running, the figure appearing and disappearing through the windows. Someone was sounding the alarm. A short yelp made its way to Rohan's ears, followed by a feline yowl. Trepidation began creeping up his veins.

Then he heard the front door slam shut, and Iago swooped back down toward the ledge.

Rohan supposed that was Jafar's signal. Maybe. It didn't matter. He didn't plan on being a tiger's snack. He whirled and ran back for the ledge, which was almost invisible amidst the houses and sand dunes spreading out before him except for the red speck where Iago was already waiting.

Rohan dropped beside him, panting and panicked, trying not to feel bad about the mess the tiger was inevitably creating in the caliph's house.

"You're dreadfully out of breath for someone who ran downhill," Iago snarked, hopping on Rohan's bent-over back.

Rohan was hot and sweaty and agitated, and Iago's words and talons stabbing needles into his spine weren't helping. "Keep at it, and I'll—I'll—"

"Oh? You'll what?" Iago taunted. "You can barely stand on your own two feet, and I don't mean that literally."

Rohan knew exactly what he meant. "I'll kill you."

He couldn't fully control what jumped out of his mouth sometimes.

"Those are some real bold words to say right after your father died in a mysterious fire," Iago said ominously.

Rohan froze and then desperately tried to unfreeze so that Iago wouldn't feel the muscles in his back tense. How did Iago know of Rohan's terrible deed? Rohan thought back to a time several years ago when he'd bribed a servant boy to keep quiet about the pony who had died of a fever brought on by Rohan's lack of care. What kind of bribe would Iago require?

Before Rohan could craft a response, Jafar materialized

beside him, not a hair out of place. He hadn't even broken a sweat.

"Everything all right over here?" Jafar asked, narrowing his eyes. He had a cloak slung over his arm. "I expected a little more excitement due to the fact that I was not eaten by the tiger."

"Just making conversation," Iago said cavalierly, hopping off and squinting at the cloak. "Glad you weren't eaten alive. Are we off to phase two now?"

The fact that Iago could switch emotions so quickly was not lost on Rohan. He eyed the parrot but said nothing, following Jafar as he took the lead. Rohan decided then and there that he hated Iago. He hated that the parrot had survived the fire, and he hated that he'd ever bought it in the first place.

"Yes," Jafar said, and began walking down the ledge as the alarmed shouts of the caliph's staff carried on behind them.

"And what's phase two?" Iago asked, flapping along beside Jafar.

"Impersonating the caliph," Jafar answered, detouring through an alley to avoid the hubbub of the bazaar. Rohan hated how cheerful the people seemed, how no one seemed to be mourning Baba.

"Hey!" Iago protested. "You said no imitating! No confuddling!"

Jafar nodded. "During phase one. For phase two, we'll be getting aboard that caravan by impersonating the caliph."

Iago harrumphed. "Which means you two would fail without me."

"Which means you two would fail without me," Rohan mimicked in exactly the same cadence and tone.

Iago's wings stopped working for a beat, sending him plummeting. As Jafar laughed, the bird righted himself and gaped at Rohan in surprise.

"Exactly, parrot," Rohan said, finding himself growing more and more bitter with every passing second.

They passed through an empty plaza, where a water fountain gurgled forlornly, the stone crumbling, the few decorative tiles dull and chipped. Baba had been trying to change that. To improve their tiny village.

"This way," Jafar said, squeezing into a gap between two large buildings to a clearing where people had gathered, camels idling and cart coverings flapping. The caravan. Rohan, Jafar, and Iago ducked behind the cover of a few overgrown shrubs.

"We don't need you at all," Rohan added. "I have more abilities than you can dream of."

"Ability," Jafar said, correcting him. He turned and readjusted Rohan's keffiyeh, tightening it against his protest. "Not plural. And the ability to mimic someone is hardly uncanny. That goes for both of you."

Voices stirred with the breeze. The camels grunted,

stomping their feet, their backs piled high with parcels and packages or fitted with little tents over cushioned seats. One of them spat and another snorted. Most of the travelers were already settled. Some clutched bags, others held children tight. Rohan spotted someone with a goat, and another with a bird in a cage.

"We should get Iago one of those," Rohan said, gesturing to the cage.

"Focus," Jafar said, draping the caliph's cloak over Rohan's shoulders. "Ready?"

The cloak stank of old closets and tickled his nose, but he held back a sneeze.

"Ready," Rohan said, and marched toward the caravan leader while Jafar and Iago remained at a distance.

The leader held up a hand. "Passage isn't open to all."

Rohan was melting under this thing, and the sooner he was out of it, the sooner he would stop wanting to lie down in the sand and drown in his own sweat.

The camel train was more lavish than most that traveled through their village, the animals draped in jewel tones and beaded reins.

"I should"—Rohan paused to make his voice a tad more gummy, waiting for the rumble of a fruit cart to get closer and help his facade—"hope not."

The caravan leader stiffened. "Caliph Cassim! Oh, I—I

did not know it was you! You've lost weight, my friend." He bowed and gestured to the nearest camel. "Please! Have your servant let you atop my finest."

Servant? Rohan followed the man's gaze to . . . Jafar, who looked more dejected than a monkey who'd just had his banana stolen. *Oh.* Even with the sorrow and grief weighing heavier than this cloak, Rohan had to bite back a laugh.

"You heard him!" Rohan called.

Jafar's glare was priceless, but he didn't waste any time. Though they'd caused enough of a ruckus in the real Caliph Cassim's house, they could not risk the caliph's showing up regardless. Jafar bent near the camel and interlocked his fingers for Rohan to use as a step.

"Oh, brother, if only you could see the look on your face," Rohan whispered when he got close.

Jafar gritted his teeth. "You're not going to be seeing much longer if you keep this up."

"Want me to bite him?" Iago asked, clacking his beak together.

"My servant has teeth!" Rohan said with a laugh that died as quickly as it had come.

For a moment, impersonating this esteemed and respected caliph, he felt as powerful as his father. His father, who was now in a grave identical to every other. Rohan put a cork in his thoughts. He didn't want to think about his dead father. He didn't want to think about him burning to death, suffering in those last, helpless moments. He didn't want to think about how they had nothing left to their names—and no one but each other left to speak them.

"Rohan," Jafar said from the ground. His expression was hard to make out under the harsh glare of the sun, but his tone was soft. He knew what Rohan was thinking, and here, amongst all these people, Rohan was selfishly happy he wasn't alone.

If only Jafar knew it was Rohan's fault they were in this predicament to begin with. That he had killed Baba and, more than a decade before, Mama.

"Rohan," Jafar said again.

Numbly, Rohan reached down and helped Jafar atop the camel behind him.

"Tell him to hurry up, or at this rate, we may never leave this place," Jafar whispered as Iago settled on his shoulder.

"Yalla!" Rohan called to the caravan leader. The rest of the camels carried wares and other passengers. He saw a group of uniformed girls his age, students, he presumed, piling into a covered cart, too. The caravan leader had just been waiting for Rohan and Jafar.

They were already off to an excellent start.

The caravan leader liked to talk. He transported a great deal of people in a short amount of time regularly, so he was privy to gossip. He had once helped the son of a sheikh escape an overbearing family. Another time, he'd carried a woman who was married to caliphs in two different kingdoms back and forth between her spouses, and neither caliph knew it.

Rohan could tell that Jafar listened to every little bit intently, and because he was a "servant," his keen interest was easy to explain away. Sometimes Rohan wondered if coincidences ever really occurred when Jafar was involved. With every new story Jafar guzzled, he whispered something to Iago. Rohan couldn't always hear what was said, but he would notice Iago leaning toward Jafar or the other way around, and it irked him.

He was Jafar's brother. *He* was the one with whom Jafar shared blood and history.

Iago was just a talking bird only someone who loved garish color and constant companionship would want.

And Rohan wanted Jafar to know that. If he could get his brother alone, that was. It was a struggle, but he finally got his chance when the caravan stopped for a break and Iago disappeared into a grove of date palms. Rohan hurried to Jafar.

"I don't trust him," Rohan said.

"The caravan leader?" Jafar asked, scrunching his brow.

"No, Iago," Rohan gritted out.

"Is this because he's been making fun of you?" Jafar asked.

Rohan glared at him. In most cases, Jafar had trouble trusting anyone, even his own parents. Why did that not extend to the wretched bird?

"How did he escape the fire?" Rohan asked. Jafar paused, something flitting over his features—that darkness Rohan didn't like. He didn't like how it matched Jafar's clothes so well, too: he always wore some variation of crimson and black, as dark as the facial hair slowly shading the planes of his face.

Rohan wished he could take the words back. Were they too bold? Too out of character? He was trying to make Jafar suspicious of Iago, not *himself*. That was the last thing he needed at the moment.

Jafar's brow furrowed, and Rohan braced himself. He supposed this had been inevitable.

"Are you saying he might have caused Baba's death?" Jafar asked with care, as if he were treading dangerous ground.

Yes! Rohan felt lightheaded with relief. He didn't like lying to Jafar, but he had to do what was best for the ones he loved.

Home for Rohan was wherever Jafar was. He had never faced the same torment Jafar had, for Baba always directed his ire at Jafar. Or Baba would compare the two of them and declare Rohan superior, when he really wasn't. He was quiet, compared to Jafar. He had no opinions or objections. Baba didn't care. He loved making Jafar feel inferior.

It all served to make Rohan feel terrible, which in turn made him wallow in guilt for feeling bad when his brother had it worse. Sometimes, when Rohan was feeling especially helpless, he would blame Mama for the way Baba was. If only she'd been better about putting Baba in his place. If only she'd lived longer so she could be there to counter him.

Rohan didn't think parents understood how deeply their children were affected by their actions.

"It's very likely," Rohan said.

Jafar closed his eyes for a brief moment—the shortest of moments, and yet long enough to flood Rohan with guilt.

"At the very least, we should be more wary of him," Rohan added.

Jafar took a deep breath and released it. Rohan thought it was in relief, that somewhere in his mask of emotions, he was trying to stifle a smile, but *he* had no reason to be relieved. Did he?

"Agreed," Jafar said at last. "He's a tool, nothing more."

Rohan smiled, victory flooding through him. He'd successfully planted the seed of suspicion against Iago, and Rohan was free. For now. He vowed then and there to do better. To be more like Jafar, to *do* more for him as his brother deserved.

He froze at the sound of sand dipping under footfalls. Someone was approaching from behind him.

"The caravan leader," Jafar whispered.

Rohan quickly tugged his keffiyeh back over his face.

Jafar lowered his head, the picture of an obedient servant. His voice was a low murmur when he said, "Get back to the camel."

"And leave you here? What are you going to do?" Rohan asked under his breath, turning around.

The caravan leader sauntered over with a bright smile and eyes that were eager for news to spread. His dark hair was dusted in sand, much of it covered by the green headdress wrapped around his head.

"I'm going to get answers," Jafar hissed. "He won't talk with you here, and nor can I. Now get back on your camel before your *servant* causes a scene."

9

JAFAR

The moment Rohan disappeared, the caravan leader turned to Jafar like a rat to cheese, and Jafar bit back a smile. Some people were far too easy to predict.

"Very good weather today, no?" the caravan leader asked.

Jafar squinted up at the sky through the woven leaves of the date palms. It wasn't anything out of the ordinary. "I hope it's just as nice in Maghriz."

He didn't think he'd ever used the word *hope* before.

"Around this time of year? Definitely," the caravan leader said. "The sun is kinder to us bedouins, and the sands are softer."

"I've never been," Jafar said in as dreamy and wistful a

tone as he could muster. He felt like Rohan just then. "Are they still at war? I thought I heard that somewhere."

"War?" the caravan leader asked, propping a hand against a date palm. The midafternoon sun fell through the leaves, painting him in dappled light. "No, no. They haven't been at war in so long!" He lowered his voice. "Are you waiting for your caliph?"

"He's returned to his camel, why?" Jafar asked.

The man stepped awfully close, and Jafar had to resist the urge to step away. He was still playing the part of a servant, and a servant could have no such grievances.

"Can't speak so freely in front of a caliph, can we?" the man asked.

Jafar pulled a laugh. "Unfortunately, no."

"See! You understand me!" The caravan leader chuckled. "As I said, Maghriz hasn't been at war in many moons. That sultana knows what she's doing, but"—the man looked around them, even though the majority of the travelers were by the watering hole a good distance away—"you are right. I've heard the whispers, too. Something is in the works."

Jafar gasped. The sound was foreign on his tongue, but he knew what the caravan leader wanted, and a gasp it was. Jafar leaned closer. "Like what?"

"I heard that the Sultana's son went off on an expedition across the sea, by ship," he said, pausing to crunch loudly on some candied almonds, "and never returned."

The prince of Maghriz. Interesting.

Iago flapped over and perched on a boulder. Why *was* Rohan so wary of him? Did he fear Iago might have overheard Rohan talking to Baba about the scholarship, and that Jafar might trust Iago? Jafar still didn't know if he trusted Iago, but Rohan wasn't doing himself any favors by acting so suspicious himself.

"Did you hear me?" the caravan leader asked.

Jafar shook away the errant thoughts.

"So he . . . he . . ." Jafar left the end of his sentence hanging as if he were too frightened to say the word.

"Yes," the caravan leader whispered loudly. "He *died*. No one has seen that ship in months."

"That's horrible. Surely word would have spread," Jafar replied. "There's no reason to keep silent about the prince's death."

The caravan leader shrugged. "Could be rumor, could be an opportunity."

Iago squawked. "Opportunity! Opportunity!"

The caravan leader turned to him in awe. "You're a funny little bird, aren't you?"

Jafar inched closer to Iago and glared. It took everything in Jafar's power not to clamp his beak together to keep him quiet.

"Opportunity," Jafar repeated. "That's an odd way to view a missing prince, no? Was he not liked?"

And what relation did any of this have to whispers of war?

"Oh, he was *loved*," the man said. "And so it begs the question: Why remain silent about his death?"

"Because he might not be dead," Jafar said. "The ship might not have sunk. Perhaps they are mired in a storm and their voyage is delayed. There's still hope of his return."

It wasn't as if they had *proof* of his death. Jafar studied the caravan leader. There came a point when gossip veered into scandalous and shocking falsehood. Jafar didn't know how much of what the caravan leader spoke was actually true, and how much was the conspiracy of a man who guided camels through the desert all day.

Still, he pocketed every word he'd collected. He never knew what might prove useful.

They spent days on that caravan, and from there, Jafar and Rohan hailed passage on a boat, losing their dinners and turning green as the sea stole their legs. Iago barely said a word, clamping his wings tight and coiling his talons around anything that kept him steady.

With nothing but the endless sea to distract them, there was more than enough time for Jafar to relive every moment that had led to the destruction of Baba's manor while Rohan shed more tears about the debris itself. Jafar often felt he was two disparate halves of a whole constantly at war with each other: one nurtured by his mother, the other battered and bruised and tormented by his father.

One evening, when Rohan dozed off against his shoulder, Jafar carefully pulled the scraps of his scholarship out of his pocket, wishing he could show them to his father and tell him, *See, I'm going there anyway.* Nothing could stand in the way of what Jafar wanted. When he closed his eyes, he saw the House of Wisdom. When he closed them tighter, he saw those rubies he was going to find, bright and red and powerful.

Oh, the power he would have after a lifetime of having none, like a starved animal finally freed of its shackles.

Jafar lost track of the days—had it been five nights? Ten?—before the crew spotted land, and amidst their triumphant shouts and ululations, he saw it: Maghriz. The kingdom shone like an oasis, shimmering in the midday sun, gold sparkling like magic. Jafar felt Rohan's gaze on him, his judgment, and Jafar masked his excitement. He couldn't be too happy when he was supposed to be mourning his father.

Jafar couldn't leave the boat soon enough. He hobbled on weak legs, grateful, in more ways than one, for the sand beneath his sandals. Iago wobbled along a small dune and collapsed on his face.

"I'll suffer a lifetime of bland crackers if it means never having to ride in another boat," he groaned when he finally righted himself.

"We're here," Rohan breathed. "We made it."

"The kingdom of Maghriz," Jafar said with the same hushed awe. "At last."

He couldn't quite believe he was here. Everything felt richer, better. Even the air tasted of success. A bazaar spread ahead of them, and it was alive in a way the entire village of Ghurub was not. Vibrant and at once homey. The Sultana was imposing to the world as much as she was compassionate and caring to her people—tales of Maghriz were carried far and wide, and it seemed without exaggeration.

"I can almost see the golden scarab, Jafar," Rohan said, barely containing a grin.

It took Jafar several tries before he could meet his eyes. "It'll be ours, brother."

Maybe. Perhaps after Jafar secured those rubies and the knowledge of every scroll he could hold—or never, if Rohan realized Jafar's way, grounded in the science of alchemy, was the more viable one.

Or, if Rohan didn't realize it on his own, maybe Jafar could make him.

A medley of people dotted the streets ahead, and Jafar could hear the liveliness in their voices, see it in their gait as they bartered for produce and silks, new rugs and fresh spices. It stirred something inside of him just the same.

Rohan looked down at the creased, half-torn map. "This must be the Sakaka Bazaar." He gave their surroundings a good sweep and turned the map upside down. "Oi. We're at the wrong end of the capital city—look, the palace and the House of Wisdom are way up there. We can't walk that far."

"This is very nice for a bazaar on the outskirts," Iago said, circling them.

"Better than the bazaar we found you in before we gifted you to our father," Jafar pointed out.

"Don't remind me," Iago said, and swooped ahead with a squawk.

Jafar observed the way the people of Maghriz moved and behaved. He studied a man buying an apple, placing his own hand just so over his robes, tightening them in his fist to hold it together. He pulled his shoulders back the way a woman perusing jewelry did, her chin high as if she were royalty. He saw another man with an orange headdress wrapped around his head, a jewel set in its center, making Jafar's dusty keffiyeh seem ratty in comparison. He needed one of those. Preferably in black.

The people of Maghriz walked with pride, with the knowledge that the land beneath their feet was something earned and special, and Jafar was smitten. He tried picking up as many little quirks as he could—the slight jut of a jaw, the tilt of a chin, the way they accentuated each word as if it were a dish to be savored.

"See? That's how we need to . . ." Jafar stopped and whirled around. A family carrying fresh produce stared at him blankly. A girl around his age smiled coyly. Rohan was nowhere to be seen. Nor was that vermillion-red parrot. "Rohan? Iago?"

Jafar stepped into the bustle of the market, passing stall after stall. The crowds were thick, the bazaar labyrinthine. The smells, sounds, and sights assaulted his senses. At last, Rohan's voice came from the other side of a booth, just out of sight behind rolls of colorful fabric.

"—but she's my sister," Rohan was saying. "She's bound to go into labor any moment now, but she's on the other side of the city. My brother and I have no coin to hire a ride."

"And her spouse?" asked a voice.

Iago was observing Rohan's antics from a nearby post. He noticed Jafar and fluttered to his shoulder. "Get a load of this guy."

Was . . . Rohan trying to secure them a ride? Jafar didn't know if he should be proud or worried. It was like earlier, when he'd suddenly decided to follow Jafar to the tiger's cage.

Jafar paused and listened, estimating that his brother would stammer out two more attempts at being persuasive before he shifted to full-out begging. He rounded the stalls in time to see Rohan pull a most miserable expression.

It was almost believable. If one were closing their eyes and looking the other way.

"Fallen in a skirmish," Jafar said, rearranging his own features with ease.

Rohan, it seemed, had been trying to persuade an old merchant packing up his wares into taking the three of them across the kingdom. His face was leathered from the sun, but his features were kind. *Good catch, brother.* Rohan, for all his displays of innocence, could be a hawk when he wished.

The merchant looked up at him, hesitant. "You must be the other brother. And what an adorable parrot! Isn't she a beauty."

"She?" Iago spat, just out of earshot. "Are you listening to this? I'll show him adorable."

"Soon-to-be uncle, thank you," Jafar said to the merchant, grinning as wide as he could. He lowered his voice and spoke behind his teeth to Iago. "You'll do no such thing."

The merchant smiled. "The new baby will be lucky to have such a devoted uncle, I am certain." He glanced at Rohan as if he'd forgotten he was there. Jafar felt Rohan's annoyance at the intervention loud and clear. "*Uncles.* Though I am sorry for the loss of your brother-in-law."

Jafar looked as sorry as he could. "It wasn't too long ago, unfortunately. Bandits can be horrible."

"Bandits! Why didn't you say so?" the merchant exclaimed, and Jafar knew he'd struck gold, for there was nothing merchants hated more. "Oh, those rascals. Get on! I'm taking you both right away." He peeled back his cart's rough covering and looked inside, then back at them. "I've sold most of my baubles today. It won't be the comfiest of rides, but you are welcome to sit with them."

There was just one last thing Jafar and Rohan needed to do to secure passage.

"Remind him that we can't pay," he murmured to Rohan, who worked his jaw at the instruction. Where was this pride coming from? He'd certainly had none of it when he would beg their father. *"Do it."*

Rohan sighed and straightened. "Oh, sayyidi, we couldn't even pay for you to take us all—"

"Nonsense!" the merchant said, and Jafar saw the decision finalize in the man's dark eyes. His donkey brayed, and the man gave them a smile. "She says it's settled. Now help me finish loading my cart. Yalla, yalla!"

It was scarcely an hour before they were on the road again, the merchant's cart barely big enough for the two of them and a parrot. From his seat in front of the cart, the merchant hummed a tune while he guided his donkey, his silhouette marked by the sun against the dusty white canopy separating him from the brothers.

Rohan and Iago clutched what they could to ward off motion sickness, Rohan's knuckles white against the worn wood while Iago hopped from one rolling trinket to the next. The merchant made short work of the journey that would have taken far too long on foot, and Jafar watched as the man's silhouette lengthened with the shifting sun. When Rohan gagged for the thousandth time, Jafar pulled back the covering at the back of the cart and gazed outside. His heartbeat quickened as the donkey slogged on and their surroundings grew louder and denser. Beat by beat, the heart of Maghriz's capital city enveloped them.

Jafar couldn't stop the smile that curled his lips. This was the kingdom he had traversed the sands to see. This was what he'd left his father behind in a pile of ash to experience. A place worthy of Jafar's presence. He paused at the thought. That wasn't right. It was a place worth *being* in.

He already felt as though he belonged here. Back in their village, when he'd speak before Baba and his men, telling them of his ideas and countering theirs, he'd felt out of place. As if he spoke a different language. As if they embodied the sleepiness of the village of Ghurub.

Maghriz was the complete opposite.

The change was gradual. Smaller houses surrounded them at first, dainty and quaint, but as the merchant and his donkey began an ascent, the buildings rose, too. Taller, fancier, decked with tiles and glass and shiny stone. Outfits became more regal, mannerisms more royal. There were fewer merchant carts, and more shopfronts with beckoning doors. And there, at the very center of it all, was the Maghrizi palace, standing atop a hill, with wide domes of glittering gold and minarets rising to the dusty skies. It truly was a sight to behold.

And as they neared the palace and Jafar fell more and more in love with it, he remembered what the caravan leader had said about the missing prince.

An opportunity.

"What happens when the House of Wisdom leads us to the golden scarab?" Rohan asked loudly. Did he think the merchant's being on the outside of the cart meant he couldn't hear?

Jafar dropped the canvas flap and picked up a tiny brass vase etched with ornate lines. "Let's not yell, but . . . supposedly, we'll put the pieces together and it'll lead us to the genie who will grant us three wishes."

As simple as that. Jafar didn't know if he believed it yet. Then again, what the rubies promised sounded just as impossible and outlandish, didn't it? *No,* Jafar told himself. That was Baba getting into his head, stirring up uncertainty. The rubies were nothing like the genie lamp. They would be his to control, allowing him to control others.

Why put his faith in a genie when he could hold all the cards himself?

Rohan sighed as the cart rolled to a stop and they heard

the merchant shuffling outside. "We'll have to get *into* the House of Wisdom first."

"A pity I don't have a scholarship," Jafar said, watching Rohan closely, but his brother simply fiddled with one of the trinkets.

"Pity indeed," Iago echoed, and Jafar gave him and his red feathers a look. Clearly parrots weren't made for subtlety.

"I—" Rohan began, and stopped. His brow furrowed, but he said nothing more. Jafar waited. The remains of his scholarship were still in his pocket, crushed even further and slightly damp from their journey across the water.

He had wanted to pull them out and show them to Rohan more than once. Sometimes, he imagined his brother's face breaking out into a wide grin, beaming and proud. Other times, he imagined a shadow crossing over it, distress and discontentment souring his features.

Jafar didn't know why he cared for his brother's opinion of him so deeply.

"Anyway," he said, moving his hand from his pocket. "We'll be fine. There's more than one way to get into the House of Wisdom."

Maybe. But he *was* counting on being able to work with the shreds in his pocket.

"And you know this how?" Iago asked.

"He knows everything about the House of Wisdom," Rohan replied, almost triumphantly. Oh, *now* he could speak?

It sounded as if Rohan and Iago were competing somehow—for Jafar's attention? For his favor? Ridiculous.

Jafar liked it.

But it was a reminder, too: Rohan cared. Jafar realized just then that Iago had been an observer of their lives for months. If he wanted Jafar's undivided attention, he very well might have been trying to sow discord between the two of them all along—like with the scholarship.

"You're not planning on breaking into it, are you?" Rohan asked. "I doubt they have a caged tiger you can use as a distraction."

Jafar shook his head as the cart trundled to a stop. He needed to make sure Rohan knew that Jafar cared, too—that everything he'd done, even the less than savory bit, was to help them both. He exited the cart and stretched out his legs, scanning the desert while inhaling deep. The smell of hot and tarnished trinkets was worse than he'd expected. "No, we'll be marching straight up to the House of Wisdom itself. I applied, didn't I? I'll tell them as much."

Iago pulled a face. Rohan paled. Jafar bit back a wicked grin and turned to the merchant with as warm a smile as he could muster. The man looked taken aback for a moment.

"Shukrun for the ride, sayyidi," Jafar said, placing a palm over his heart. "Your kindness will not be forgotten."

"Oh—" the merchant stammered out. He looked a little starstruck. "It was—it was my pleasure."

Jafar inclined his head again and turned away. Part of him waited for a slap across the cheek or a slew of reprimands attacking everything from his physical appearance to his audacity to speak. His father didn't like when Jafar spoke to people, for they had a tendency to listen.

To obey.

Jafar didn't realize until now that he had taken Baba's criticism to heart. *No more,* Jafar told himself. He answered to no one but himself now.

He began walking up the street, jaw set and memories of Baba streaking through his mind, one after the other. Rohan struggled to keep up, bickering with Iago about something Jafar tuned out. It didn't yet feel like Baba was really gone. He was an entire realm away now, but at times, Jafar felt worse than when he had known Baba was a room over.

He couldn't let that feeling hinder what he had already accomplished—and had yet to achieve.

Buildings rose to either side of them, some with carvings etched into stone, others with fancy moldings that jutted out at intervals. Some tapered to pointed domes, while others were flat with rooftop terraces.

Jafar had never seen anything like it. He'd never seen a city that had been built for *leisure,* rather than necessity.

He pointed at Rohan's map. "Let's head to that bazaar first. We're going to need better clothes and a few other things. And then a place to stay for the night."

As occasional passersby became small crowds and busier storefronts, Jafar spied a sweetshop. *Perfect.* Rohan would love that.

"Jafar, we really need to—" Rohan began.

"Come on," Jafar said.

Rohan ran to catch up. "We need to talk about your plan. You can't go up to the House of Wisdom and expect to be let in simply because you've applied."

"There's a sweetshop just up ahead," Jafar singsonged.

"Did you hear me?" Rohan asked.

"Relax, Rohan. I'll buy you qatayef," Jafar said.

"Hey, I deserve a little something, too," Iago said. Jafar ignored him and looked at Rohan with a mock pout.

Rohan sighed. "And cardamom tea, too? With your imaginary money?"

"Of course," Jafar said, hopes rising as they ventured deeper into the capital city. Date palms swayed, fountains gurgled.

"Are you actually— With what money, Jafar?" Rohan asked in hushed panic as Jafar neared the sweetshop.

It was a stall, really, run by a girl, with a sampling of sweets inside a glass case. Behind her, a woman who might have been her sister poured orange blossom syrup over a fresh batch of basbousa, the buttery and nutty aroma spiraling around them. Cozy cushions had been arranged out in front of the shop, occupied by men sitting cross-legged and chatting in boisterous tones without a care in the world, pouring fragrant streams of tea and passing glasses around.

"A plate of qatayef, please," Jafar said. "And a glass of cardamom tea."

The girl behind the glass case blushed when he pulled out a handful of coins with a flourish.

"You had money this entire time?" Rohan sputtered. The men burst into laughter at something completely unrelated.

"If I had used it sooner, we wouldn't be here right now, would we?" Jafar asked.

Rohan grumbled, and then when Jafar winked, a laugh sputtered out of him. Jafar, despite everything looming ahead, warmed inside. This was what he lived for: his brother.

And when Jafar wasn't careful, it was easy to forget.

10

JAFAR

Jafar counted the last of the coins he'd brought from home and set off with Rohan and Iago for the bazaar. Their clothes were dusty and worn from their travels, and though Rohan argued that the gatekeepers of the House of Wisdom wouldn't care, Jafar believed otherwise.

While Rohan perused the stalls, Iago fluttered to Jafar's shoulder, nails cinching tight.

"When I have new clothes on, we'll have to revisit where you sit, because it won't be on my shoulder anymore," Jafar said, eyeing his talons.

"Sure it will," Iago said. Jafar enjoyed their raillery. It was different from his back-and-forth with Rohan, and strangely, the fact that it was less sincere and intense made it feel more natural. "We need to talk about your idea to walk up to the House of Wisdom."

"As I already told my brother, it's not up for discussion," Jafar replied, narrowly avoiding a child running across the street, waving a brand-new doll.

"Your brother doesn't know you ever saw the acceptance letter," Iago said.

"And?"

"Don't tell me you don't care about hurting his feelings."

Jafar glanced at him sidelong with a pause. He didn't think the parrot cared either way. "He won't have to know."

"You still have the scraps in your pocket," Iago said, fluffing his feathers. "You're planning on showing them at the House of Wisdom's door."

Jafar gritted his teeth. He didn't like that Iago had been watching him and knew his plans. "Why do you care about how Rohan will feel? You don't even like him."

"I don't," Iago said matter-of-factly as Jafar balked at the price tag on a blacker-than-black set of robes. "But you're brothers. He can be as sinister as you, and I'd be careful about betraying him when you're all he has. In case you haven't noticed, we're short on allies."

"Wait, *betraying* him? I'm not—"

"Jafar, when you're a parrot like me, you learn people. There's a lot going on in that boy's head, and he'll see anything you keep from him as a betrayal. And you've got a list of secrets and lies, don't you?" Iago asked.

He had a point. Rohan *was* easily disquieted. He had always tried so hard to please everyone around him, including unworthy people like Baba. Perhaps Rohan had some of that same ruthlessness in him that Jafar had recognized in their baba . . . and himself.

Jafar didn't fully know why Iago cared. Why was he on his side? Jafar wasn't used to anyone doing anything for him without expecting something in return, without a motive that wasn't immediately clear.

Still, Jafar wasn't sinister, and Rohan surely didn't have a sinister bone in his body. He was a daffodil abloom in the carnage.

"Stop thinking you know me. And him," Jafar said, annoyed that Iago had thoroughly messed with his head.

Iago shrugged. "Oh, *I'm* sorry I was looking out for us."

Us. Jafar didn't know where this sense of companionship had sprouted from, but as sounds of the bazaar rushed back between them, he realized he didn't want to refute it.

"Fine, then tell me this," Jafar said, stepping to the side to let a family pass. "What reason would Rohan have had for not wanting me to apprentice at the House of Wisdom?"

Iago looked like he wanted to say something but decided against it. "Did you ever think about how leaving your baba behind meant leaving Rohan, too?"

Jafar's suspicions over Iago's withheld response were quickly overshadowed by what he did say. Jafar had toyed with the idea, sure. He would be leaving Rohan behind, but for better things, knowledge that would soon distract him, a pair of rubies that would alter the very foundation of his world.

He hadn't thought about how his brother would feel.

Rohan waved him over to a shop amidst the stalls. Jafar pushed past a man carrying fresh fruit and a woman counting her change with confusion, biting his tongue when a boy and his friends nearly tripped him.

"Oi! Watch where you're going," Iago snarled, and the boys looked at Jafar like his voice didn't quite match his body because they didn't realize it was Iago who had spoken.

When Jafar finally made it to the shop, Rohan pulled open the door, and the three of them stepped inside to find it hot and crowded. Robes in every color hung from the walls, rich and vibrant, fit for royalty.

"Are we supposed to be able to afford something?" Jafar asked with a laugh. The place *smelled* expensive. Like heady musk and crisp sandalwood.

Rohan leaned close. "We don't have to. The shopkeeper can't keep a close eye on everyone."

"Did your fresh start already die?" Iago exclaimed before Jafar could.

Rohan shrugged. "It's like Jafar said. We have to find our footing first."

Jafar was fingering the fabric on a set of decadent ink-black robes. *Or,* he thought, *it's acceptable when it's Rohan's idea, and immoral when it's mine.*

It was a very Baba thing to do.

Iago said nothing, but Jafar got the sense that he was thinking the same. He was dreading the inevitable moment when the parrot would speak to him about it.

"Can I help you, young effendi?"

The three of them turned to the shopkeeper, a tall and slender woman, her lips bright as Iago's feathers. She seemed unbothered by the heat in the tight space, but Jafar was starting to grow a little faint.

"We are only looking," Jafar said.

"Our mother might need help, though," Rohan said, and pointed to where the crowds were the thickest. "She's over there."

The moment she turned away, Rohan began rolling up the ink-black robes.

"What are you doing?" Jafar asked.

"Hurrying up," Rohan said, shoving the bundle against Jafar.

Jafar glanced at the shopkeeper in alarm, but she was pressing deeper into the crowd, her voice rising above the din. He couldn't protest now that their countdown had begun, and besides, the robes *were* exquisite. If he pilfered a new headdress in a deep shade of crimson while he was at it, oh, it was only because he was passing time until Rohan picked out his own clothes.

"Uh, boys?" Iago asked from atop Jafar's shoulder. "We have a bit of a problem."

Jafar followed Iago's line of sight. The shopkeeper was coming their way, and she didn't look too happy. Jafar slipped his hands and the robes behind him, pressing back against the shelves with various decorations for sale.

"I didn't see your mother," the woman said, a little suspicious.

Rohan fumbled. "Are you—"

"She might have left without us, then," Jafar replied, oozing dismay. "I told her we needed new clothes for my brother's betrothal, but she rarely takes him seriously. We'll go find her, though."

Jafar was proud of himself when sympathy softened the woman's features. Another beat more, and they would have been free.

If Rohan hadn't failed.

He dropped the robes he'd chosen for himself.

The shopkeeper looked at the pile of clothes at his feet and then behind him, where the robes had been hanging neatly, realization slowly dawning on her face. Jafar met her eyes with a guilty laugh.

She didn't waste a beat. "Guards!"

Of course a store like this would have its own guards.

"Run!" Jafar shouted. He tossed the dropped robes at Rohan and darted for the exit, squeezing between two burly men who had just stepped inside. He shoved the door open with his shoulder and leaped into the street, sinking into the sand before he found the paved road. Rohan was on his heels. Iago took to the skies. Shouts rang out behind them. Jafar ducked past a sweep of fabric draped over a stall and glanced back, heart dropping to his feet.

An entire *platoon* of guards was on their tail.

11

ROHAN

While Rohan bounded after Jafar, he thought about those qatayef again, mostly to keep his mind preoccupied, but also because he truly couldn't stop thinking about them. The pistachios were crunchy, the ashta cream thick and dreamy with just the right sweetness, the coned pancakes soft and fluffy. Food had a way of settling his nerves. This place did, too.

The beauty and wonder and magnitude of this kingdom had given him the confidence to act like his brother, to be more brazen and bold. But he'd still gone and ruined it.

"This is going great, isn't it?" Iago simply could not let

Rohan linger in his own thoughts. It was impossible enough that he was a talking parrot, but to talk more than the average human? Sorcery, really.

They ran, boots beating the sandy ground. The people meandering through the bazaar fled, dispersing like a bag of marbles as Rohan and Jafar neared. A spear slammed into the bench beside them. Rohan yelped.

"What are they, clothes made of gold?" Iago exclaimed.

"This is all your fault, Rohan," Jafar yelled back, but he was laughing. They wrenched to a halt when they came to a crossroads where throngs of people were pulling carts or children, carrying produce or their own purses.

"Which way do we go?" Rohan asked.

"You were the one studying that map," Jafar sputtered.

"I—I did," Rohan stammered out. He shoved the robes under his arm and pulled the map out of his pocket, trying to make sense of it. But his hands were shaking too hard and his brain was in a frenzy as the guards clamored behind them. "Let's go—"

"Right," Iago squawked.

Jafar hesitated, and Rohan didn't know why that made him feel so good about himself. Jafar considered the path to their left, which was darker but seemed linear, and then he looked to the right. "But it's a maze."

"And I can guide you two through it," Iago replied.

Rohan could see his brother considering the parrot's route. "Jafar, I—"

Iago swerved between them, flapping his wings at eye level with Jafar. "Do you trust me?"

Jafar took a deep breath, and Rohan couldn't see if he nodded, but he heard his decision loud and clear: "We don't have time. Iago, lead the way."

He disappeared into the fray, Iago's bright red form guiding from above, zooming through date palms and hanging laundry.

Rohan gritted his teeth and followed, trying to stay on Jafar's heels.

Jafar veered right, between two posts carved with attempts at inspiring inscriptions, and Rohan struggled to keep up. He might have been more muscled, but Jafar was far taller. At a particularly gruff shout, some part of him seized up, thinking of Baba. Thinking of the fire. Thinking of death.

I killed him. Rohan didn't welcome the thought, but he had no power to stop it.

If only he were more like Jafar. Certain and calm. Confident and fearless and—

"This way!" Iago yelled, leading them through a massive hole in the wall.

— stupidly never questioning that bird even when Rohan wished he would. Jafar toppled an abandoned cart behind them to slow the guards even further. They finally came to a wide alley, clear of people and secluded from view.

Iago landed on a window ledge. "You're welcome."

"Well done, Iago," Jafar panted, and Rohan hated the grin that spread across the parrot's face. It was also a little terrifying.

Iago rose to the skies and returned, nearly diving into a line of laundry dancing in the dry breeze. "It looks like they're catching up."

The alley stretched to either side of them. Jafar looked over at Iago. "Which way?"

Rohan stepped between them with the map in hand and squared his shoulders. "Left."

"Are you sure?" Jafar asked, eyeing the rubble in their path.

"Yes, Jafar," Rohan said, not the least bit certain, but he wasn't going to let the bird take any more credit or any more of Jafar's attention. Baba was gone, Jafar was all he had left, and if Iago kept at it, Rohan would take care of him, too.

Rohan paused but didn't have time to dwell on his dark thoughts before Jafar took off to the left, glancing back only to make sure Rohan was keeping up. Iago flew away with a loud harrumph, but Rohan couldn't have cared less. He and his brother ducked through clothes hung to dry, darted past a man slipping a woman coin, and then meandered through barrels waiting to be toppled.

Until they skidded to a breathless halt.

A dead end.

The alley ended at a building, tall and imposing. There was no way around it.

"There they are!"

And the guards had found them again.

"Well," Jafar mused. "Too late to go right."

"Too bad you two can't fly," Iago snarked.

Rohan wanted to crush the bird's skull. He wanted to be swallowed whole by the ground and freed of this embarrassment. He wanted—

"Wait. Jafar! There are plenty of footholds," Iago called from the sky. "You can make the climb if you hurry."

The building was lined with windows, worn wooden pegs, deformed stones, and tiny windcatchers. And if they could climb the precarious stack of crates in front of them, they would get halfway up the building.

Jafar turned to Rohan and paused with a wistful smile. "Just like old times, eh?"

Rohan immediately felt a little better. He watched Jafar leap atop the first row of crates, slowly making his way up the teetering pile. Back in their village, the two of them would sometimes scale an old apartment building and share ma'moul. It was a secret treat whenever their father sent them out on errands and Jafar would get the task done in record time, always bartering for a dinar less so he could spend it on the sweet date-filled cookie.

This was a little less leisurely, but at least Rohan wasn't alone. He paused when he spotted something shiny between two of the crates. He reached for the dull end of it and pulled out a sword.

"Oi!"

Rohan turned at the voice, sword in hand. The guards froze, staring up at him.

"He's got a sword!" one of them exclaimed.

The others looked as stunned as Rohan before another one of them yelled, "Idiots, so do we!"

They brandished their own swords as one and began running for him. Rohan couldn't climb with a sword, nor did he have a desire to use such a thing. He chucked it off the crates and hurried after Jafar.

The guards were getting closer, and Jafar was nearing the top.

"Hurry!" Iago shouted.

"Oh, shut it, bird!" Rohan shouted back as he picked up the pace. Splinters in the old crates nicked his skin, and he nearly lost his footing one too many times before he reached the top.

But the tower of crates had already survived one boy and wasn't eager to sustain another. It groaned in warning and teetered toward the alley, threatening to pull Rohan down, too. With a shout, he jumped to one of the wooden beams, swinging his legs out of reach when a guard tried grabbing him. He swung to another beam with all his weight, then used a windcatcher to climb higher.

The guards were on his tail.

"Faster, Rohan!" Jafar yelled from the top. Rohan leaped to another windcatcher, feet scrambling for purchase in the grooves of the stone.

A hand clamped around his leg before he could pull himself up to the next window ledge. He looked down, head spinning.

A guard was grinning toothily up at him. "I've got you now, boy."

The rest of the guards were crawling up the wall behind him. Rohan threw a glance up, but Jafar was nowhere to be seen. Panic squeezed his lungs, making it hard to breathe. Had Iago convinced Jafar to leave him? Another thought shot through him like ice, unwelcome and unbidden: Had Iago convinced Jafar to leave *Baba* behind?

No, that was all you, Rohan told himself. He was confused and lost and *why* was he in his head when he was fighting for his life?

Rohan tried shaking the guard off, but his grip was iron tight. It was hopeless. Rohan was doomed. All for a set of robes he didn't even want.

Something zoomed past his cheek, hitting the guard on the head with a thwack. Rohan stared, certain he'd imagined it. Even the guard looked just as stunned.

"Take that!" Iago shouted, followed by Jafar's whoop from the rooftop. He was there, more rocks in hand.

Another one struck the guard. He yelped, his hold loosening enough for Rohan to yank free. He pulled himself up to the next ledge before the guard could grab him again. Sweat was trickling down his back, slickening his grip, but he was almost there. He swung his legs to the side, throwing his arm out to grip the nearest post. The wood, baking in the heat of the sun, scorched his palm, and then Jafar was reaching for him, pulling him up as the guards continued clamoring beneath them.

At last, Rohan was on his own two feet beside Jafar.

"Good?" Jafar asked. The dry breeze ruffled Jafar's hair and whipped at his clothes, but his eyes were steady on Rohan, attentive and caring.

"Good," Rohan replied with a nod, even as he wobbled on his feet.

A hand grabbed the edge of the rooftop. The guards were truly relentless for something as trivial as clothes. Rohan and Jafar glanced at one another and took off across the rooftops, leaping from one to the next. Jafar laughed again, and Rohan came alive at the sound.

He wasn't in danger then; he wasn't running for his life.

They were eight and six years old again, and Jafar would protect him. Rohan found himself giving in to the moment: the wind running through his hair, the freedom of being on top of the world, the glee when they finally lost the guards.

It made him feel as if the past was still possible. Mama, laughing. Baba, brightening at the sound of it. Jafar, spending hours with Rohan.

A family.

For the first time since he'd smelled smoke, he felt hope. Jafar straightened out their new clothes, panting when he ruffled Rohan's hair like they were still children. Rohan felt, just then, like a stray cat suddenly overwhelmed by attention.

"I did it," he blurted out on the rooftop. The sun was dropping lower, burning a line of red along the horizon.

Jafar tilted his head at him. "Did what?"

"I killed Baba," Rohan whispered. "And before him, Mama. I'm cursed, can't you see?"

Jafar narrowed his eyes, considering him. "You killed Mama when you were six years old? You made her sick enough to cough up blood? Where is this coming from?"

He said nothing about Baba, but then again, Jafar didn't care much for Baba. Iago settled on Jafar's shoulder, quietly watching the exchange.

"I— She told us about the genie," Rohan stuttered, "and then I made wishes, and they came true years later, but—but don't you understand? *She* was the cost."

Jafar smiled. The desert breeze rustled his hair. They were free here, above the world, and Rohan's emotions felt different, almost outside of him. "You always did like looking for signs. There's nothing wrong with that, but at some point, you'll begin creating signs yourself."

"It's true," Iago piped up, and for once, Rohan didn't immediately sour at his voice.

"So no, you didn't kill Mama," Jafar said, crossing the rooftop over to the ladder at the end. "Besides, Mama was too strong to die by a measly six-year-old's hand."

Rohan lightened at Jafar's teasing tone. "Yes. She was."

"Then there you have it," Jafar replied. "You're not cursed."

Jafar's words loosened a knot in Rohan's lungs, but he still didn't think it was that simple. He felt as if his emotions had trapped him in a maze with no way out. He didn't know if Jafar was simply placating him, or if he truly believed Rohan had no hand in Mama's death. It had been so sudden, so immediate, how could Jafar know for certain?

"But what about Baba? The same happened to him," Rohan ventured.

"The same?" Jafar asked, pausing at the edge of the rooftop.

"I wasn't there for your mama's death, but it sounds to me like your baba died a lot more violently," Iago piped up.

Rohan didn't know how that was supposed to make him

feel better. He hadn't mentioned specifics when he'd made his wish. He'd been desperate, hurting. As he was now—*always*.

"Violent, indeed," Jafar said, and when he faced him, Rohan wished the sun weren't to his back, stretching shadows over his face, darkening the pools of his eyes. "There are deaths, and there are punishments, Rohan. Now come, we have a big day tomorrow."

Rohan followed, pretending Jafar's words hadn't chilled him to the bone.

12

JAFAR

Jafar woke to aching bones after tossing and turning on a thin mattress all night. His dreams were tormented fragments, from stepping into a golden mansion of knowledge to seeing it aflame. From finding comfort in Mama's voice to cowering from Baba's scorn. He was glad when dawn crested the horizon.

If Jafar were to sit with Mama right now, he would have much to tell her.

Your stories didn't inspire only Rohan, Mama. I'm here in Maghriz, so close to the House of Wisdom, like all great men. Despite Baba's attempts to stop him. Despite years of Baba's acting as if he might have cared enough to let him go, giving

Jafar tiny morsels of hope to keep the starvation at bay. *Rohan thinks he killed you and Baba.* As wrong as it felt to refuse Rohan a concrete answer and leave him wondering if he'd had something to do with Baba's death, Jafar needed Rohan compliant, and that uncertainty and regret would help. *Baba can't bother me anymore.* He was dead. Gone. Violently, as Iago had said, but it was also fitting.

Jafar didn't even feel bad.

Death was an end, and if one had nothing more to offer the world, then death was all they deserved. Mama's face, and the faces of their servants, materialized in his mind, as if asking if the words applied to them, too, but he pressed his eyes closed and made them disappear.

He smoothed out the qamis over his chest and knotted the salwar around his waist. They were a tad too large for him but still fit well. He tugged on the robes, running his fingers over the fine gold embroidery, and stood before the room's mottled mirror beside Rohan. His brother's robes were dove gray and vibrant with accents in jewel-toned teal. The color matched the wide grin on his face and brightened the grief that was a constant in his eyes.

"You look good, brother," Jafar said.

"And you look regal," Rohan commented.

Jafar smiled. He did look regal. He looked *ready* for the new life he was making for himself. He could almost feel the rubies weighing deliciously in his pocket. Control just within reach. He could almost smell the ink of the secrets etched for eternity within the archive's walls. Knowledge just within reach.

"Shall we?" he asked. *Shall we venture to the House of Wisdom, where I'll distract you?*

"I suppose so," Rohan replied.

"Yeah, yeah. I'll just fly in naked, I guess!" Iago groused, and flapped after them.

Anticipation thrummed through Jafar's veins as the sun rose fierce and bright, eager to witness all that was about to happen. They detoured around the bazaar, wary of any guards who might recognize them, and passed a bathhouse, finally coming upon the path leading to the palace grounds. With every step, the palace grew larger and larger, and soon, he saw the House of Wisdom just beyond it.

When they reached the top of the incline, Jafar turned, facing the rest of Maghriz. From here, the kingdom unfurled like the petals of a rose arranged with beautiful precision, and unlike many places, it didn't darken with decay the farther out from the city one went. As evidenced by the bazaar they'd seen at the outskirts of the capital city—it didn't reek of a place left to rot, it didn't look abandoned. Even the dark alleys between streets beckoned with the promise of shade, not a lurking foe.

Jafar and Rohan stopped at a crossroads and a sign. A guard stood beside it, watching them with stoic features. An arrow pointing to the left said *Grand Palace*, and another pointed to the right, saying *House of Wisdom*. Jafar's pulse quickened. He nodded at the guard and carried forward on the mostly barren road. The few people present were either deep in hushed conversation or rushing past with their heads bowed low.

There were, however, a great many guards.

"Stop fidgeting," Jafar said. "I can *hear* your fingers twiddling."

"There's so many of them," Rohan said beside him.

"Because we're near a palace," Iago deadpanned. He was a welcome weight on Jafar's shoulder today. Strangely comforting.

Jafar nodded. "The *Maghrizi* palace at that."

"I guess I'd hoped a library wouldn't be as patrolled. Are you sure we can walk in through the front door?" Rohan asked.

"I have more faith in my ability to charm than in my ability to sneak through a window of the palace's neighbor."

The caliph's house was one thing. A library as lauded as the Maghrizi palace? Jafar's pulse raced even faster. He knew his limits.

Jafar looked behind them to where the sands swirled

along the path leading to the palace. It was a lot less vibrant than he had anticipated. A lot quieter. The silence was eerie, filled with a sense of foreboding. Mourning, almost.

Just as he was about to turn back, he saw a young woman with midnight hair and tantalizing curves crossing into the walled gardens behind the palace. There was something about her bold gait that made it hard not to stare.

"Something feels wrong about that place," Rohan said, picking up on what Jafar had been thinking before he'd gotten distracted.

Right. Focus.

"I know," Jafar replied, facing the House of Wisdom again. "It feels like someone's dead."

The very air reeked of it. He hadn't shared with Rohan what he'd learned from the caravan leader, mostly because he wasn't certain it was true, but also because Rohan would be even more hesitant to go through with the plan.

Rohan paused midstep. "Then this is probably not a good time."

Like that.

"Relax, brother," Jafar said, glancing back to the palace again. The girl was gone. "Gaze to the oasis. We're going to the House of Wisdom, not the palace. And we need that lamp, remember?"

That was what made Rohan immediately relax, and for once, Jafar was more relieved than guilty. Rohan had always trusted him. Enough that he had followed Jafar across the cruel sands and braved the perilous seas. Eh, perhaps he ought to feel a little bad, but he was too excited at the moment.

A pair of guards were stationed at the intricate archway ahead. Beyond them, an enclosed walkway meandered to a towering structure, welcoming and imposing at once. The House of Wisdom. Its large domes sharpened to spears cutting through the clouds, and wide windows were set with panes of glass telling a tale of their own.

"Smile," Jafar said.

Rohan started to protest.

"Don't think, *smile*," Jafar insisted.

Rohan smiled his innocent, boyish smile, and as Jafar expected, the guard on the right softened.

"Marhaba," the man said.

"Shukrun," Rohan replied with just as much ease. Jafar hadn't expected *that* to come so easily when a smile couldn't.

He continued without breaking stride, compelling Rohan to do the same. The guards said nothing more, returning to their quiet conversation as if nothing were amiss.

Not that anything *was* amiss.

"See? That wasn't so hard now, was it?" Jafar asked. Rohan rolled his eyes.

The walkway was wide and airy, columns holding up a roof of stone latticed with the sky and its scattered clouds. Potted palms swayed in the breeze, corridors branching off to various doorways, all of them connected to the House of Wisdom.

"The sky is brighter here," Rohan said.

"The absence of smoke will create such a thing," Jafar said.

"So will not having an old man shoving stale crackers down your throat all the time," Iago added.

Rohan's eyes dropped to the worn leather of his sandals and the ornate stones beneath them, no doubt slipping into a memory he had no reason to dwell upon.

"That was our father. Have a little respect," Jafar said, and Iago lifted a brow at him, but Rohan cracked a wistful smile. *Success,* Jafar thought.

They turned the corner. Dust gritted their footfalls. The air turned drier and warmer as the sun shook off the dregs of her slumber. The doors to the renowned House of Wisdom approached, and Jafar tightened his fingers around the scraps in his pocket.

Rohan released a slow breath. "For the lamp. For Baba."

Jafar couldn't bring himself to lie. Especially not with the way Iago was looking at him.

The House of Wisdom had been constructed with the sun in mind. The rising rays painted the stone in gold, sand glittering like embers in the wind. When they cleared the glare of the sun, it was to find a guard in white robes standing before a pair of massive carved double doors.

Jafar swallowed his anxiety and straightened his shoulders.

"That's a very pointy weapon for a man guarding books," Iago remarked.

Books that had the power to change the world.

"Remember the plan," Jafar whispered.

Rohan drew a shaky breath and nodded.

"State your business," said the guard, spear glinting.

"We're House of Wisdom acolytes," Rohan said in a voice much more believable than Jafar had expected.

The guard laughed. "Every street rat from here to Agrabah would say the same."

Iago ruffled his feathers. Jafar soured at the words, fighting a wave of anger when Rohan flinched. *Rat.* Jafar's hands itched, something feral coming over him, but he was the elder, the first. He couldn't allow his emotions to best him.

He took the slightest step forward. "Do we appear to be rats, *guard*?"

The guard swept a better look down their clothes: the finely embossed sashes around their middles, neatly hemmed robes, supple leather for their gauntlets. It was only their sandals they hadn't been able to spruce up, but no one would look that far.

Except this guard did.

He glanced from Rohan's feet to Jafar's, brow wrinkling. Iago's talons tightened. Jafar homed in on the guard's every move: the way his mouth straightened and his fingers tightened around the spear, a decision settling into his shoulders.

Jafar held his breath. A whine was slithering up Rohan's bare throat. The guard looked up and licked his lips, setting Jafar's teeth on edge.

"You two have had quite a long journey," he said at last.

Jafar exhaled long and slow, but he couldn't let his relief show. "And you're making it much longer."

"Yes, yes—of course." The guard tapped the ground with his spear. "If you can hand me your scholarship, you'll be on your way."

Jafar stilled. This was it. He supposed he had hoped they would be allowed inside before he was asked for proof. Somewhere such as a receiving room, so that he could put a little distance between himself and Rohan before opening his mouth.

Rohan beat him to it. "We journeyed—"

Iago leaped to Rohan's shoulder and shoved a wing over his face, muffling the rest of his response.

The parrot's words from before were thunder in Jafar's ears. He needed access; he couldn't set off the guard. He needed his brother; he couldn't set off Rohan.

Jafar reached for his pocket and then paused, reaching for another, pretending to search for the scholarship in a way that said he was oh so certain he had pocketed it but had clearly misplaced it in all the excitement.

"Hmm. See, I applied for admission about eight weeks ago," Jafar said, straddling that line of being confident yet humble. Honesty was a good way to begin, wasn't it? He continued searching, and his heart skipped a beat when he brushed against the torn scraps of his scholarship.

A last resort, he told himself.

The guard narrowed his eyes. The breeze carried the din of the early crowds flooding the bazaar from just beyond, further cementing the quiet of the House of Wisdom, the otherworldliness.

"As did thousands of others," the guard said slowly.

It wasn't the time and place, but learning that he had succeeded in being accepted from a pool of thousands sent his spirits soaring—and quickly flaring with rage as he remembered, yet again, what his father had tried to steal from him.

Which made it all the more imperative that he get inside.

"I'm sorry, I seem to have misplaced my acceptance letter. Do you have records?" Jafar asked. At this point, it would feel ignoble to pull out the shreds. Who ripped up a scholarship? Who disrespected the written word in such a way? It couldn't even be brushed off as a mistake. The shreds were deliberately created.

The guard did not look pleased.

"I wrote about improving routes used for trade and transport. Incorporating the use of reeds—"

"To keep goods fresh?" the guard finished, his demeanor shifting from irritated and annoyed to piqued and . . . excited? The change was instant, in the blink of an eye. Jafar glanced behind him, sure the guard's zeal was directed at someone else. "You're the one who came up with the idea?"

"You know of it?" Jafar asked slowly.

The guard laughed and dipped his head. "Guards aren't typically a part of the application process, but it was the talk of the staff! Brilliant idea, truly. Jamal, isn't it? No, no, that isn't right. Jafar!"

Jafar's eyes widened and he nodded, taken aback by the guard's enthusiasm. He'd never experienced anything like this before. He looked over with a stupid goofy smile to find a shadow crossing Rohan's face and a regretful expression on Iago's.

I told you so, Iago's look said.

It sent a zing through Jafar's heart, but he ignored it. He wouldn't allow himself this confusion. This befuddlement. Not when he finally had a reason to feel proud of himself.

"Yes, I am Jafar," he said.

The guard laughed uneasily. "I'm certain, but I'm also good at my job and must verify that you really are you. I'll need other details from your application. Your age, full name."

As Jafar listed out the details, that he was nineteen years old and that his full name was Jafar ibn Ali al-Abbad, he also found himself slipping into an explanation. ". . . because the village of Ghurub is so far from here. It was a long journey with no shortage of chaos."

The guard laughed again, this time in understanding. "I do not doubt it! This is precisely what I needed, though, as I know for a fact that you were accepted. Why, you're all but a prince within these walls."

From street rat to prince in a matter of one conversation.

The doors opened with a deafening groan, a glorious sound, somehow symbolic of the journey it had taken Jafar to reach the grand entryway. "Right this way."

They entered a hall, their footsteps echoing on the dark tiles. A word was painted in calligraphy over and over on the walls, scribed in a pattern that flowed from one end to the other: *ilm. Knowledge, indeed,* Jafar thought, reminding himself to breathe.

The guard glanced at Rohan. "You're the brother he mentioned, aren't you?"

Rohan gave an embarrassed shrug, as if he hadn't known he was in the application. Which he hadn't.

"It was quite the essay," the guard said with a tight smile. His gaze darted between Jafar and Rohan. "But unfortunately, apprenticeship was only granted to Jafar, and that doesn't extend—"

"He's only visiting," Jafar said, leaving no room for discussion. "He didn't want me to travel on my own, especially across the sea. Once I'm settled, he'll return back to our village."

The guard didn't seem too pleased but finally obliged,

turning to lead them through. "If it was up to me, he'd be allowed to stay as long as he would like, but rules are in place for a reason." He glanced back and paused at the sight of Iago hopping onto Jafar's shoulder. "Now pets, I'm afraid, are not allowed inside the premises at all."

"Oh, the bird won't be apprenticing," Jafar said, and nearly flung Iago off when he tensed up, prepared to protest Jafar's calling him a bird.

All the guard ever did was laugh uneasily.

"I'm aware," the guard said, "but pets aren't allowed because they're animals, not—"

"My *pet* is pertinent to my work," Jafar said tersely.

The guard looked from Jafar to Rohan to Iago and back, his brow and mustache furrowing in tandem. Jafar recognized the pause, the way his lip twisted, just barely. He saw the unrefined village in them, the destitution from whence they'd come.

And then, the guard laughed yet again.

"What am I thinking?" he asked. "You of all people understand the importance of keeping history safe. I know you'll keep an eye on her. She is a beauty, by the way."

Iago straightened. "I'm a—"

Jafar squeezed his beak shut, hiding the move with a quick stroke down his head and neck and a flitted smile. Iago shuddered.

"Thank you," Jafar said, holding back a shudder of his own.

And then, at last, the guard led them inside.

Jafar's pulse pounded in his ears, thrummed in the palms of his hands. Excitement ramped up with each step, the guard an amplifier. The hall opened to a wide foyer with a table in its center, ebony dark and rich, carved by a careful hand.

Beyond it was a sight to behold. The floor was a map of the known world, routes twisting like fissures in the earth, painted in bronze upon tiles of earthy, glossy stone. Shelves fanned out, reaching into the shadowed ceiling, made to look as if they rose up forever, a reminder that what the written word promised was just as limitless. He saw towers of scrolls and plaques of bronze. He tried not to gape at the countless artifacts housed in cases, each one displayed on a stone plinth. He even caught a glimpse of the famed laboratory.

"I find it funny, however," the guard said, slicing into Jafar's awe. "I recall a messenger picked up your scholarship about three weeks ago. We expected you a lot sooner."

There were far too many emotions rolling through him. To know that he could have been here, witnessing this magnificence and not sitting idle in the shadows of the broom closet, made his anger thrash anew.

"Our village is a long ways from here, remember?" Rohan

said. Jafar glanced at him. Not a word all this time, but when it came to defending Baba, Rohan leaped at the chance.

Again, Iago gave Jafar a look that said *I told you so*.

"Indeed," the guard said, pausing in the foyer. "The head librarian has not arrived yet, but I will send for him immediately. He'll proceed with initiation and give you a tour of the library and your lodgings at the back of the building. In the meantime, stay here. Soon you'll be free to peruse the collections that are now yours."

With that, he turned and left.

"That's it?" Jafar asked, aghast, but the guard was gone, the doors groaning behind him.

"What's it?" Rohan asked tightly. He was a completely different boy from this morning, or even yesterday atop the roof.

"He left us here unattended," Jafar said. "No escort, no safety measures. We can do as we wish."

"First of all, the guy was clearly a fan," Iago said, hopping off his shoulder to poke around. "And second of all, who wants to steal books?"

"Third of all, he told you to stay put until the head librarian arrives," Rohan pointed out.

Jafar supposed they were right. The guard trusted him. But as quickly as the concern had come, it left. Jafar was here, *here!* Standing in the House of Wisdom. Soft murmurs trickled from the stacks, scritching pens in the hands of scribes. There were pockets built into the walls where cushions were arranged with slates to prop on a lap and use as a desk. He even smelled fresh coffee.

The atmosphere was hushed, the walls enveloping a space of perpetual awe. He ignored the guard's instructions and made his way past the front desk to the shelves. Along with the ones that disappeared into the shadowed ceiling, there were short bookcases, too, round tables stacked with resources waiting to be cataloged, and scrolls that had no place as yet.

Jafar didn't know where to begin.

Yes, you do. The House of Wisdom might have recognized his worth, but his goal was still more important: he needed to secure those rubies. Then he would take a look through the laboratory and proceed with his dive into alchemy. And then—

"Where do you think we'll find what we need for the golden scarab?" Rohan asked, not at all fazed by the wonder around them.

Jafar held back his sigh and studied the markers hammered into every few shelves. "Lore, perhaps. It could also be under Artifacts over there." Which was conveniently located beside the section titled Al-Kimiya. *Alchemy.* "We can split up—I want to check out the laboratory later, but I'll head to Artifacts."

"Shouldn't we wait for the head librarian?" Rohan asked.

Jafar pursed his lips and pulled a grin. "No."

Rohan nodded, gave him a smile that was as lackluster as meals with Baba, and walked away.

Jafar felt his brow furrow, and for a moment, he could only stand still as a heavy, unwelcome sorrow thrummed through his bloodstream. He'd been worried Rohan would question him and he'd have to shy away from a response, but this was somehow worse. This sadness was foreign, a rare feeling. Baba had kept him bubbling with other emotions: anger, dismay, the overwhelming desire to be free of that place.

And now here he was, excited, jubilant, victorious—and lonely.

"Get a load of this place, huh?" Iago said, swooping closer and tugging at his attention. "It's huge."

That pulled a smile out of Jafar. An understatement, but some appreciation at least. "Indeed."

"So why are you just standing there?" Iago asked.

"You're welcome to hunt around for anything that might give you the answers you need about your . . . predicament," Jafar said. "Since you can read."

Iago deadpanned a laugh. "Very funny, Jafar. But if it's all right with you, I'll stick around a little longer."

Jafar lifted a brow. "To spy?"

"For whom? Your baba?" Iago asked, a note of betrayal in his tone. "Can a parrot not be excited for your new adventure?

I just don't think I'm ready to go soul-searching yet. Besides, I know you've got no interest in that genie lamp."

Again, the words pulled a genuine smile out of Jafar. He was surprised that Iago had noticed.

"What makes you think that?" Jafar asked.

"You were a little heavy-handed when you delivered your pitch to your brother," Iago said. "I'm not so easily distracted, though. So? What are we really here for?"

Jafar appreciated good perception. "We're searching for a pair of rubies."

Iago dropped to Jafar's shoulder. "Never took you for a guy who wears earrings."

"Oh, I have something else in mind," Jafar replied, lips curling in a wicked smile. Iago took flight again, and the two of them passed display case after display case, glass cubes presenting the most unexpected of artifacts, from shimmering gold cuffs to a headdress that seemed to change color as Jafar stared at its rich fabric. "The stories say that the rubies were gathered just like the rest of these artifacts and stored in the House of Wisdom, and judging by the way these are arranged, someone likes to organize by color."

"Too bad the head librarian isn't here to lead us to it," Iago said, reading each of the little placards with interest. He fluttered higher. "Hey, there's a line of pink stuff that way."

He immediately dove back down with a hurried whisper. "And someone's over there."

Footsteps tiptoed on the other side of the shelves. They were trying to be quiet—and not in the way warranted by a library.

"It's not Rohan," Iago said.

Jafar held a finger to his lips, pressing against the shelves and creeping ahead with a terrible, sinking feeling. Someone else was getting to his rubies first. He knew it in his bones.

He rounded the bookcase.

It was a woman. Regal and tall, a cloak on her shoulders. Gray streaked her dark hair. Nothing about her suggested a life dedicated to reading and befriending the written word. The glass case in front of her was empty, as Jafar had feared. But none of this made sense. She didn't look like a thief—she was dressed for attention, not obscurity.

Iago knocked into a vase, and Jafar caught it before it crashed to the floor.

Oops, Iago mouthed.

And the woman whirled. Jafar froze. Her features were delicate, with a sorrow carved into the bow of her lip. She truly was dressed in finery. Dainty cuts of topaz were threaded throughout her gown, sharp facets catching the library's warm light. Fine gold chains shimmered from her cloak, which was as dark as Jafar's robes. He saw a glint of scarlet red in her hands before she tightened her fist and pulled her hands behind her back. His rubies. For a moment, she looked as if she recognized him before her gaze drifted to a figure behind him.

Jafar looked back to find a man in sapphire-blue robes, his dark eyes piercing Jafar as if he'd seen a ghost.

He looked to the woman. "Sultana?"

Iago squawked. *Sultana?* Jafar dropped to his knees, his heart launching into his throat.

The queen of Maghriz had stolen his rubies.

13

ROHAN

Rohan should have been happy to shed the anxious dread that had piled on his shoulders. He was finally on his way to bringing Baba back from the dead. But when that guard had praised Jafar and Jafar had smiled, his eyes glowing red from the sun reflecting off the mosaicked glass, as if he'd never known praise before, Rohan had felt . . . odd.

He wondered what Jafar had written about him in his application. Could that have been one reason the House of Wisdom had even accepted him?

The shelves towered, daunting and dull. Every spine looked the same, a drab stack of papyrus shoved between two covers with a title stamped into the linen. How was he to find anything related to the golden scarab without falling asleep? How did Jafar find any of this exciting?

He could only hope his brother would find what they needed first, sparing Rohan the trouble. *As he always does*.

Iago's annoying laugh cut through the library's hushed silence. He hated that parrot.

Rohan recognized many of the names in the Lore section from Mama's tales, from the Dendan to the Ebony Horse. He smiled when he spied an account of a magical carpet that was as trusty as a steed and capable of soaring through the skies. He flitted from memory to memory, back in that cocoon of magic Mama would weave around him, transporting him away for just a moment. Shielding him from the world.

As Jafar did now.

Contrite, Rohan traced the ornate rug with the toe of his sandal. He was witnessing Jafar's dream come true and had decided to be bitter about it. Someone had praised his brother's intellect, and he'd decided to grouse.

He was behaving like Baba just then, and he despised himself for it. What was the point of finding the golden scarab and tracking down the genie and making a wish to not only return Baba to life but *change* him, when Rohan was becoming just like him?

The golden scarab could wait. Rohan had a brother to

celebrate. But when he crossed to the other side of the House of Wisdom, Jafar and Iago weren't reading or browsing the shelves as he had been.

They were being escorted away.

14

JAFAR

Jafar gave the man in the sapphire-blue robes his name but received no excitement or recognition. If they didn't know him as the boy who had stirred the House of Wisdom with his application, why *were* they treating him as though they knew him?

"Follow us," the man said, and Jafar began to refuse before he saw the light bounce off the rubies one last time as the Sultana slipped them into her dress pocket. He needed those rubies. Obeying the man might be the only way to retrieve them. "Come, Sultana."

The Sultana nodded, and though Jafar recognized the man as her royal vizier, he appeared to be more like the queen's keeper. Jafar had never before considered that though a king or queen might seem supreme, someone else might pull the strings from the shadows.

It was an interesting distribution of power, one it seemed the vizier enjoyed, for there was cunning in the man's dark gaze, a sternness about him that Jafar couldn't tell if it was being used for the Sultana, or against her.

"Where are you taking me?" Jafar asked.

The royal vizier looked back at him, his lips pressed into a thin, hard line. "The palace."

He had only just arrived at the House of Wisdom and didn't want to leave just yet. He certainly never thought he'd be escorted away by the queen of Maghriz and her royal vizier. Or find himself at the whim of another man old enough to be his father, but he needed those rubies.

"You're not really going to let them order us around, are you?" Iago snapped in his ear.

"I am indeed," Jafar said with a sigh.

"Why I oughta—" Iago began grumbling beneath his breath, but took no initiative to leave. Jafar hid a smile.

He steeled himself with a heavy inhale, and as the two of them followed the Sultana and the man in the sapphire-blue robes toward the great doors of the House of Wisdom, movement caught his eye. Rohan! He was emerging from the shelves.

"Wait!" Jafar said, albeit a little too loudly. Iago cleared his throat. Jafar swallowed. It wasn't every day one met a queen, let alone the queen of *Maghriz*.

Both she and her vizier halted and followed his gaze to Rohan.

"There are two of you?" the vizier asked, sounding perplexed.

"He's my brother," Jafar said, confused. "Can he visit the palace as well?"

He didn't know why he was being escorted to the palace, but that was the most neutral way to put it. He didn't think he was in trouble. After they'd stumbled upon him and stared like he was a dead man returned, the Sultana had said a single word.

Him.

And the vizier had understood exactly what she'd meant.

At Jafar's question now, the vizier deferred to the Sultana, who studied both Rohan and Jafar with a furrow in her brow. A sorrow, he wanted to guess. She wasn't wholly present, as if part of her had been left behind and was yet to catch up. He didn't fully know what was happening, but he wanted the rubies and Rohan wanted the genie.

And until Jafar retrieved the rubies, he couldn't risk Rohan's learning what he needed to about the golden scarab and dragging them away to find the two halves.

The Sultana pulled her royal vizier behind one of the round tables with precariously stacked scrolls. Her voice was low, but Jafar had grown up in the silence of Baba's presence. His hearing was better than most.

"We will have our pick," she said to him.

The vizier didn't seem so certain. "People will know, Your Highness."

The Sultana shook her head. "It's been years."

Iago leaned closer to Jafar's ear. "I can't tell if they're talking about cooking us up, or the rubies you're sure she stole."

"I can't, either," Jafar said, and beckoned Rohan closer.

"Now's our chance to make a run for it, then," Iago replied.

"No," Jafar said. "Not without the—"

"The whereabouts of the golden scarab," Rohan finished, overhearing them. Jafar gave him a tight smile. "So why are we trying to visit the palace?"

"Because we can't say no to the queen," Jafar answered matter-of-factly, touching the back of his neck.

Rohan's eyes widened. "That's the Sultana of Maghriz?"

"Yes, it is," the Sultana replied, returning to them. She laughed at his shock. "And I hear from your brother that the two of you traveled long and far to reach us. Please, allow me to properly welcome you to my kingdom."

Rohan opened his mouth to protest.

"Ah," she said, stopping him with a raised hand. "It's impolite to refuse."

Jafar held very still. He couldn't place her tone, but he was certain a threat was to follow.

It did not come.

She turned and glided away in the direction of the exit, in the direction of the Maghrizi palace, her cloak stretching a dark reflection in the gloss of the wide tiles. It looked like an oasis, one Jafar wasn't certain he should follow, but he understood: she was a queen, and the threat was implied. They had no choice. He stared after her, a nervous Rohan beside him.

For the rubies, Jafar tried to convince himself. The only difference between the moment he'd met the Sultana and now was the illusion that he *had* a choice.

"Look at the bright side," Iago said. "At least the two of you are dressed the part."

15

ROHAN

That eerie silence grew louder and louder as Rohan and Jafar neared the palace. That sense of mourning settled over him like rare, sticky heat. He remembered what Jafar had said: it felt as if someone was dead.

Rohan knew how that felt. He'd experienced it twice. Once when he'd found Mama's body cold and unmoving on the kitchen floor, and again when he'd lost his house, his father, and his life in one fell swoop.

"You find it odd that I insist upon your visit," the Sultana said, glancing back at them. The sunlight glinted off the lemon-drop jewels that dangled from her ears. Her azure gown was as bright as the sky, but it only served to make her look paler. Sadder, somehow.

Rohan stumbled on a reply.

"Admittedly, yes," Jafar said. He possessed an innate charisma. Rohan thought again how his brother had been born to the wrong class, even if Baba's later riches had eventually raised them higher. He wasn't meant to be poor or even middle class. He was destined for greater things. He could call himself a prince in the streets, and no one would question it—the guard earlier had said as much.

The Sultana smiled. "It's been long since we've had such young acolytes. The world is not as it used to be."

Her gaze darkened, or perhaps that was the sun disappearing from view when they stepped under the shade of the palace entrance. They climbed the low, crescent-shaped staircase that led to a pair of wide, dark wooden doors that must have taken months and skillful talent to carve.

The guards pushed them open as the four of them neared. The Sultana didn't even pause her stride as she entered, her royal vizier following her inside like a loyal tiger, Jafar and Rohan at their heels.

They passed an exquisite foyer, in the center of which was a large plant that looked as if it held a significance Rohan didn't understand. The entirety of the palace oozed extravagance, and not in a lavish, overstated way. It was subtle, well done. Even the air here tasted different, like magic.

The Sultana and her vizier didn't pause, carrying on to another pair of doors that guards leaped forward to open. Rohan felt important as he passed them, and tried not to gape as they entered the throne room. The floor lightened to polished alabaster, brilliant and bright. A massive bronze throne sat at the other end, bejeweled in rubies, pearls, and other gems Rohan had never seen before. He was in awe but also torn between wanting to give in to this unexpected adventure and wanting to return to his search for the golden scarab.

Notes of citrus and clove filled his lungs, a blend that reminded him of those first promising drops of rain on the sun-scorched sands, but the scent felt off. Wrong. As if they were trying to mask something with it.

"Here we are," the Sultana said, sinking into her throne. There were others in the room, more advisors who didn't seem to hold the same status at the royal vizier, and guards stationed by every elaborately carved window. "Welcome to my palace."

Her tone was less queenly now, more battered and bruised. She looked at Jafar in a way that was almost yearning, and Rohan couldn't fathom why. It was an odd expression, as if they were kin. As if she were his mother.

"You will be fed and led to your rooms, and—"

"Rooms?" Jafar asked, cutting her short.

Everyone seemed to hold their breath at the interruption. Rohan had heard one too many stories from Mama about royalty who had beheaded commoners for less, and a fresh sweat broke out along his brow.

"Forgive us, Your Highness," Jafar quickly added, "but I must say that we are not here to stay."

The Sultana tilted her head. "You'll turn down an offer to stay in a palace? To live as princes?"

Jafar had stiffened. Rohan knew that stance and expression well: he wanted to pull Rohan behind him, but the Sultana had just offered to let them live as princes, not threatened to kill them.

"The head librarian is expecting me," Jafar said, his voice tight.

"And I'll send word of your new arrangements. You will no longer be a traditional apprentice of the House of Wisdom."

Jafar was still stiff, that dreaded darkness shrouding his gaze, his brows dropping low. "All of this at what cost?"

His pride could get them killed one day.

"What my brother means to say, Sultana," Rohan started, "is that we can't understand why such a generous offer would be presented to us, a pair of village boys." He smiled. "And a parrot."

"Ah, he speaks," the Sultana said, turning her scrutiny to Rohan. "You sound like a boy accustomed to being a diplomat."

Mama had always been the diplomat. Rohan had never

considered that after her death, he had taken her place. He was the one who would step between Baba and Jafar, persuading Jafar to relent, begging Baba to forgive. He had only a moment to dwell on that fact before the weight of the eyes in the room threatened to crush him. Now would have been a good time to disappear into the stone beneath his feet. Was he supposed to respond? He didn't know. Expectations were rarely ever placed on him.

The Sultana clucked her tongue and waved to the royal vizier, sparing him the trouble, and Rohan realized he was getting a glimpse of what she was like as queen. "Harun, take them away. I have other matters to attend to."

16

JAFAR

The royal vizier took Jafar and Rohan to a hall lit with sconces secured at intervals, each flicker illuminating the rich carvings along the stone walls. In the room's center was a table with ornate legs and a wide surface, and it was full of food. Columns formed a sort of perimeter around the central part of the hall, darkening it and giving the illusion of a more intimate setting, but light from the hall's windows found its way between the columns, dousing the food in golden warmth.

The smells were rich and layered, spices balanced just right with the bases they accentuated. There were lamb ribs slathered in the seven-spice blend known as baharat, hummus bejeweled with tart sumac, rice bright with saffron. Jafar, unfortunately, knew food. He'd been there in Mama's kitchen, helping her cook, knowing what spice complemented what vegetable or meat.

"Our cuisine is unlike what you're used to," Harun said, as if he could read Jafar's thoughts. The man eyed them with disgust and curiosity, a strange combination.

Curiosity was fine, but Jafar wouldn't allow him to think of them as lesser. He gave Harun a tight smile. "A bribe is a bribe and food is food."

With another pinched look in Jafar's direction, Harun turned and glided out of the room.

"He wears those robes so they don't need a maid to dust the place," Iago snarked.

Jafar snorted. They did look like they needed hemming.

"Why would you say that to him?" Rohan hissed.

Jafar gestured to the array of food that had been spread *just* for them. "Are you not seeing what I'm seeing? I'd be less concerned if the food were poisoned."

Iago dropped a falafel midchew.

Rohan stiffened. "Could it—"

"No, it's not," Jafar replied with a sigh. The Sultana was far too interested in them to get rid of them. Something else was at play here. Rohan's stomach gurgled, and Jafar sat down on a dark cushion threaded with Maghrizi blue so he'd follow suit.

"I didn't realize how hungry I was," Rohan said, sitting down beside him.

"Eat up, then," Jafar said. He had yet to tell Rohan about what he'd learned from the caravan leader: that the prince of Maghriz was likely dead. It hadn't seemed important at the time, but everything had changed in the past hour.

Now they were to *live* in the palace. Almost like princes. *Maybe* like princes. For reasons still unknown. Jafar wondered if there was a correlation there, but he was too frazzled to see it.

All he knew was that he needed those rubies, and that Rohan was looking at him like it was his fault they hadn't found the golden scarab yet.

"We'll return to the House of Wisdom once we are situated," Jafar promised. "I have no notion of what's to come."

Everything about this felt like he was under Baba's control again, and he had to shake his head more than once to remind himself that no, he was free, he was no longer trapped. But he didn't yet feel as though he could safely deny—and therefore *defy*—the Sultana any more than he had just attempted.

His appetite disappeared when his worries filled his belly, and he didn't hide a smug look when Harun returned and saw his untouched plate.

"Where to now?" Jafar asked, and Rohan dug his elbow into his side, but Jafar couldn't care less.

Harun ignored him and turned for them to follow. As

Rohan licked pomegranate molasses off his fingers, Iago snatched up one last lauzinaj in his beak, rose-sweet syrup dripping down his chin. He bit into it as discreetly as he could—which was not at all, considering its many thin layers of flaky pastry—before hopping back on Jafar's shoulder. It took everything in Jafar not to fling him and his sticky feathers off.

As much as Jafar would have liked to demand answers from Harun, he didn't want the royal vizier mistaking his curiosity for fear, and so he kept quiet. After a winding walk through the halls of the palace, Harun paused before a door, waiting for a guard to open it even though it would have taken him about the same amount of time to do so himself.

"Here are your quarters," the royal vizier said, brandishing a hand toward the open door. "I'm certain you're accustomed to sharing, but there are separate bedrooms."

Condescension oozed from his tone, and Jafar loathed the way he'd said "accustomed to sharing" with the assumption that they were poor and had huddled in a hut. He looked the royal vizier straight in the eye, raising a single brow. He wouldn't even bother talking to him. Iago cleared his throat imperiously.

"Thank you," Rohan said, squeezing between them and heading inside. When he stepped out of Harun's line of sight, he pulled a face bidding Jafar not to lash out.

Jafar worked his jaw. *Fine.*

He walked past the vizier and closed the door behind him. The antechamber comprised a short hall with carved tables against the walls, cushioned seating with a collection of pillows beneath sconces, and doors on either side leading to matching bedrooms, with a third door leading to a bath at the end of the hall.

"And thank *you*," Rohan huffed, slumping back against the wall. "First you disrespect the Sultana in her own throne room, then irk that man. Are you trying to get us killed?"

Jafar exhaled. He remembered Rohan's being overly cautious after Mama had died, too. Death came with a shroud, an aura of foreboding that blanketed the ones it left behind. They might have survived the fire that took Baba, but nothing could save them from the reminder of how fragile life truly was.

"We're safe," Jafar said. "I'm not callous, but I won't allow them to order us around when we owe them no allegiance."

"He has a point," Iago said.

"Oh, don't run your mouth," Rohan snapped.

Iago mimicked him and hopped off Jafar's shoulder, flapping around the antechamber and ducking his head into the rooms. Jafar did the same. Each of their beds was big enough for four, the cushions piled upon them enough for a family back in Ghurub. The bath smelled fresh and clean, and looked just as tidy.

"At least these are rooms meant for guests and not

servants," Jafar said. "That's promising. We should probably settle in."

Rohan didn't move. "I don't—"

A knock sounded at the door.

Jafar glanced at Rohan, ignoring a waver of uncertainty before he answered it. The Sultana stood on the other side.

"I am thrilled you decided to stay," she said, as if she'd given them much of a choice.

She stepped inside, setting a plate of pistachio-topped cookies and garnished dates on the sideboard table. Rohan's eyes lit up.

"And what do you think of the House of Wisdom?" she asked.

"I barely had time to explore," Jafar said, and then pursed his lips. He still needed his rubies, and for that, he needed to be more . . . what had the Sultana called Rohan? Diplomatic. "But I don't think I can put my feelings into words."

He could not wait to return, once he'd picked the Sultana's pockets and secured the rubies. He didn't know how, exactly, he'd overcome the Sultana's desire to keep them here, but that was a problem for future him.

"I feel the same. We are nothing without the written word," the Sultana agreed, giving him a smile that said she appreciated his attempt at being civil.

"You say that with sadness," Jafar observed. Trepidation crept into his heart. He could only hope the House of

Wisdom's collection hadn't been promised to another kingdom in some political struggle. He'd only just arrived, and their wing on alchemy was large.

"Did you know that the process of making paper is a secret that could put us all at war?" the Sultana asked.

Rohan looked confused. "I thought paper came from the South."

"That's papyrus," Jafar replied before she could. Rohan's jaw flickered in annoyance, and he wasn't certain why.

The Sultana looked impressed. "Indeed so. And there is only so much one can do with papyrus in this day and age. The people of a kingdom far east are the only ones who know how to make paper, and they hold the world in a vise because of it." She laughed. "Can you imagine? We bow to them because of paper. Something we don't even see as necessary to live." Her gaze darkened. "But no secret can be kept forever. I'm close, I know it."

It seemed like information she wanted them to be aware of, but Jafar didn't understand how any of this pertained to either him or Rohan.

"Close to uncovering the secret?" Jafar asked.

She nodded and leaned toward them, lowering her voice with a lopsided smile. "I have a prisoner, and he'll break soon enough."

The words sent a chill down Jafar's spine. She smiled and

spoke and behaved like she could do no harm. She acted, in every respect, like a doting mother.

One who was ready to "break" a man.

"Is he from the East?" Jafar asked. He'd never met anyone from so far away.

The Sultana shook her head. "A Maghrizi traveler, if you can believe that. We're under the assumption that he picked up the secret during his voyage."

"Why are you doing this?" Rohan asked, harsh and sudden. "Giving us rooms; letting us walk about like we live here—why?"

Jafar went still as the Sultana turned to his brother.

"You do live here now," the Sultana said, tilting her head. She paused a moment, as if contemplating her answer. "Maghriz isn't short on bright minds, but ambition is harder to come by. You two came from so far away for the knowledge the House of Wisdom holds. It would be a disservice to my kingdom to *not* allow you to stay here."

Something about the Sultana's words struck Jafar as strange. As if she was trying to butter them up with praise. Jafar loved to question everything—why the sky was said to be blue, why water was a commodity, why their father was so cunning and hateful—so not having answers was gnawing at his soul.

Get the rubies and you'll be free. Then he could even get her to stop talking in circles and tell them what she really wanted with him and Rohan. When the rubies were in his hand, he could simply ask, and people would answer. Truthfully. He could tell them to walk into the river, and they would.

"There is one condition, however," the Sultana said.

Rohan made a sound in his throat. Jafar braced himself.

"You are to shed your identities," she said.

For a moment, neither Jafar nor Rohan knew how to respond to the strange request.

"With respect, Sultana, *you* do not even know who we are," Jafar said.

"And so it will remain," the Sultana said. "If you are asked, you are neither your name nor your birthplace."

Jafar didn't know what to say to that. He had no ties to his past, not even to his name, but he was hesitant to make any promises to the Sultana. Not without knowing her motive.

He waited, hopeful she would leave and allow them to settle in. As much as he wanted to return to the House of Wisdom, standing within reach of a bed with fresh linens and cozy cushions was making his limbs lethargic, his mind slow.

The Sultana didn't press for an answer. "I'll leave you to rest, but don't forget: tell no one your names. We will talk again."

With that, she exited, instructing the guards at their door to escort them when required and to tend to their needs as if they were her sons and not a pair of waifs she had pulled from the shadows of the House of Wisdom.

Rohan whirled to Jafar. "How are you all right with this?"

"We're a walk from the House of Wisdom, exactly where we want to be," Jafar said.

"We should be lodging *in* the House of Wisdom," Rohan said.

"Funny, you weren't interested in the House of Wisdom at all earlier today," Jafar mused. "Nor did you seem as concerned when you were gobbling down food meant for royalty."

"That was before she threatened us," Rohan snapped.

Jafar was fully, wholly, painfully aware. He'd been cautious of the Sultana from the moment she'd set eyes on him and regarded him, well, differently. He dragged a foot along the plush rug. "Is this not the finest wool we've ever seen?"

Rohan growled. "We need to find the golden scarab, Jafar. We need to find that lamp and bring Baba back to life. Mama, too. We need to get back to the House of Wisdom right now."

Jafar tried, he really did. He tried to remain calm, to keep the ruse going. He tried to hold back, to not break his brother's heart, but at some point, one had to stop being a child and grow up. Rohan was all over the place, almost as finicky as Baba. One moment he wanted to find the genie lamp, the next he wanted nothing to do with its search. One moment he refused to let Jafar question the Sultana and happily gorged on her food, the next he was hissing in Jafar's ear for *not* questioning the queen—and then questioning her himself.

It appeared to Jafar that Rohan was more concerned with opposing Jafar than anything else. And Jafar decided he'd had enough.

"Did you want to bring Mama back so you could count the ridges in her spine?" Jafar asked. "See her mottled, dirt-dredged skull?"

Bile rose in his own throat at the words. Iago croaked and disappeared into one of the rooms. Rohan took a step back, disgust curling his upper lip, horror bright in his eyes.

"How could you?" he asked.

"It's the truth, Rohan," Jafar spat.

"What—no," Rohan breathed. "What do you mean?"

"Say we learn of the golden scarab's whereabouts. Say we find both halves and find the lamp and summon your genie. Say we wish Mama back to life—did you ever think about how that would work? She's been dead for more than a decade. She could very well rise out of her grave as she is. A soulless corpse."

Rohan was breathing hard and fast. "Then—then I'll wish her soul back."

"The lamp only offers so many wishes, Rohan."

"No," Rohan whispered again. "No, no, no. You said—"

"I said we could get our lives back. You decided the rest," Jafar said, the fight leaching out of him. His anger winnowed into nothing. This wasn't Baba. This wasn't one of Baba's advisors laughing in his face.

This was Rohan.

Jafar softened. It was easier without Iago here. "We can still—"

"Stop," Rohan hissed. "Stop spinning words in circles. Stop twisting things. Stop acting like a caged animal let loose simply because Baba isn't around to stop you anymore."

Jafar's laugh was mirthless, hiding his shock as best as he could. "I'm sorry I was trying to protect us."

"Us?" Rohan bit out.

"Us, Rohan," Jafar bit back. "I've been trying to do what's best for *us*. I'm sorry if being fed and housed in a palace is inadequate for you."

His brother said nothing, but his hurt was loud enough as he stormed into one of the bedrooms with one final look at Jafar and slammed the door closed.

17

ROHAN

Rohan pressed his back against the door and sank to the floor. The tile was cold beneath him, and the sun wasn't as hot anymore as the day neared its end. His brother had been lying to his face the entire time. And Rohan, worst of all, had followed him without question.

Now that the truth was out, Jafar hadn't even tried to apologize or explain, or to pretend. He'd spoken of their parents like someone would speak about glasses that had shattered or trinkets they'd bought in a shop full of a hundred others.

Rohan thought back to when the guard had praised Jafar for his application, and when Jafar had sent him to the section on Lore, saying he would look through the section on Artifacts. Right in front of the section titled Al-Kimiya.

Alchemy. The word transported him back to their house and their mother's stories that spoke of alchemy. And then, another recollection: their father, yelling and shouting and the word *al-kimiya*.

Rohan couldn't remember much of the conversation—up until he recalled the word now, he hadn't even known of the memory. What he did remember was Jafar's fascination with alchemy, even as it straddled the line of the dark arts. Was that what he had always intended to do? Come here and learn alchemy? Rohan should have realized it from the start. Jafar had never cared for their father. He wouldn't want to bring him back to life.

Jafar hadn't come here for the lamp.

Rohan ground his teeth. He didn't need Jafar. He didn't know if the genie could revive the dead, but it didn't matter now.

He was going to find the lamp anyway.

If only he weren't trapped in a palace. A strangled laugh tore out of him. *Of all the problems to have.* The room was spacious and luxurious. Rohan sank into a bed that was plusher than anything he'd ever felt before.

It made him feel lonely. Baba was gone, and he felt Mama's absence even more now that he had not a single possession to his name. Jafar had all but crushed his trust, and the Sultana's kindness was alarming. As alarming as the cavalier way in which she spoke of the prisoner kept somewhere in the palace.

But you're *not a prisoner.*

That was a welcome thought. He might have been trapped in the palace, but the Sultana had given them free rein *of* said palace. Rohan could explore as he pleased, without Jafar. Or better yet, he could find a way to cross over to the House of Wisdom and continue his search for the golden scarab. It was still on the palace grounds, after all.

Rohan eased the door open, listening for any sound of his brother or the ruffle of a parrot's feathers. He picked up one of the ghorayeba cookies from the platter the Sultana had brought them and bit down. The single pistachio in its center rolled between his teeth as buttery flakes melted on his tongue. The antechamber was quiet, and the door to Jafar's room was ajar. He peeked inside at the untouched bed and still-full pitcher of water on the low table beside it.

Jafar wasn't there.

Rohan opened the door to the palace hall, jumping at the sight of the guard standing beside it. The man stared down at him.

"Hello," Rohan said.

The man said and did nothing. *Well then.*

"Do you happen to know where my brother went?"

The guard shuffled, readjusting the menacing spear in his

fist. Rohan couldn't tell if the spear was meant to protect him or keep him in line.

"The House of Wisdom," the guard said.

Rohan bit back a growl. *So much for that plan.* He didn't want to see Jafar's face right now. He didn't want to hear his voice. Nor did he want to be alone when Jafar was out doing something.

He looked down the corridors outside their rooms. Somewhere, a fountain gurgled. A group of women giggled. The breeze whistled through the latticed windows, evening sunlight slipping in with it.

"Explore it is," Rohan said, with a nod at the guard.

18

JAFAR

"Can I talk now?" Iago asked as he and Jafar crossed the open sands to the House of Wisdom. Jafar was certain they were being watched in the palace, by Harun most likely, and he hadn't wanted Iago squawking about. Keeping the parrot in line was akin to trying to keep a child from a bag of dates. Endlessly futile.

Jafar turned his gaze to the sun, breathing in the warm sands and the fresh breeze. Before them, the House of Wisdom was still as breathtaking as the first time he'd seen it. Immense and vast, sheer power to behold.

"Go ahead," Jafar said.

"You sounded a little breathless there," Iago said with a tilt of his head.

Jafar glared at him. "Is that what you wanted to say? I'm going to start carrying around crackers to shove down your throat."

Iago scowled as the guard let them through with a nod, and Jafar paused to breathe it all in. That *smell*. Jafar wished he could inject it into his veins. He would kill for the smell of ink, for the preservation of the written word, for books. Rolls of papyrus were layered as delicately and beautifully as baklava beside books in every size and shape, worn covers humming a tune, enticing him to part their covers and hear their songs.

"I thought we already established that the Sultana has the rubies," Iago eventually said.

"We did," Jafar said. It was a struggle to keep his excitement from bubbling into his voice. "But who knows where she's keeping them now."

"Exactly," Iago said haltingly, not following his logic.

He couldn't waste time dawdling at the palace, especially with the Sultana being cagey and strange. Jafar didn't know what she wanted from him and Rohan, but he didn't intend to stick around long to find out.

"First, I want to take a look at something," Jafar said. "Then, we'll whip up a finder's spell."

He strode past the shelves to the western wing of the library, separated by a wide, ornate arch that led to something he had been as eager to see as the library itself: the laboratory.

The House of Wisdom was funded by the Maghrizi palace, and though much of their resources were clearly dedicated to the preservation of the many books and scrolls in the library, they did not scrimp here, either.

There were complex distillation sets and vials storing a multitude of gases, elixirs, and potions. Well-made tools hung from the walls, neat and orderly, above sheets of metal that could be sculpted however one required. Jafar suspected he'd be spending a good amount of time in here when he began dabbling in alchemy.

He almost laughed at the idea that was once so far out of reach.

"And where will you find your finder's spell?" Iago asked, grounding him.

Jafar made his way through the shelves. "In Alchemy."

"I see," Iago said with a note of trepidation. Jafar realized then that whatever had made Iago the way he was had to be related to alchemy. The study was innocent enough, but it was a narrow path, easy to veer off into the dark arts. And create something like a bird who spoke and acted like a man.

Jafar couldn't keep looking with Iago here. That would be disrespectful, dismissive. He opened his mouth to tell him to embark on his search.

Iago spoke first. "Well, get on with it, then! I guess I'll hunt around for answers of my own."

The parrot hopped off his shoulder and flew to the shadows above the shelves with a whistle, leaving Jafar before the section he'd only ever dreamed of seeing with his own two eyes. He drew a careful breath to steady himself and the rush of emotions flooding through him. If only Mama were here to see him now. To see *this*—the House of Wisdom and the artifacts she'd spoken of; to feel the air that shimmered with the same mystical magic of her tales.

He didn't know where to start. He stepped closer, awestruck and ecstatic, perusing the spines and scrolls and an endless string of words listing out ways to evoke and persuade and alter. There were infinite uses for elements like brimstone and quicksilver, even for water. Then there were other, more obscure elements he'd never heard of, like bloodstones and tin salts, and the strange, eerie symbols used to represent them. He hadn't realized the magnitude of what alchemy had to offer. All he'd ever known were Mama's stories and the handful of books she'd once owned. This was tenfold. This was more than he could ever ask for.

But he could barely concentrate.

Every time he blinked, he saw the hurt crushing Rohan's features. He dragged a hand down his face. *Why do I care so much?* Rohan was acting more childish than ever, slowly becoming a hindrance as Baba had been.

Jafar set a bundle of scrolls aside and sighed, leaning back against the bookshelf. He would make things right with Rohan first and return with a clear mind.

"That's quite the sigh," someone said. "Whatever you're worried about might just not be worth the trouble."

Jafar started, nearly toppling the scrolls piled precariously on the shelf as someone rounded the aisle to stand before him.

It was her. The girl he'd seen walking to the gardens.

She was even more tantalizing up close. The picture of beauty, with doe eyes encased by lashes as lush as her curves, irises a lovely shade darker than her silken hair, and a smile that could only be described as wickedly sweet. Her gown clung to her as keenly as a lover, exuding opulence with faceted garnets dazzling in gold-threaded florals, vibrant against a landscape of black gossamer.

The potted plants scattered amongst the shelves leaned toward her, and the featherlight curtains rustled for her attention from the library's windows.

"It's bad manners to stare," she mock-whispered. Her gaze was alight with mischief under the library's many candlelit sconces.

"As it is to take someone by surprise," Jafar replied just as quickly. Her grin widened.

She hummed. "You got me there."

Her eyes were like ink, eager to tell a story, drawing him into their depths. She was curious, he could tell. He wondered if she was one of the scholarship students the House of Wisdom had taken in this year. No, she was dressed too finely for that, and the Sultana didn't have a daughter, as far as he knew. Then again, very few even knew of the prince's current situation.

"I see we're one and the same," the girl said, and Jafar blinked at her, eyebrows lifting in question.

"Are we?" he asked.

She nodded. "You want to know who I am, and I want to know who you are. Though there's something thrilling about meeting a person wholly unaware of who you are, no? To be a stranger is often a gift."

That, Jafar could agree on. It was refreshing. It was *freeing*. His entire existence had been associated with his father's for so long that it sometimes felt as if he was only ever a son and never his own person.

For a moment, Jafar thought that meant the girl *was* a secret Maghrizi princess, but a girl who was kept hidden wouldn't find it thrilling to meet someone who didn't know of her. Jafar imagined she would feel quite the opposite.

"And I see no reason why that must change," Jafar replied, because he knew it was what she wanted him to say.

She was distracting him from his task, but Jafar was as intrigued by her as she appeared to be by him. Did she wear kohl for beauty or protection? Was her sun-kissed skin an indicator of a girl who preferred the outdoors? *What are you doing, Jafar?* Why did any of this matter?

Please don't come back yet, Iago.

"And *I* see no reason why we can't have both," she announced and lifted her head with a flourish. The fine silver chains threaded through her hair swayed, tiny pearls dotted throughout shimmering. "Tell me something about you that won't give you away."

Jafar didn't have to think long. "I adore the scent of ink."

"You're fast," the girl said with a surprised laugh. "Hmm, I adore the sight of a black moon."

Both ink and a black moon were the same: dark and full of possibility, promising something new. And she was quick as a viper. He liked that. Her laugh made his heart quiver, a feeling not too different from when Baba would snap at him, or when Mama had been on the floor, gasping her last breaths. He'd never felt the same quiver for something *nice*, and he liked that, too.

"Careful," Jafar said. "I'll start to think we're the same person."

The girl studied him a long moment, something like remorse flickering in her eyes.

"No," she said, tilting her head. The light glazed down the side of her neck, and warmth washed down Jafar's body. "We're too different for that."

And then she was sauntering away.

"I'll leave you to your scrolls, then," she called, "but do steer clear of the forbidden, hmm? Until next time, ink boy."

He watched her leave, her walk as proud as her words. She hadn't even told him her name. The village of Ghurub had its fair share of pretty faces, but none of them had ever sparked Jafar's interest. It was hard to find someone alluring when they were dull, their minds as small as their town. This girl was different. She walked as though she'd seen the cruelty of the world and remained headstrong regardless.

Jafar started to follow her, but he . . . *couldn't*. He didn't make it far from the section on alchemy before invisible hands gripped his arms and a fog drifted over his thoughts. The books hummed and beckoned until he couldn't remember the girl. The scrolls held him in place. *We understand you,* the shelves seemed to say. Unlike everyone else. Unlike Baba. Unlike Rohan. His brother could wait—he wasn't ready to listen.

And Jafar needed to find those rubies.

Light spilled from the windowpanes, casting the shelves

in a blood-like hue. *Strange.* Jafar might not always heed the commands of people, but when the written word spoke to him, he listened. Always. He turned back to the pyramid of scrolls and plucked the first one.

19

ROHAN

Though the Sultana had given them the freedom to explore the palace, Rohan knew everything came with limits, and he wasn't going to traipse about with reckless abandon. Still, there was a benefit to being a shadow. No one noticed him. Not servants, not guards.

Baba would have liked the palace. Even when they'd been poor, he walked—or strutted, as Jafar put it—as though he had far more in his pockets than lint, as though there were jewels in his headdress and not holes. He would attempt to speak like royalty, and dress like it, too. Now that Rohan thought about it, he was somewhat happy Baba wasn't here to make a fool out of himself, and by association, Rohan as well.

Maybe he was more like Jafar than he cared to admit. Maybe it was for the best that genies couldn't revive the dead—if that really was a stipulation. He didn't know if he could trust Jafar, or if he even wanted to.

This is confusing. Very, very confusing.

Rohan didn't want to stand still and think about the fact that he'd killed his father and was now finding ways to justify the fact. Maybe he'd ask the genie to make him forget. Maybe all he needed was instruction. To be told what to do so he wouldn't have to do anything himself. He walked on, marveling at how the palace was a small world of its own, from social structure to culture.

He passed a group of women giggling on their way to the courtyard, excitedly chatting about the prospect of watching guards remove their shirts and spar in the sun. He passed a pair of servants talking about a girl who had been staying in the palace for the past several days. He didn't know if she had anything to do with the Sultana's tense and frazzled state— a state that seemed unusual, if the way the rest of her escort behaved was any indication.

And then he paused, a chill creeping up his spine when he heard a tune, a lullaby Mama would hum while she coaxed him to sleep as a little boy. It was a Ghurubi classic that he hadn't heard in years. *A sign,* he thought, ignoring Jafar's warning about looking for them.

He followed the tune to an attendant carrying a tray of steaming food down a hall, her hair bound by a shawl. She struggled with the large satchel at her side until she paused near a guard at the mouth of a corridor. It was darker here, quieter, the air eerie.

The guard sighed. "Food for the prisoner?"

The girl nodded and passed him the tray and the satchel, too. "And a medical kit. They want him clean and lucid for more questioning."

Prisoner? Questioning?

Rohan felt his pulse in his ears, panic rising. They had to be referring to the prisoner the Sultana had told them about. The one guarding the secret to papermaking. Curiosity tried to spur him forward, out of the shadows and onto the guard's heels, through that iron door to see the prisoner for himself.

A diplomat, the Sultana had called him.

The Sultana might not have given them reasons to trust her, but she was still a queen with favors to grant, and what if Rohan could make himself useful to her? What if he could get her the information she needed? If only Jafar were here to — *No,* Rohan thought. He was mad at Jafar and this was his chance to do something on his own.

But then a loud *clang* echoed in the silence, followed by an angry hiss and several angry voices, making it clear Rohan should not be here.

Never mind, then. Rohan hurried back down the maze of halls, hiding under an archway at the sight of another approaching guard and berating himself for ever leaving Jafar and— *No, no, no.* He stopped those thoughts in their tracks.

He needed to formulate a plan. *Together, you are both as powerful as the golden scarab.* Mama had always emphasized working together, as a team. He backtracked through the hall, pausing when the weight of eyes bored into him. He glanced around, seeing nothing until a shimmer of sapphire blue caught the light. The royal vizier. He was standing at the end of the hall, silent as a pillar, watching him with an unreadable expression.

Rohan wouldn't let the man intimidate him.

He straightened his spine and squared his shoulders, turning his back on Harun as he returned to their chambers, where he would wait for Jafar and then use him for once.

That night, Rohan waited in Jafar's room, listening through the crack of the door while his brother tiptoed past the antechamber, both he and Iago murmuring low to avoid Rohan. When Jafar stepped inside the room, his eyes were bright and a little starry. Rohan knew his brother loved knowledge, but he didn't think he loved it *that* much.

"About time," Rohan said.

Jafar startled and Iago screeched like a ghoul. Jafar exhaled and lit more lanterns, letting the silence stretch between them, likely waiting for Rohan to speak first.

"I was lonely without you," Jafar finally said.

Apologies were not in his nature, but Jafar could be convincing and persuasive, and Rohan was as much a victim to his powers of charisma as anyone else. Awareness was a step, he supposed.

"Did you know a new moon is sometimes called a black moon?" Jafar asked.

At least he wasn't lecturing him for storming out.

Still, Rohan gave him a look. "Did you know that the Sultana's royal vizier spies on us?"

"I did, and can't imagine why he wouldn't. They know nothing about us," Jafar replied. Of course he knew. "Is that why you're in my room?"

"I was waiting for you." Rohan rose from the myriad cushions. He wanted to be angry at Jafar, but he couldn't. He'd spent enough time away from his brother that his anger had faded like the sunlight, and now he was more relieved to see him than anything else. "Did you find what you were looking for?"

He didn't know if Jafar had been in search of something in particular, or if he was simply in pursuit of any and all knowledge. He didn't know his brother much at all, he realized.

Jafar removed his robes and hung them on a hook. He straightened his shirt and poured himself a glass of water. "I don't think I'll ever finish looking. There's so much out there. A way to make a woman love you, a way to make you stronger, a way to find anything your heart desires, which I'm certain a hunter would find useful."

"Or huntress," Rohan said.

"Indeed," Jafar said. "The House of Wisdom even has a laboratory for alchemical use. And I found several interesting scrolls, like one detailing how to rid someone of anything, which I certainly see uses for, and another that causes memory loss. If only we'd had that ridding spell when we found out you were allergic to figs and had to suffer for a month."

Rohan made a face. "Ha, ha."

He noticed that Jafar hadn't collected notes or anything of the sort. He could read a page and recall it by memory — every word, every quirk of the script, every tear in the papyrus. As if his brain painted a replica in his head.

Rohan merely *hmm*ed at it all as Jafar continued speaking, not wanting to hear any of it but not wanting to shut Jafar down, either. He had always been a good listener. "So one can combine ideas or spells, too, then?"

Jafar's brow furrowed. He seemed surprised at Rohan's interest. "Which ones?"

"The first ones you mentioned."

"The spell for memory loss and the one for ridding someone of anything? To make them vomit the memory instead of losing it? So it would make them vomit . . . words?" Jafar considered that as he sat at the foot of the bed across from Rohan. "I suppose it might be possible to make someone spill a secret."

Rohan nodded as if that were what he'd been going for all along. "We could have learned how Baba really felt."

Jafar made a face that told Rohan he knew very well how their father had felt. He touched the gossamer curtains rustling at the window and stared out in the dark gardens for a long moment. "We still know nothing about why the Sultana wants us here. I'm starting to wonder if we should leave."

Rohan scoffed. "You decided when to come here, so you can leave whenever you want, too."

"Don't speak like that," Jafar said softly, defeated. He turned back to him, his features awash in gold from the lantern light. "I apologize."

"Apologies are for when something happens that's out of your control, or when you make a mistake," Rohan said. He'd come here for the genie and the lamp and the scarab beetles. He'd come because Jafar had lied. "Not when you lie for your own personal gain, Jafar. But all right; I won't speak like that. If you want to leave, feel free. I'm staying."

He would get his wishes, even if it was the last thing he did.

Jafar pressed his lips thin and nodded. "Then you should also know that the Sultana's son is presumed to be dead."

"The prince?" Rohan asked. "That makes little sense. If the prince was dead, the entire kingdom would know about it." He laughed dryly. "Yet another thing you've kept from me."

"That's cold," Iago said, inserting himself into their conversation.

Cold was what he'd be when Rohan inevitably locked him out of the palace in the dead of the night.

"Did you not notice the air of mourning when we arrived? I didn't *keep* anything from you," Jafar retorted with a tone of ice. "I simply learned of it ahead of time from the caravan leader."

Rohan resisted the urge to call out the fact that he'd known for so long. At this point, he was beginning to sound as though all he did was whine.

"And it wasn't important to impart," Jafar continued. "We were heading for the House of Wisdom, not the palace. But think about it, Rohan. Does it not strike you as odd that the Sultana would keep that a secret?"

All Rohan heard were excuses.

"And you decided now was a good time to impart this knowledge, because I've decided to stay," Rohan said.

Jafar sighed. He could be a lot like Baba when he wanted to. "I'll leave you alone. It's getting late and I think I'll explore the palace a little."

Rohan didn't want him to leave. He didn't want Jafar to have the satisfaction of evading Rohan's scrutiny, nor did he want Jafar exploring the palace and acting like he was the first to make discoveries.

"I already did that," Rohan said, following Jafar out to the antechamber. "Even found where they're keeping that prisoner with the papermaking secret."

Between being angry at Jafar and concurrently missing Jafar, Rohan hadn't put much thought into it, but something about the whole ordeal with the prisoner didn't tally. It didn't make sense to Rohan why the prisoner was Maghrizi and held a secret of the East. It didn't make sense that the Sultana would tell the two of them about it when she knew nothing about them. *They* could be spies, for all she knew.

"Oh," Jafar said, hurt crossing over his face.

Now he knew how it felt.

"Did you . . . speak to the Sultana, too?" Jafar asked haltingly.

Rohan studied Jafar. It didn't take long for him to realize: Jafar cared what the Sultana thought of him. Or rather, Jafar cared about how she might feel about *Rohan*.

"A little," Rohan said. It was a bald-faced lie; he hadn't even seen the Sultana. He could only hope he was selling his false words. "We shared honey cake. It was probably the best I've ever had."

Jafar didn't care for food as much as he once had, but honey cake was the exception—it was on Jafar's list of beloved things, very likely right under alchemy.

"Very nice," Jafar said softly, quiet as the serpent he wanted to be, and opened the door to the hall. "Good night, Rohan."

20

JAFAR

Helping Baba thwart Jafar's scholarship was one thing, but lying about honey cake was going too far. Jafar knew that Rohan was hurt and grieving and that Jafar was in the wrong for lying himself, but he was doing what was best for them. He wasn't trying to sabotage his brother.

Unlike Rohan.

And Jafar needed to do something about it. He thought back to what Rohan said, about combining the two alchemical spells to create a new one, to make someone *vomit* words.

Someone like the Sultana's prisoner.

"You're sure interrogating the prisoner will get us the

rubies?" Iago asked as Jafar paced the hall by their rooms just out of earshot from the guards.

Jafar had used the finder's spell, which required less work than he'd been looking forward to for his first dabble in alchemy—and with disappointing results that gave him a headache, because the rubies kept moving. Which meant they were still on the Sultana's person. Short of picking her pockets, which Jafar didn't trust his ability to do, the only way he could get his hands on the rubies was if she gave them to him herself.

"She wants the prisoner's secret and we want the rubies," Jafar said. "It'll be a solid trade, no?"

"And you think Rohan is going to be all right with all of this?" Iago asked, flying up to eye one of the elaborate sconces lining the hall.

Jafar wanted to stop worrying about Rohan and think of other things. Like the girl from the library and how beautiful she would look in a swathe of fabric he'd seen at the bazaar. It was the color of the sky where it met the sea, brilliant and bright, just like her.

Jafar cleared his throat. Iago lifted a brow.

"The longer we stay here, the more I lose her—*him*," Jafar quickly corrected. It was true. They hadn't been here a day and Rohan was already becoming Baba. Jafar saw the signs. He hated them. Once he had the rubies, he would leave—as much as Jafar hated leaving all those scrolls and stories untouched. As much as he yearned to see that girl once more. And he would take Rohan with him, whether his brother wanted it or not.

Iago nodded. "So much for shedding light on my past."

"Ah, I might have done some sleuthing," Jafar said, stopping to face Iago in the eerily still palace hall. Moonlight slipped through the latticed wall, spotting Iago's red coat in vibrance, the rest of him in the shadows of his unknown past.

"There are spells by which a human can be transformed into an animal, anything from tigers and elephants to creatures as small as mice," Jafar began.

Iago was quiet for a moment. Jafar tried to imagine how it would feel to learn, without warning, that he was once a different species entirely. Seeing the shredded pieces of his scholarship was painful enough.

"Even parrots," Iago said slowly.

"Even parrots," Jafar said with a nod.

"So I wasn't always like this," Iago said, quieter than Jafar had ever heard him.

"It's quite possible," Jafar said. "That said, the spell is dark and no easy task to complete. It requires materials from vastly different terrains as well as something dear to the person being transformed. Certain spells take their toll on the caster. There's no telling how it affected the one who did this to you."

Iago shifted uneasily, and his silhouette stretched ahead

of him as tall as a man's. "So what you're saying is whoever did this to me was dedicated."

"Indeed," Jafar replied. "Are you sure you don't remember anything from before the bazaar?"

Iago shook his head, beak glinting. "I've tried, Jafar. I really have. Does that—does it mean—"

"Yes," Jafar said softly, surprised by how much sympathy he felt for the bird. "It is permanent."

Iago dropped his head and then immediately fluffed his feathers, flying up beside him. "Well, that was fun. Don't we have some rubies to retrieve?"

Jafar didn't move. The desert was quiet, the night calm. It reminded him of nights in Baba's house, when Rohan and Jafar would speak freely, when the moon in the sky meant emotions weren't bottled so tight.

"It's all right to mourn what you once were," Jafar said.

"Can't mourn what I can't remember," Iago said, eyeing him.

He pushed on Iago's little head until he sat back on the windowsill, talons scraping the stone. Jafar wasn't used to praise—neither receiving it nor offering it—and so it took him a moment to piece together what he wanted to say. Iago had proven to be a better ally than Jafar ever anticipated, and in this place where allies were few and far between, Jafar did not want to lose him.

"And there's nothing wrong with being a parrot," Jafar

said. "And a princely one at that. You're still a worthy opponent to your foes and, well, a fine partner to have."

The words simmered between them before Iago squinted up at him.

"Are you commending me, Jafar?"

"Seems as though I am," Jafar said.

"I like you, too," Iago said, and with a squawk, he hopped to Jafar's shoulder. "To the prisoner, then? Wait, we don't even know where the prisoner is. Are we going to try the finding spell one more time?"

He shook his head. The finding spell was so lackluster that Jafar had decided to never use it again. He had a better way in mind. He glanced back down the empty hall to where his and Rohan's rooms were.

"We'll know where he is soon enough," Jafar said, and the shadows swallowed them whole.

21

ROHAN

Rohan couldn't stay still. His leg kept wanting to twitch in irritation and impatience and annoyance. He hadn't wanted Jafar to leave. He didn't know what he wanted, but he certainly didn't want Jafar going out and finding that prisoner.

Because that was what Jafar would do. Caution? He didn't know it.

Rohan had been so eager to hurt Jafar that he hadn't thought of anything else. He tried sinking deeper into the bed, hoping the lush sheets and feathery cushions would hold him captive and lull him to sleep. He tried listening to the night, facing the open window and the breeze rustling the curtains.

With a growl, he threw off the covers, pulled on his shirt and then his robes, and slipped into his sandals by the door. The guard was nowhere to be seen. A palace at night was a lot like any other place at night. Dark, quiet, lonely. Lit sconces were few, and the moon could slip in through only so many windows.

Rohan retraced his steps with care, and after several detours because it was sometimes too dark to see where he was going, he found the corridor where he'd seen the attendant girl hand the guard the food and medical kit.

He didn't know what lay through the corridor. His teeth were on edge, his limbs even more restless now. What if Jafar was in trouble? Rohan took a careful breath, wishing he had thought to bring a lantern from their rooms.

And then he froze. A hand clamped down on his shoulder, and his soul nearly left his body. A long silhouette stretched in the dark. Shadows painted his face gaunt and the parrot on his shoulder in black.

"Jafar! What are you doing?"

Jafar lifted a brow. "Following you. Did you think I'd know how to get in there?"

The pounding in Rohan's chest careened from fear into anger—at himself. How could he have been so stupid? Not only had he been used *again*, but he'd done exactly what Jafar had thought he would.

"Now come," Jafar said.

"Come?" Rohan seethed, his voice so hushed that it sounded like a rat skittering in the dark. "You can't just take over—"

"I didn't," Jafar said. "It's no one's fault you're being pre-dictable, and *you're* the one who told me about the prisoner. I did nothing but pay heed to what my brother had to say, and now I want to see him. If you don't want to come, you're more than welcome to sit this one out. Iago, will you help my brother find his way back?"

"I don't need your pet's help," Rohan snapped. "Let's just go."

He stomped ahead of Jafar, still squinting through the shadows. The floor disappeared under his next step and he nearly plummeted down a set of stairs. *Gah!* This was all Jafar's fault. *I'm behaving just like Baba,* Rohan thought, *blaming others for the consequences of my own actions.*

And yet, he was surprised to find he wasn't as bothered by that realization as he would have expected to be.

There was a door at the very end of the steps, heavy and black. Rohan knew this because it was ajar, because there was a line of light slipping from its other side, flickering in shades of orange and red. Like the fire that had taken Baba from them. The one Rohan had wished for.

His throat closed, cinching his lungs tight, denying him another exhale.

"Breathe," Jafar whispered to him kindly, gently. It took everything in Rohan not to step closer to him, back in his shadow, in his protection.

Baba was gone; there was no use blaming himself for it. No point stifling himself with his fear.

Rohan opened the door. More stairs. Shadows grew and folded, dragging a shiver out of him. It was desolate and pitiful, a cold that dug into his bones.

"I was thinking," Jafar began. He sounded distant and unaffected. "Baba was most horrible *with* a soul. Imagine asking a genie to bring him back. Imagine Baba *without* a soul."

A chill crept down Rohan's spine, freezing into the divots. Was Jafar trying to make him uneasy?

"Hmm?" Jafar asked when Rohan didn't respond. "Let's see your prisoner."

A low keening reverberated through the walls. Rohan shivered. Iago didn't look too happy to be here, either.

"He isn't *my* prisoner," Rohan said, glancing back. His voice caught when the keening sounded again. "Maybe this was a bad idea. We probably shouldn't be here."

Jafar was utterly unfazed. "I thought about what you said. About combining the spells to make someone speak."

Rohan took a careful step back, but Jafar didn't move. His eyes took on a reddish hue, his features still as stone.

"I think we can use that to get the Sultana her secret," Jafar said.

Whatever happened to wanting to leave the palace? Rohan didn't know what Jafar was planning, but *he* wanted to be useful to the Sultana. *He* wanted to be the diplomat and question the prisoner.

Not let Jafar do it.

That was Rohan's gift to give, but Jafar was already squeezing past him, sweeping down the stairs as if he owned the place.

"What for?" Rohan asked

"We could use it to barter, I'm sure," Jafar answered without breaking stride. It was a guarded response, mired in another secret Jafar was clearly keeping from him.

Rohan stared after him. This was beginning to feel less diplomatic and more reckless. He wanted no part in the cold hollow in Jafar's voice. Jafar was scaring him, and he was ready to run back to their rooms and burrow back under the covers.

But like any good shadow, Rohan disappeared after his brother.

The walls pressed tight. Rohan stretched his arms, and stone greeted him on either side, rough and damp. His footfalls echoed behind Jafar's until the stairs spat the three of them out into a large room. Slowly, his eyes adjusted to the dim, greedily seeking out the lone lantern. It cast off the metal bars that formed cell after cell. A forlorn leak squeezed into a tin pail somewhere in the darkness, and that low keening began again, so helpless that Rohan wanted to cover his ears.

This was the dark side of running a kingdom.

A single guard leaned against a small pillar of stone near the lantern. His legs were crossed, his head tipped.

"There's a gua—"

"Shh," Jafar whispered, pulling Rohan deeper into the shadows as Iago shot past, wings an almost silent rustle.

Moments later, a voice called from the stairs: "Which one of you is down there? I need you in the banquet hall at once!"

The guard straightened, blinking groggily and wiping drool from his beardless chin with the back of his hand.

"Yes, Sultana!" he called back, and Rohan pressed himself flat against the cold hard wall as the guard sprinted past them and out the door.

And then they were alone.

"You're welcome," Iago said in his normal voice, fluttering back to Jafar's shoulder.

Jafar was waiting for him by the guard's lamp. The lamplight cast half his face in shadow, the other half in starry-eyed mischief. "Good job."

Rohan could have done that. Jafar only had to ask.

"He'll come back when he sees the empty banquet hall," Rohan said, hoping to wipe the victory from Iago's face. "We need to go."

"No, he'll try to find the Sultana and then question why he heard her voice in the first place," Jafar countered.

Iago harrumphed. "Yeah, stop being such a killjoy. This was your idea, remember?"

Rohan gritted his teeth. He'd told them *about* the prisoner, not that he wanted to interrogate him. Jafar was staring at the prison cells. Despite its size, the dungeon housed no more than ten cells as far as Rohan could tell. He guessed that the Sultana only locked the more important prisoners here. The ones she needed to keep close.

Jafar stepped in a puddle of something dark and questionable. He didn't even flinch. He was too cavalier. Too at ease.

Rohan's next inhale was deep, and the dank odor of the prison assaulted his senses. It was sour and musty, combined with the sweet and sickening stench of rot. He barely stopped himself from retching right there in the middle of the place.

And that was when Rohan saw the cell with the tray of food and that medical kit outside of it.

The papermaking prisoner.

"That's him," Rohan whispered.

"Odd, he doesn't look too bad," Jafar said, and Rohan had to agree.

The man wheezed, leaning his head back against the stone wall, but even barely illuminated and striped in the shadows of the cell bars, it was clear his clothes weren't too worn, his beard and mustache still relatively trim. But his knuckles were dirty, and the hair by his ears was matted with something dark.

Rohan choked. *Blood.* They were torturing him.

" 'No secret can be kept forever,' " Jafar said, repeating the Sultana's words and looking at Rohan.

The prisoner was clearly Maghrizi, as the Sultana had said, but why would he protect the secrets of another kingdom? Why would he risk his own life for a place he had no allegiance to?

The Sultana had said his secret could start a war and change the course of the future—that for as long as the kingdoms to the east held a monopoly over papermaking, they also held great power. By that reasoning, Rohan thought those kingdoms must be dangerous, which meant any number of deaths to protect against them could be justified.

Still, something was off about this.

For the Sultana had also claimed papermaking wasn't a necessity. And those kingdoms had no reason to come for her with swords if she left them to their own devices. They were flourishing, as she was. Rohan might even argue they were at peace.

Unlike the man in front of him now.

"He's—he's *bleeding*," Rohan said with half a sob.

"And we can make that stop," Jafar said.

"How?" Rohan asked. Ah, the kit! They could—

"We'll make him vomit words," Jafar said, turning to

Rohan with a smile. It was his usual smile, a gesture that normally set Rohan at ease. But here, half bathed in shadow, in the presence of someone's suffering, it was sinister.

And as fear coiled tighter and tighter around Rohan's limbs, Jafar seemed to grow less and less concerned. Less himself. Less worried over consequences and what "vomiting words" might do to a starved man who had been shoved in a dank, dark prison cell.

Rohan peered closer. The man was awake, but barely. He didn't seem to notice them.

"Jafar, this is wrong," Rohan said, shocked by his apprehension toward his own brother.

"What is?" Jafar asked. "Using alchemy to get an answer out of him? I'd say it's better than whatever they've been torturing him with to get him to speak."

"His *being* here is wrong. And I don't know if the Sultana is someone I want to barter with."

Nor was Rohan so sure he wanted to help the Sultana anymore. A queen who could recklessly torture her own subject wasn't one whose favor he wanted to earn. Was *Jafar* trying to gain her favor after Rohan had lied about eating honey cake with her? He had lied to make Jafar jealous, not spur him to do *this*.

Jafar tilted his head. "Mm, we might not be Maghrizi, but we can both agree that we'd rather see the Sultana win than some other kingdom, no?"

"Win? This isn't a war. They're not hurting us," Rohan said.

Not once in Jafar's life had he cared for politics, and while they might have been in a palace, Rohan still didn't think that was enough reason for Jafar to begin now.

"That's how it always begins," Jafar said, and Rohan had the sense he wasn't talking about wars or queens, but their past. "And the only way to ensure you don't get hurt is to hurt them first."

Jafar pressed his eyes closed for a long moment, and when he opened them, Rohan imagined that red glow again. A dagger of fear sliced through Rohan.

"Get me that lantern," Jafar said, picking up a coil of twine from the medical kit. "We'll need to borrow some oil. Then gather three stones, and we'll need something that he's touched—ah, yes, and grab his empty plate from over there."

Before Rohan could even think of a response, Jafar pushed past him, snatching up the ring of keys that had sat on the pillar where the guard had been resting. He stopped before the man's cell and peered inside.

"Marhaba," Jafar said to him.

The lantern lit the caution in the man's dark eyes.

"What is your name?" Jafar asked.

The man said nothing.

Jafar was unfazed—no, he almost looked satisfied that the man wasn't answering. "I know why you're here and the pain keeping your secret will cause our world. You have no reason to keep it, you know. Divulge your knowledge and you will live as a free man."

The man only drew a stuttering breath. If he felt even half of Rohan's desperation, he didn't show it.

"You owe them no loyalty," said Jafar. "Speak, man."

The man remained silent, watching through dead eyes as Jafar dipped the twine in oil and lit it aflame, twisting it into a strange symbol, placing the stones just so, picking up the plate, his eyes sharp with intent. If Rohan hadn't been uneasy to begin with, he was wholly so now.

He thought he saw the hint of a smile flit across the prisoner's face. A pitiful one. If this had been any other cir-cumstance, that defiance would have rattled Rohan's pride.

As it did to Jafar's.

He rose, the keys jangling hauntingly, and the lantern stretched his shadow to something frightful. "Very well, sayyidi."

22

JAFAR

Jafar had not anticipated the screaming that reverberated from the dungeon's stone walls or the blood the lone lantern illuminated quite well. He had never seen so much of it.

Dead bodies, yes. He'd seen flesh charred and blackened, bubbled and crisp from merciless heat, when he'd gone back to the remains of their home, unbeknownst to Rohan, to make sure his father really was dead.

His past life had ended with that massacre.

But alchemy was words and ideas, not knives against flesh. The man who had refused to speak was supposed to speak, nothing else. Instead, he had forced Jafar to press and then press a little more, and by the time the prisoner spoke, he had heaved so much that his insides had already begun leaching outside.

"The papermakers . . . in the East," the prisoner said, trembling, his voice no more than a quivering mumble. "They mixed bark an-and shredded rags and hemp." He broke off with a rattling cough, blood gurgling from his lips.

"With what?" Jafar asked. As Iago turned away in pity, Jafar belatedly realized this should be affecting *him* just as much. But all he saw was Baba in the prisoner's place, and any sorrow he might have begun to feel was quickly overtaken by pure elation.

"Water. Strained"—more coughing—"it. And then . . . pressed the pulp flat t-to dry in the sun."

"Incredible," Jafar said. The human mind was incredible. The ability to create something from nothing fascinated him to no end. He glanced at Rohan. "Did you hear that?"

Rohan was pale and shivering, fixated on the depthless pool slowly widening by their feet. He nodded, but Jafar didn't think Rohan had heard anything at all. The blood was sticky and dark, and almost made him nostalgic, reminding him of cooking with Mama and her precious pomegranate molasses.

The girl's voice echoed in his ears: *Steer clear of the forbidden.* He wondered if she would be horrified right now or share in his captivation.

"Is he—is he dead?" Rohan asked.

His voice was like a hand reaching into the abyss of Jafar's mind, pulling him out of a trance. Jafar's breath caught. He stared at his hands, his arms, the veins stark against his skin. He was shaking, he realized. He was shocked. Alarmed. *Numb*.

Rohan sobbed.

"No—no. He's still alive," Jafar said, trying to calm him down. Trying to calm *himself* down.

Not because he'd done something terrible. Not because he'd caused suffering. But because he had enjoyed it.

"He's bleeding out of every orifice," Rohan argued, his words punctuated by his chattering teeth.

Jafar was still shaking, still trying to make sense of the emotions coursing through him. He pulled Rohan behind him and out of the cell, leaving the stench and the quivering prisoner behind. The dungeon was silent as a tomb. The guard had never returned, likely keeled over in a corner wondering if he'd imagined Iago's impersonation of the Sultana.

Jafar could almost *smell* the fear from the other prisoners until he slammed the iron door closed behind him.

He liked it.

Rohan wrenched himself free and sank to his knees. Drenched in moonlight, he stared at Jafar as if he didn't recognize him. As if he was . . . afraid of him.

"That was too far," Rohan bleated. "Too far."

"I didn't know that would happen," Jafar countered. "But it might have gone a lot faster and smoother had you helped me rather than whimpering like a child. And let's not forget that this was your idea."

Rohan shook his head. There were oil spots on his robes and soot was smeared on his hem. He was gasping for air as if he were an unseasoned bedouin floundering under the desert heat.

"And now we have something that can change Maghriz forever," Jafar said.

Ever since Baba's death, Jafar had felt a restlessness that wouldn't abate no matter how many nights had passed or how long a journey they'd put between themselves and their old village.

Now he felt calm.

Rohan threw a finger at the dungeon door. "And that was the cost."

Jafar leaned against the wall. Moonlight glistened on his fingers. Red. He hadn't even noticed the blood staining his hands, painting each whorl in stark relief. *Bah.*

"And—where's Iago?" Rohan asked.

"Here," came the reply. Iago crept from the shadows, a tiny figure in the vast blackness of the space. Apprehension stilted his steps, his wings cinched tight against his body. "I don't know if that was the right thing to do."

Rohan released a long, slow breath. "It wasn't."

Jafar rubbed the red between his fingers, watching it tint more of his skin, until something moved out of the corner of his eye. He looked up furtively, certain it was the royal vizier spying on them again, but it was her.

Moon girl.

Jafar froze. How much had she heard? *Seen?* Had she crept into the dungeons with them? No, Iago would have noticed her. She was at the far end of his peripheral vision in the adjacent hall, heading toward them, not away. Her hair was bound in a bun, stray strands framing the soft, iridescent planes of her face. He couldn't see what she was wearing, but he was certain it was lovely. It was a strange feeling for butterflies to flutter in the exhilaration already pumping through his veins.

"Did you hear me, Jafar?" Rohan asked, thankfully unaware. "We need to get back to our rooms and wash our hands of this." He winced. "Literally."

The girl's lips curled into a grin. She, on the other hand, was wholly aware of how she was distracting him.

"We're in no rush, brother. It's the middle of the night," Jafar replied, dismissing his concerns. "Everyone important is asleep."

He snuck another glance in time to see her lift a brow before she seized up at the sight of something behind them and slowly backed away, disappearing into the shadows. He heard a door click closed, and then—

"Boys?"

Jafar, Rohan, and Iago went stock-still.

The Sultana.

Jafar's mind was still racing with all that had transpired in the prison, with the sight of the girl and her lifted brow, but his mind was working enough to know that the Sultana shouldn't have been up and about at midnight. Near the dungeons, no less.

Iago quickly hopped onto Jafar's shoulder, and the three of them turned to face her and the lantern she held high, dousing the place with light. Harun stood just behind her, more vigilant than anyone should be at this hour. Jafar tried to shove his bloodied hands behind him and failed.

The Sultana saw.

With a cry, she rushed to them. She brushed Rohan's damp hair from his brow, sparing him heartbeats of motherly attention before turning fully to Jafar. She swiped her thumb down Jafar's cheek, and he had to stop himself from leaning into it. How long had it been since he'd felt a mother's touch? Since he'd been the subject of another's concern?

"You're bleeding," she said, and for a moment, she wavered in Jafar's gaze. He was a little boy again, watching the sun warm the worn lines of his mother's face.

Through it all, he could feel Rohan's ire. His unhappiness, scrubbing Jafar's skin raw. Maybe that was the reason for what Rohan did next, because Jafar could not fathom any other.

Rohan cleared his throat and said, "We have something to tell you."

23

ROHAN

Rohan was certain the Sultana would wait until morning before granting them an audience, but she whisked them away at once. He was still wary of her after how quickly she'd arrived at the dungeons, and with her royal vizier, too. Rohan had thought, at first, that it was because of Iago's impersonation of her, but it couldn't be.

Something was amiss, but all Rohan saw was the attention she'd given Jafar, like a doting mother who suddenly forgot that she had two sons. *She's not your mother,* Rohan told himself. It was the late hour, he decided, toying with his mind.

The Sultana marched through the halls in relative darkness, Harun following behind her, enveloping Jafar and Rohan in flickering light. She led them to a wing of the palace they'd never been to before and pushed open a pair of doors to a receiving chamber with ease. It was a majlis, with low seats wrapped in brushed bronze, plush and inviting, centered in the room with little else of note.

She sat first, her legs crossed, her gown a river of pale pink silk around her. The lantern flickered, catching the strands of gray running through her hair.

Rohan carefully sat to her right, Jafar to her left. She summoned a servant with a bowl of water, and watched as Jafar scrubbed at his hands without a hint of disgust on his face—or hers. The royal vizier, on the other hand, had enough for both of them, revulsion twisting his features into something sour.

Rohan was starting to wish he hadn't spoken so brazenly outside the dungeons. He was surprised he could even speak for the way his teeth wouldn't stop chattering. Another servant brought in a tray with food and drink, setting it on the low table between them. Rohan could barely look at it.

Were they going to be punished for sneaking around the palace? Did she know the two of them had found the dungeons? And *why* were they awake and alert at midnight— almost as though they'd been waiting for this moment?

"Drink," the Sultana said, nodding at the tray and the little handleless cups on it.

They were glass, the liquid inside amber and fragrant.

Cardamom tea. Rohan didn't need to be told twice. He gulped it down, even as the glass burned his fingers and the tea scorched a path through his throat.

He stopped shaking.

His head cleared.

The majlis cushions were palatial beneath them, embroidered in tiny flowers of vermillion and white, fine vines intersecting one another. The intricacy of the seating was contrasted by the minimalist beauty of the floor. Wide tiles in creamy onyx cascaded to plain walls accented by simple wood carvings hung at intervals. He set his empty glass on the ebony table beside a still untouched plate of those buttery ghorayeba cookies with perfectly centered pistachios.

"Now, what is it you wish to tell me?" she asked.

She looked to Jafar, even though it was Rohan who had prompted this meeting, Rohan whose idea it had been to put two alchemical texts together and create what they had created.

Rohan heard Jafar's inhale, the teetering pause as he gathered his words.

But if it was Rohan's idea to combine the spells and Rohan who had found the prisoner to begin with, had Jafar really discovered the secret to papermaking? Was it Jafar who had unearthed the Maghrizi kingdom's salvation?

Rohan didn't think so.

"We explored the palace," he said before Jafar could speak.
The Sultana looked to him at last.

As did Jafar. His gaze was heavier than an anvil. This
would be easier if Jafar didn't look at him. Jafar hadn't cared
when that man was vomiting blood. Rohan needed to be just
as uncaring.

"First, I saw an attendant taking food to the dungeons,"
Rohan continued, "and later, I found the iron door."

Beside him, Jafar tensed when Rohan shifted from *we* to
I. Just as Jafar had when he'd lied to Rohan and brought him
all this way.

"I found your Maghrizi prisoner," he continued. Iago
made a sound. Rohan ignored him, because he wanted to say
more. *You tortured the prisoner. You hurt your own people. You're
not worried about war, you're greedy.*

But weren't they all?

Rohan took a deep breath. "And then, I found your
secret."

24

JAFAR

Jafar had watched a man retch his secrets while spewing bile and blood. He had looked at his father's corpse and he had run for his life from guards. Yet it was only now that he felt sick to his stomach. Why was Rohan doing this? Every *I* that escaped his lips was a blade nicking Jafar's skin, a slap across his cheek.

Jafar tried taking a sip of tea, to busy himself, to do *something*, but it was cardamom and only made his stomach churn more.

"You can't just sit there, Jafar," Iago whispered in his ear. If the Sultana had heard, she didn't react.

But Jafar had no choice. He couldn't denounce Rohan's claims, not without condemning him to the sword for lying to the queen. *An important oath,* Mama had said long, long ago. It stuck with him mostly because *oath* was a funny word, and he didn't learn what it truly meant until he was much older.

An oath was solemn, protected, sacred, and as the adults in his life violated them time and time again, it became increasingly imperative that Jafar never did.

"Our rubi—" Iago began.

Jafar shook his head. He couldn't even think of the rubies right now, he couldn't even worry about the fact that Rohan was going about it all wrong by not attempting to set up a trade first.

"My secret?" the Sultana asked Rohan, brow creased.

Rohan didn't pause, he didn't look to Jafar, he didn't even let a beat pass before he volleyed his response: *yes.* That one word became two, then ten, and even as Jafar's blood heated and simmered and eventually boiled, Rohan didn't stop.

"The secret to papermaking that you so desire."

The Sultana whirled to Harun. He gave her a small, almost imperceptible nod. His stern scowl softened. His cold gaze warmed. Their joy and pride was directed at Rohan, despite the blood on Jafar's fingers, despite the words that had been hoarse in his throat as the prisoner had gone from smug to alarmed, despite the way something in Jafar had broken while he followed through with the alchemical experiment.

Jafar finally locked eyes with Rohan. *Why are you doing this?*

Rohan stared back coolly, and his response was clear. *Did you not do the same?*

He sat back, realizing he had given Rohan too much credit. It wasn't that he was inept and going about it all wrong by not demanding to barter with the Sultana—he was punishing Jafar.

This wasn't like Rohan. He was never vindictive; he never held a grudge. He was forever doting, forever fascinated by anything and everything Jafar had done. But ever since setting foot in the palace, Rohan had been different.

He had dissuaded Jafar from interrogating the prisoner. He had done worse than just stand there as Jafar extracted the secret—he'd tried to make him feel horrible for looking out for their best interests. For *helping* them.

He had wanted to make Jafar feel like he was in the *wrong*, just as Baba would, time and time again, and now he was claiming Jafar's deeds as his own.

The Sultana turned back to them. "This is not what I wished upon you. The young must be allowed to be young, even those in a palace."

The royal vizier cleared his throat.

The Sultana looked chagrined. Was she speaking of her

son? Jafar was sorting through too many of his own emotions to decipher hers.

"How did you do it?" she asked, glancing from Jafar to Rohan. Did she suspect the lies? Could she see right through them? Jafar latched on to that glimmer of hope.

Still, he said nothing. He couldn't tell them the truth without vilifying his brother.

"By combining two well-known alchemical findings," Rohan said, and then smiled. Confidence dripped from his every word, because he knew Jafar. He knew Jafar wouldn't betray him the way he'd just done. "The words spilled out of him."

As they were spilling out of Rohan now, as if Jafar had ceased to exist. He didn't tell her the secret itself, his burgeoned pride likely waiting for her to ask him for it. Or maybe he hadn't heard it at all, too frightened by what he had been seeing to hear anything.

The Sultana laughed, still a little uncertain. For her, this was likely too good to be true.

"We've been at our wits' end for months," she said.

"I'm currently at my wits' end myself," Iago groused in Jafar's ear.

Jafar couldn't dwell on it anymore. His focus was on the wall that had risen between his brother and himself. He didn't feel angry, he didn't feel that insult to his pride Rohan often did.

He felt sad, but he remained silent.

Whatever you're worried about might just not be worth the trouble, the girl had said, but she was wrong, wasn't she? The worst part of betrayal was that it never came from an enemy.

An oath was an oath, even when it was a burden.

25

ROHAN

Rohan returned to their chambers with a silent Jafar. His brother's dark eyes were shattered, mistrust and hurt dragging the proud line of his shoulders down. Rohan had wanted to show him what it was like to feel the pain that he did. To trust in someone completely and learn they'd been selfish. To be used by someone he loved.

He'd thought it would make him feel better.

It had not.

When Rohan tried to speak, his tongue tied itself in knots, but it didn't matter, for Jafar stalked into his room and slammed the door in Rohan's face.

It was long past midnight, and as tired as Rohan was, he was also overwhelmed—from the voices and the blood and the fact that he'd opened his mouth. As he lay in bed, tossing and turning, the distance between him and Jafar more than an antechamber, he realized something far more horrifying than anything that had happened tonight.

The Sultana hadn't asked for the secret.

26

JAFAR

Jafar could not sleep. The sheets were a tangle around his legs, and he'd memorized every pattern in the detailed ceiling above him in the hours since he'd crawled into bed. In the long list Jafar had to describe his brother, *rival* was never a word he thought he'd choose. Rohan had abysmal confidence on a good day, but he had somehow *known* Jafar wouldn't call him out. He had exploited him. He had *used* him and made him feel lesser, inferior.

Rohan had behaved exactly as Baba would have.

"That's enough with this moping," Iago quipped, hopping onto the cushions.

"Because you told me so?" Jafar asked, and he had. Iago had warned Jafar when he was still locked in the broom closet, when he'd first held the ripped remains of his scholarship.

He braced himself for Iago's gloating.

"For someone who was plotting how to steal a pair of mind-controlling rubies from the Sultana of Maghriz's pocket, you crumble fast," Iago said instead.

Jafar didn't want to hear it. There was so much else about their meeting with the Sultana that gnawed at him, namely the fact that she hadn't asked for the secret itself. It was all too much, and he couldn't stand to be in the presence of Iago or Rohan, stark reminders of Baba, stark reminders of everything that had gone wrong. He threw off the sheets and retied his loose trousers, not bothering with a shirt before pulling on his robes and leaving their rooms.

The halls were dark, the palace still asleep. Even now, it struck Jafar as peculiar that the Sultana had arrived to the dungeons so quickly, with her royal vizier at that. As if she'd plotted the entire event—from disclosing knowledge of the prisoner to gathering them all for a meeting.

Jafar's brain hurt. His shoulder felt bare without Iago. In the middle of the hall before one of the trellised windows, he sank to the floor with his back to the wall. His fingernails were rimmed in blood where he couldn't scrub it away. The life had drained out of him, leaving nothing but weak limbs and a mind too numb to think.

"Hello, ink boy."

Jafar looked up, quickly shifting his hands from the light. He didn't have an explanation for how the lovely cadence of her voice made him feel. "Are you spying on me, moon girl?"

She laughed, and he could have sworn the hall brightened. Her existence was sorcery, and Jafar was thoroughly under her spell.

He could see her gown now, a deep blush that was almost purple, black filigree forming thick, stiff cuffs around her wrists. When his gaze returned to hers, it was to find her studying him just as diligently, and he remembered that his chest was bare and his robes only covered so much. A hint of red colored her cheeks. Jafar swallowed and saw her gaze follow the bob of his throat.

She chewed the inside of her lip and glanced down the hall. "You're a great deal sadder than the last time I saw you."

"My melancholy ebbs and flows with the tides," Jafar said, his own voice a little hoarse.

"So poetic," the girl drawled. "Let's do another trade."

He liked this game. He liked *her*, even more than he did the first time. Jafar thought about it for a moment.

"I have been known to go too far," he said, rubbing at his blood-crusted nails with discretion.

"His melancholy is at its peak, everyone," she mock-announced. "Come now, get up! Life is too short to obsess over any one thing."

She reached for his hands and hauled him up, her face coming dangerously close to his chest. Wisps of her hair brushed his skin and his breath caught. It made something slither up his veins and put his lungs in a vise before she let go as if his skin were coal.

Her gaze swept to the floor, the first instance of reserve he'd seen in her. Her chest heaved just as heavily as he felt his own did. When she crossed her arms, he noticed how she slid her hands up them, as if she too had felt that unexpected slither.

"I—" Her voice cracked.

She cleared her throat with a sheepish smile. It made her look younger, softened the harshness of her features that Jafar hadn't noticed at first. Had she, too, lived a lifetime in her youth? Did she know what it was like to be subjected to subordination when she didn't deserve it?

"My turn," she said in a voice like gossamer, a little thinner but just as silky. A little unnerved, and it was because of him. It was as intoxicating as when he'd made the prisoner bleed.

He didn't know what compelled him to hold her gaze. "Yes."

She dipped her head again, flooding him with warmth and something brazen and thrilling. When her gaze went coy and her smile turned shy, it made his heart feel too big for his body. It made him forget about everything else.

He saw the ripple down her throat when she swallowed. He wondered what it would be like to brush his fingers along the slender column of her neck.

"I've been known to give in too easily," she said.

That surprised him, for she wore confidence like the heady jasmine of her perfume. "You don't seem the type."

"Are you referring to my boisterous personality?" she asked, pushing out a hip.

The warmth that was spreading through Jafar suddenly gathered and pooled low.

She gave him a half smile. "I've got to make up for it somehow."

"What—"

"Ah," she reprimanded. "No more questions. We have our agreement, remember? Why else did I refrain from asking about your excursion earlier? Pity, too. I wanted to meet your friend, but it was too dark to see him."

Jafar did not want her to meet his *friend*, his brother, his nemesis. She sauntered past, veering closer to him despite the wide expanse of the hall. Her skirts brushed his legs, and he bit back a shiver, watching as she pulled a key from her pocket. He didn't know how she managed to make something as dull as a key heat every ounce of his blood, but she did. And judging from the way her eyes darkened, she knew it.

"A key of your own," Jafar drawled.

"Because I'm here on my own," she replied coyly. "My first time, really."

But a key meant she was trustworthy enough to be given one. Jafar and Rohan didn't have keys to their rooms. Who *was* she, and why was she here alone?

She winked. "Until next time, melancholy boy."

Jafar bowed with a flourish. "Until then, boisterous girl."

Perhaps it was because of her voice, or her touch, or the fact that she was something Rohan did not and would never have, but when she left him, he did not feel particularly like moping anymore. He smiled at the guards, nodded his way to the House of Wisdom's laboratory, and busied his hands.

Just before noon, Jafar climbed to the palace's rooftop ter-race and wrapped his fingers around the banister until the sharp edges cut into his skin. He inhaled the sun-soaked des-ert air.

He could see much of the capital city from here. Dunes churned on the horizon, but the city was rife with people treading to and fro, stirring sand as they bartered and traveled and went about their day.

"Can I tell you what I think?" Iago asked, hopping along the banister. The wind ruffled the tuft of feathers on his head.

"I abhor when a question is preceded by permission to ask a question," Jafar drawled. The high of his moment with the girl was fading, spiraling him back to Rohan and the prisoner and all that had transpired the night before.

Iago tilted his head. "We're really leaning into the brooding here. I like it."

Jafar rolled his eyes. He hadn't seen Rohan all morning, though that was in part because Jafar had avoided any opportunity *to* see him.

Iago shrugged. "We need to find your rubies and skedaddle as fast as we can. Hey, will you stop moping? It's not your fault."

Wasn't it?

"Oi, we've got company," Iago whispered.

"For a boy who always has something to say, your silence last night was deafening."

Jafar stilled.

He gripped the iron railing, sand clinging to his damp

palms. The Sultana stepped beside him, her ebony over-cloak and heavy shawl rustling in the breeze. Jafar refused to acknowledge her statement, and so they watched the city in silence, voices riding the dry breeze to their ears. He held his breath. The scent of her perfume transported him back to last night in that receiving room, the walls pressing as close as the broom closet's, the eyes of her men boring holes into him.

"I know it was you," she said at last.

Iago squawked. Jafar looked at her, surprised and a little wary. Out of the corner of his eye, he saw Harun, the royal vizier, standing at a distance, his sapphire robes vivid. He looked less like he was there to protect her than to supervise.

"I knew the moment I saw you by the door," the Sultana said. "You are an extraordinary boy."

A man, his father would yell at him. *You are no longer a boy.* His surprise careened into anger when she smiled. If she knew, *had known,* why had she not confronted Rohan then and there? Why had she allowed him to boast and garner the praise and pride of her closest circle?

And if she'd never even asked for the secret in the end, what was the point, besides pitting Rohan and Jafar against each other? Almost . . .

Almost as if she wanted to test them.

Jafar knew manipulation when he saw it. He had

experience with it, after all. He just couldn't understand what the Sultana stood to gain. He swept his gaze to the palace courtyard below, jaw clenching at the sight of his brother. The terrace overlooked the gardens, where Rohan idled by the rectangular reflecting pool in its center, playing with a host of baby ducklings, yellow and bright.

He cupped the youngest one in his palms.

"If you knew," Jafar started, turning his attention back to her, "then why—"

"This is no place for those who cede to others," the Sultana said. She sounded disappointed.

She was the one who had brought them to this *place*. All he'd wanted were those rubies.

"Rohan is my brother, not my competition," Jafar countered.

"Competition! Competition!" Iago squawked.

"The parrot has the right idea," she said with a wry smile. "I've lived long, Jafar, and encountered enough people to have learned them. Men share greed, not blood. Do you think he was unaware of the penalty for lying?"

Jafar swallowed. No, Rohan was not unaware. Just as he was aware that Jafar would do anything for him.

Let go, said the girl in his mind, but she was wrong—some obsessions couldn't be helped. Some transgressions could not be forgiven.

"I do not wish to discuss my brother," Jafar said, surprised by how cold his voice was.

He wanted to know how being the better person and not outing his brother for lying still earned him nothing. A thought resurfaced, one that had been born in the shadows of the locked broom closet: What point was there in being good if he could not reap the benefit of it?

"Nor do I," the Sultana replied.

Jafar looked back down at Rohan, the turquoise depths of the pool complementing his robes. The duckling was squirming in his palms. *Men share greed.* Jafar wondered if that was why his brother had claimed the discovery as his own. He wondered if, beneath his bright, daffodil smiles, his brother had a little bit of the devil in him.

"The two of you remind me of my son," she said, seemingly unaware of the turmoil inside him. "Much of the palace agrees, as well. Those who have seen you in passing."

"Well, since you haven't told anyone he's dead, maybe one of us can take his place," Jafar said, callously disregarding her pain as she did his. Showing her that her son could be replaced, just as Rohan had taken Jafar's place.

The Sultana recoiled as if he had slapped her.

Jafar froze.

And the world slowed as he realized: That was it.

That was why she'd taken them from the House of Wisdom, why she regarded them with far more attention than two bedouin boys from a far-off village deserved, and why her palace staff were so few. The Maghrizi, like most kingdoms and tribes of the desert, weren't keen on portraits, so it was unlikely anyone would even notice.

Jafar almost laughed at her. She had planned this all along—ever since she'd pocketed those rubies and seen him behind her. That was why she had been testing them.

Which meant—

"The prisoner," Jafar breathed, his chest tightening with the realization. "He wasn't really a prisoner."

The Sultana neither denied nor affirmed his words, but her silence was confirmation enough. She looked impressed when she met his eyes, as if she had hoped to carry on the ruse a little longer. He'd lost a piece of himself inside that dungeon, and for what? He had hurt a man, made him suffer, *bleed*. Because of a twisted *test*?

And yet, the only person he was angry at, *livid* at, was Rohan. His brother, still loitering by that pool, playing with the smallest of the ducklings in the water as if nothing were awry.

"The prisoner is fine, by the way. Despite how well you did," the Sultana said, finally.

Well. She was commending the level of damage he'd dealt.

Jafar kept staring at the duckling, even as it began to squirm and struggle, his rage rising with the babe's thrashing as he imagined the Sultana in its place.

And then it stopped.

A stillness fell over the gardens, and down below, when Rohan opened his palms, the duckling was dead.

"But you must know," the Sultana continued, "that one cannot afford to be second best."

27

ROHAN

The babe lay quiet and unmoving in Rohan's palms, its warmth already bleeding into the cool waters. The other ducklings continued to splash in the pool, blissfully oblivious. His sleeves were wet, but that wasn't what chilled him to the bone.

First Mama, then Baba, now the duckling.

Jafar was nowhere to be seen—the trellised rooftop terrace where he'd stood with the Sultana was now empty—but he had been there to witness the duckling's death. And as the chick had gasped its last breath, Rohan was struck with a sense of certainty that his brother's ire was the reason for the death.

That can't be, Rohan chided himself.

Still, Jafar's rage itself scared Rohan far less than how *well* that anger suited him. As if Jafar had cultivated such fury long ago and, over the years, had mastered a way to keep it at bay. He had no reason to be that angry, not when he'd wronged Rohan just as much by dragging him all this way on false hope.

The duckling was only a weight in his palms now, delicate beak prone, feathers still softer than soft. Death was a little like alchemy. An irrefutable change, an irreversible shift from one state to another. The realization sent a surge through him. An excitement, almost. Potent and heady.

Rohan needed to hide the duckling before someone saw him holding it and assumed *he'd* killed the thing.

No sooner had he had the thought than a shadow slanted over him and the dead duckling in his palms. He chanced a look up, hoping it was a passerby, and balked.

The Sultana. The source of Rohan's problems.

"It happens," she said with a sympathetic smile. "Runts rarely make it." Would she believe Rohan if he said it was Jafar's doing? Rohan wasn't sure he believed it himself. He was the one who was cursed, who had killed his parents, but what if Jafar's ire was at the core of it? That darkness that swirled in Jafar's gaze? "Aman had a graveyard for all the young deaths."

Rohan hadn't heard that name before. "Aman?"

The Sultana looked away, but not before he caught the swallow that bobbed her throat, half obscured by her pearl-white shawl. "My son. The prince."

The eyes she turned to him were ones of torment and pain, rimmed in red. She looked much, much older then. "I do not have the freedom to mourn or tell my people. I will always be a mother, but I'm a ruler first. My son has died, but the prince must still live on."

My son has died. So what Jafar had heard from the caravan leader was true, then. But what did she mean by *the prince must live on*? Were they not one and the same?

"Why?" Rohan asked.

"Life as a queen means making endless promises. One such vow was to the kingdom of Hulum. Our lands are similar and our armies a good match. Being equally matched, however, tends to result in a great many deaths for both sides."

The Sultana faced the city.

"To avoid that, we deemed it appropriate to unite our kingdoms."

Rohan didn't know how that was possible.

She glanced at him, searching for something, and sighed when she didn't find it. "Through marriage."

Rohan didn't know much about politics, but he knew that kingdoms united by matrimony rarely resulted in happy marriages. Most parties carried on with partners they preferred over their spouses, their unions restricted to writing.

"But how can the prince live on?" Rohan asked. Jafar would know the answer, but he wasn't here right now.

The Sultana laughed, as if he was hopeless, as if his question was the funniest thing in the world.

"Why did you leave your home?" she asked suddenly.

"Our father died," Rohan said softly. *I killed him with a wish.* "In a fire. Jafar said there was nothing left for us."

"In a fire," the Sultana mused. "How did you know he was dead?"

It was an odd question to ask when Rohan held a duckling in his hands that was most assuredly dead. "Because Jafar said so."

He didn't let Rohan verify it, nor did Rohan ever check himself.

The Sultana *hmm*ed.

Rohan's fingers were shriveling from the water and the duckling's soaked feathers. He wouldn't even need a shovel to bury so small a creature.

"Can you tell me where the graveyard is?" he asked.

She studied him again, and it took everything in Rohan not to squirm under her scrutiny.

"I can take you there," she said, finally, and began walking toward the veranda. Rohan petted one last duckling before joining her.

"Do you know what you have that your brother does

not?" she asked, and part of Rohan thought this entire conversation felt orchestrated, like when Baba would bring both Rohan and Jafar into a room and begin a conversation, furtively dictating the direction it took.

Still, Rohan could not imagine. His brother had—and was—everything. Smart, charismatic, clever, fearless. Surely the Sultana could see that.

"The illusion of compassion," she told him.

28

JAFAR

Jafar spent much of the day reading in the House of Wisdom and tinkering in the laboratory and parsing through all that he'd learned. More than the rubies was at stake now. He was no longer reading simply to learn—he needed to arm himself with all that he could. He had taken the Sultana's words to mean that he had to do better. Between him and Rohan, one of them would be crowned prince at the end of this.

If she wanted a ruthless prince, she would have one.

A prince. Jafar couldn't quite believe this was his reality now.

He heard the doors open multiple times, both he and

Iago tensing every time, wondering if it was Rohan. Did he still want the genie lamp, or had he abandoned all notion of salvaging their past in favor of the Sultana's promised future?

At dinner, Jafar still didn't feel like seeing Rohan's face, so he gathered a plate of food—for himself and Iago, which was why it took them a bit longer to get out of that dining hall—and disappeared into his room, locking it tight.

"Tell me you're not considering becoming her prince replacement," Iago said, hopping off his shoulder to sit on the bed. He took one look at Jafar's face and squawked. "You are! What happened to getting the rubies and getting out of here?"

"I still want them," Jafar said, biting into an olive.

"*And* you want princedom," Iago deadpanned, snatching the rest of it with his beak and swallowing it in one gulp. "You know, if we get greedy, we'll end up with nothing."

"We'll just have to get ourselves the genie, then," Jafar said, leaning back.

Iago squinted at him. "I don't think you're taking this seriously."

"I honestly don't care for princedom," Jafar replied. For whatever reason, he saw Harun, the Maghrizi royal vizier, in his mind's eye—never too far from the Sultana, always there to give her a nod to proceed or a shake of his head. "But I don't want Rohan to become prince, either. Not after what he's done." He took a deep breath. "You were right about him all along."

Iago didn't gloat or squawk or even brush away Jafar's words. He looked pensive. "I didn't want to be."

Jafar believed him. He hadn't even wanted Jafar brandishing the shreds of his scholarship, to avoid any possibility of upsetting Rohan.

But Jafar shouldn't have had to worry about Rohan turning on him. They were brothers. It was supposed to be him and Rohan against the world, as Mama had instructed when she'd told them about the two halves of the scarab being powerful together. But the universe had other plans. When it no longer had Baba to pit them against each other, it had replaced him with a new antagonist.

Perhaps, like the two halves of the golden scarab, Jafar and Rohan should never have remained together.

"Well, then," Iago said with a sigh. "Princedom it is."

Princedom. Jafar sent his empty plate off with a servant and readied for bed, settling under the sheets with the weight of the world on his shoulders. He had gone from a fresh start to all of *this* within days.

The windows were open wide to the night above. A black moon hung in the sky, waxing the barest sliver of a crescent.

He thought of Iago, an unexpected ally who had risen from the ashes of his old life like a phoenix. Jafar almost laughed at that imagery. He thought of the girl who, despite knowing so little about him and conversely the same, understood him more than anyone else. He thought of Rohan, whom he used to know like the back of his hand and could no longer understand at all. They'd never even slept apart before coming here—it was always the two of them in their own beds, feet apart, talking about everything and nothing until sleep snatched one away and the other followed.

What he did know was this: the Sultana wanted Jafar to take the place of her son. There was no other reason why she'd all but told him of her plans.

But Jafar had come here for knowledge, not power.

Are they not one and the same? Rohan would ask. He sometimes had the simplest, most mundane way of looking at things. Ways Jafar often overlooked because he was busy overthinking them. But in this case, Jafar wasn't certain the Rohan in his thoughts was right.

Iago swooped through the curtains and landed on the bed.

"What is he up to?" Jafar asked.

"Nothing," Iago said. "He's asleep."

Knowledge was indeed power, in many circumstances, but Jafar hadn't been interested in power, not until now. *That's a lie.* He had used his little knowledge of alchemy to overpower the prisoner in the dungeons. He'd done the same to Baba, time and time again. But to one day have control over an entire kingdom, especially one as large as Maghriz, felt tantalizing. Daunting, yes, but he was capable.

He would be in charge. He would never again have to answer to anyone. Not his father, nor anyone like him in a world full of people like him. He wouldn't have to answer to the Sultana or deal with her conniving ways.

He would never again have to be second best, and that was a welcome thought.

29

ROHAN

Rohan woke the next morning as dawn crested the horizon. Birds cried out in the distance, free and untethered from the world. When his father would join them for dinners, irate and strained from his work, Rohan would always wish he could ask him *why*. He, not anyone else, had made his own life difficult, and he had continued to do so every day, tangling himself deeper and deeper into a web from which he could never escape.

Rohan understood it now.

To live was to venture into that web. The center promised the best of lives, like a mirage in the desert, and the deeper one went, the stickier it became and the harder it was to retrace one's steps. Rohan was in the thick of it now, but he was so used to Jafar holding his hand that he didn't know how to navigate any of it alone.

Rohan tumbled out of bed with the knowledge that he would have to see Jafar today. He couldn't avoid him forever. It had been barely more than a day since they'd last spoken, but it felt like a lifetime.

He brushed his teeth with a siwak and washed his face, then pulled on his robes before picking up a bottle of attar that had been left on the alabaster counter in a bathroom as large as Baba's living room. Rohan uncapped the glass vial and took a sniff of the fragrant oil: orange blossoms and sugar, two of his most favored scents. He swiped some on with a smile.

Rohan always had believed in signs.

Jafar was in the dining hall.

He lounged on the cushions as if he were royalty. Iago sat on his shoulder, snickering at something. Jafar had always been a prince without a crown, even when he was eight and Rohan was six and they'd stolen food to survive.

He looked like he'd been waiting for him.

Rohan sat down with a gulp, not the least bit hungry anymore.

"How did you sleep?" Jafar asked, as if nothing were different between them.

"Fine enough," Rohan replied. There were still bits of red under Jafar's fingernails, remnants of the dungeon's horrors.

Jafar caught him looking. "Apparently, the false prisoner is fine. They were able to reverse everything I'd done." He looked down at his hands. "Can't say the same for myself."

False prisoner? Rohan couldn't hide his confusion. "What are you talking about?"

"Oh, did the Sultana not tell you?" Jafar asked. He seemed to be enjoying this. "It was all a ruse. She's been testing us because she wants one of us to replace her dead son."

Iago laughed, and Rohan wanted to throttle him and those vermillion feathers.

"Just throw it all on him at once, I guess," Iago said.

Jafar smirked.

Everything made sense now: the Sultana's telling them about the prisoner and materializing at the door to the dungeon in the dead of the night. Asking how and why and every question *beside* what the secret truly was.

Sickening. That was the only way to explain it. Rohan had never felt closer to Jafar than when Baba had died, and the Sultana had stepped between them and torn them apart, and for what? Something they had no say in, something that would serve only her in the end.

And her people. The people of *two* great kingdoms were

counting on the treaty, on the marriage, on the prince. Rohan wondered if Jafar knew of the marriage treaty, or if the Sultana had only given them the information that she knew would speak to each of them more.

Jafar had shared his half. For whatever reason, Rohan decided not to do the same.

A sound drew their attention to the servants' door at the far end of the dining hall. A man walked through, and Rohan thought nothing of it at first, but the man wouldn't stop staring. Fidgeting. Edging toward the main exit.

Something glinted under his sleeve.

Rohan recognized the look in his eye and his dubious movements. Jafar did, too.

"Thief," Jafar whispered, rising to his feet. "That man is a thief."

Rohan didn't move. He scanned the room, only to find it empty of guards. Strange, there had been a number of them here just a moment ago—where had they all gone?

"Stop!" Jafar shouted.

The man startled and began running for the door. An odd kind of run, as if his body didn't quite match his movements. Jafar rushed forward, and Rohan felt a moment's confusion thinking Jafar might throw himself at the man. That wasn't Jafar. That was—

The man froze in place.

Jafar's right hand was raised, his brow creased. He whispered a long string of words, and the man fell to his knees, gasping for air and clawing at his throat until Jafar released him from an invisible hold.

Rohan watched as his brother walked toward the thief, chin high, nose turned in a look of disdain that was eerily similar to the way Harun regarded the two of them. Iago settled on his shoulder with the same level of scorn on his tiny face.

"You could lose a hand," Jafar drawled at the man. "Or die as pitifully as you live."

He kicked at the man's arm, and an ornament coated in gold slipped out of his sleeve.

"N-no," the man stuttered. His headdress was dirty, his robes tattered. He was clearly a servant escaping for a better life, and he reminded Rohan of the prisoner, in a way. "It won't be missed."

Jafar laughed. "And who are you to decide that?"

Rohan couldn't understand why Jafar was behaving as if he'd never done the same. As if their childhood wasn't shaped by the pair of them running through the streets, stealing all that they could in order to keep themselves and their parents alive.

"Let him go, Jafar," Rohan said, and cursed the warble in his voice.

"Let him go?" Jafar asked, turning his scorn to Rohan. "He stole."

"As did we. For years."

Jafar's eyes flashed. "Never from a palace. Never something of value."

The man would take that trinket and sell it for coin, money he would later trade for food. There was no difference between them and him—except that he got caught.

Which is his fault.

Rohan shook his head free of the thought. *They* had caught him, which meant they had the power to let him walk free. Who were they to judge someone when they'd done the exact same?

"He loses a hand," Jafar said. Interrogating a prisoner was one thing, but a thief was different. Closer to home. Why was Jafar being so ruthless? So heartless?

"No," Rohan rasped. "We can let him go. No one will know about this but us."

"P-please," the man whimpered.

Rohan couldn't stop his lip from curling. He hated begging. "Or we take him to the Sultana and allow her to decide."

"Allow the Sultana to decide? Ask her like she's your mother?" Jafar asked. He left his post towering over the man to circle Rohan. "Just a trinket, just an orange, just a bit of bread—what kind of prince would you be if you let every criminal walk free? Your kingdom would be full of rats."

Iago shuddered at the image.

Rohan had to hold back a shudder himself, because Jafar was right, but that didn't mean he was going about it the right way.

"You would kill him instead?" Rohan asked, refusing to let Jafar goad him.

Jafar studied the man, still whimpering and on his knees. He didn't even try to rise. He had accepted whatever fate was being cast upon him, and *that* disappointed Rohan more than anything else. The longer Rohan remained in the man's presence, the more he felt it was folly to compare him to them. They had been better thieves than this failure.

"I'd make an example of him," Jafar replied simply. "That could mean killing him or taking a hand, or even doing something far less permanent."

A crackle broke the silence, along with a heavy rustling and more crackling—like bones being reshaped with a series of sickening crunches.

It was coming from where the man was kneeling.

The two of them whirled to face the thief, and Rohan's jaw dropped as he watched the man transform, rising up and up and—

"Sultana," Rohan whispered.

"Alchemy," Jafar murmured.

The Sultana stood in the place of the kneeling, whimpering servant, gown and jewels intact, without a single hair out of place.

"Indeed," she said, an aura of electric blue still sizzling around her figure.

"We didn't know," Rohan said.

"As was the intention," the Sultana said, looking between the two of them. "One of you wanted to kill me, one of you wanted to send me away. You both still have much to learn, but time is not on our side.

"The crown must be donned today, and one of you will wear it."

30

ROHAN

Time had spun too quickly for Rohan in Maghriz. His next breath always felt leagues out of reach. Lifetimes seemed to pass in the span of hours; and now either he or his brother would become a prince after they'd nearly killed the queen. He hadn't wanted to believe it when Jafar had told him one of them was to replace the missing prince, but the Sultana had cleared the air without a care for how he'd take the news.

The embers of their old life in the village of Ghurub had not even turned to ash.

Harun was already in the throne room when Rohan and Jafar arrived with the Sultana. The emptiness was almost tangible. The vizier watched them with displeasure, and now Rohan would forever associate sapphire blue with disdain.

"He doesn't look happy," Jafar whispered, surprising Rohan with the commentary. As loath as Rohan was to admit it, he had missed Jafar's usual banter. He couldn't tell him that now. He couldn't even speak to him now, not without looking like he was pandering or begging or lonely.

"Never does," Iago whispered back, and only then did Rohan realize that Jafar hadn't been speaking to him.

The Sultana took a seat on her throne, staring at Rohan for the longest moment before doing the same to Jafar. Rohan noticed two men standing to the side, one with a thin strip of papyrus draped around his neck like a shawl. A tape measure, Rohan thought it was.

"I trust you ate your fill before your debate," the Sultana said.

"Yes, Your Highness," Rohan said. He thought about what the Sultana said he possessed over Jafar's long list of talents.

She smiled at him, and it might have looked reassuring, but Rohan might have imagined it.

"As you are aware, my son drowned many moons ago," the Sultana said. She'd tried to cull the emotion from her voice, but Rohan heard it. The mourning she wasn't allowed to do in public was wound tight into her every word and movement. "Rohan, you asked why I cannot tell my people of his death. Jafar, you suggested—not so kindly, I might add—the solution I already had in mind when the two of you arrived in the House of Wisdom.

"I'm not one to believe in coincidences, but a queen always has her eye open for opportunities. And when I saw you, an ambitious pair of boys who had ventured miles to learn, I knew one of you would take the place of my son."

Neither Rohan nor Jafar spoke or reacted, only listened.

"It is no small task, I'm aware," the Sultana continued, "but I've studied you both, and I've never felt more certain."

A lie, Rohan thought. She'd said they had much more to learn, but she was short on time.

"Why not tell the people he's dead?" Jafar asked. "Why not let your people mourn and allow yourself to mourn?"

"You speak as if it is so simple. I've long had a treaty with Hulum," the Sultana explained. "Our children were sworn to each other."

"Sworn," Jafar said slowly, "as in to be married."

The Sultana nodded. "If the treaty fails, there's every likelihood the Hulumi will leap to arms."

The royal vizier barked a dry laugh. "Their king has been eagerly waiting for an excuse to pick up another sword."

Rohan wondered if he preferred a peaceful resolution or one that led to battle. War was part of his job, after all.

"A queen must always do what is best for her people," the Sultana said. "And if that means forgoing the act of mourning my son, then so be it."

"What's in it for us? What if we don't want to be your prince?" Rohan asked. When he'd first arrived, he had only ever wanted his three wishes. He didn't know what he wanted anymore, but he didn't think he wanted to marry a princess sworn to a drowned prince. Rohan didn't even think Jafar would want that.

"Is that not the dream of the common boy?" she replied.

Jafar laughed bitterly. "Do you believe every common boy to be the same? That we have the same desires and dreams and wishes, like we're a colony of ants doing the queen's bidding? For a ruler who claims to love her people, that is a very selfish way of thinking."

For a moment, the Sultana looked taken aback, but she recovered quickly. "You are right, but it is clearer now more than ever that there is no better future for our kingdom than one ruled by a sultan who has experienced life at every level."

Rohan thought back to when they had huddled in Baba's old storeroom, plotting their journey to Maghriz. Jafar had promised a life where they would live as princes, and now, mere weeks later, one of them was going to be *crowned* a prince.

He felt faint.

"Jafar, you are dedicated and relentless, ready to do anything to protect those you love," the Sultana said. "Rohan, you are kind and possess the patience of diplomacy, a rare trait. Together, you make a formidable pair."

Together, as Mama had stressed.

"But I have only one crown, one heir, and after much thought," the Sultana continued, looking from one brother to the next, "Harun and I have come to the conclusion that you are to take my son's place."

31

JAFAR

When the Sultana had said she needed to choose between them today, Jafar hadn't thought that meant this instant. He saw the words directed at Rohan and wanted to tell the Sultana she was mistaken. Jafar was standing *here*, not *there*. She could not have meant his younger brother, who knew so little of the world, who would never step out of the shadows without coaxing but would happily take credit for deeds beyond his capabilities.

Jafar had known the Sultana for less time than he'd known anyone in his life, and yet the betrayal rippling through him was startling.

Rohan balked. "Me?"

The Sultana's quick laugh was muffled in Jafar's ears.

"Yes, you, Rohan," she said. "But from this point forward, you will be known as Aman."

Her voice cracked when she spoke her drowned son's name, as Jafar's heart already had.

"I don't know how to feel," Rohan said while a pair of dressmakers swept toward him. He was lying—he knew exactly how to feel. Jafar recognized that trill of excitement in his brother's tone.

His own blood roared. He could barely comprehend his surroundings, so full of noise and hurt and anger that he wanted to scream. He couldn't breathe. Couldn't think. Couldn't focus.

Later, he remembered turning his back to the Sultana and her vizier. He remembered Rohan calling his name, the marble floors unforgiving beneath his feet, the morning heat surrounding him like a blanket against his cold reality.

It wasn't that Jafar would not be crowned, but that *Rohan would be.* He hadn't come here for power and a throne, but he could not stand for his brother to have both or either.

"Jafar."

The world spiraled into focus. He opened his eyes and stared straight into Iago's golden ones. They were outside in the gardens. When had he stumbled out here?

"Don't make me slap you," Iago squawked, settling on a plinth by the reflecting pool. The water rippled ever so slightly as a pair of birds flitted in and out of the roses.

Jafar was still finding it hard to breathe. Rohan was being crowned prince. Rohan. His—his—

"Do you know what we have that Rohan doesn't?" Iago asked.

"An uncrowned head?" Jafar asked.

"Well, at least you still have your wits about you," Iago remarked. "But no, a plan. We still need to get those rubies."

He'd momentarily forgotten about the rubies.

"For what? To control the chef as he cooks?" Jafar asked.

"You know what, I think I will slap you," Iago replied cheerily.

"I don't even know where the rubies are," Jafar said.

"In the Sultana's pocket," Iago said. "I saw her fiddling with them. I can't tell if she's using them."

"She isn't," Jafar said, pressing his eyes closed until his head cleared. Somewhat. He'd read that there were indications when the rubies were being used, subtle enough that it wasn't fully noticeable to those who didn't know where to look.

"I think she was trying to use them to buy more time for her prince problem before she saw us. Maybe persuade the Hulumi king or something," Jafar rambled as Iago lifted a brow. "I don't know. Desperate minds rarely think things through."

"Well, there you go, then," Iago said.

"There we go what?" Jafar asked. "Are we just going to reach into her pocket and pull them out?"

"Yes," Iago said, and rolled a pair of cheap red glass orbs in his talons. Jafar didn't know when or where Iago had found them. "She's frazzled and as anxious about everything as we are. We'll swap them, and she won't notice a thing. Desperate minds, remember? You said it yourself."

"Oh, goody," Iago said, "she's alone."

The throne room was indeed empty. Rohan was nowhere to be seen, nor was the royal vizier, but the Sultana was waiting for Jafar.

"He was taken to be fitted for a wardrobe," the Sultana explained before he could ask. "You will be fitted for a new collection as well."

"For what?" Jafar asked, his voice tight. The throne room felt larger than when he'd first arrived, or maybe it was just he who had become smaller, something *less than* without his brother's company.

"For a life of luxury as a companion to the prince,"

she said, but Jafar wouldn't fall for that again. He'd always known the Sultana was cunning, yet somehow he'd arrived in Maghriz and ignored the fact.

Jafar scoffed. "Advisor, you mean, because 'together, we make a formidable pair'?"

"If you would rather leave the palace, you are welcome to, but Rohan must be made presentable for the princess and her father tonight."

Tonight. Jafar felt cold all over. Iago's talons tightened around Jafar's shoulder.

"Will there be no swearing in or ceremony?" he asked, grasping at straws. Trying to delay the inevitable.

"Aman has always been prince," the Sultana said. There she was again, manipulating words and the world, renaming his brother like he was a pet fish she'd come to own.

"Do you really think the people will look at him and believe he's your son?" Jafar asked. "No alchemy can alter that many minds at once."

"We're changing guards as we speak. Those who will patrol inside the palace will never have seen the prince before. As far as officials go, my son was rarely present to discuss matters of state. Believe me, Jafar, I have thought this through."

Jafar scoffed. "No matter what your kingdom might believe, Rohan will always be my brother first—and a commoner."

Then he leaned closer to Iago, biting out a single word under his breath to signal the start of their plan. *"Now."*

The Sultana smiled as Iago leaped off Jafar's shoulder. "I expect nothing less. Do you know why you were not chosen?"

There were too many bitter ways to answer that question, and so Jafar remained silent.

"You possess far more qualities worthy of a king than your brother ever will," the Sultana said as Iago rounded behind her. For a bright red parrot, he could be subtle when he wanted to be. "But there is a darkness about you, a beast you keep hidden. And you hide it well."

Jafar's pulse thrummed beneath his left eye, at the swell of his cheekbone. "That same darkness lives in his blood."

"You were prepared to kill that prisoner, and the thief," the Sultana said.

"Prepared to," Jafar parroted her words back at her, half his focus on Iago dipping his beak into her pocket. "He killed an innocent, helpless duckling."

She held his gaze. "As you did your father."

Behind her, Iago's beak fell open with a soundless croak, just as surprised as Jafar that she'd somehow learned the truth. Jafar could only stare.

"No retort?" she asked. "Am I wrong to assume that days after you are accepted into the House of Wisdom, your father destroys your scholarship, and so he dies in a mysterious fire?

Why else would you arrive here with no scholarship in hand?"

It was true, and no one but Iago knew of the fact. Baba had deserved every moment of his suffering, every lick of the fire that burned him to a crisp. The only remorse he had ever felt about the fire was because of Rohan's suffering. His pain, his self-blame.

Now, Jafar regretted nothing.

She lowered her chin to look him straight in the eye. "Something tells me his death was due to more than the scholarship. Was it to protect you and your brother, or was it to unleash your anger?"

"Are they not one and the same?" Jafar asked. He couldn't stop his eyes from widening when Iago's talon hooked in the Sultana's cloak. He quickly whipped his gaze to the window as if he'd seen something flit past, and the Sultana looked, too, her cloak shifting with the movement. Iago pulled free and hopped to the back of the throne.

The Sultana *hmm*ed in answer. A thrum spread to Jafar's veins, beating beneath his skin, begging for release.

"I will not have a woman who lies to her people wielding judgment upon me," Jafar said. "You know nothing of my life and my suffering. Or Rohan's, for that matter. Do you think he can take the place of a son you had groomed for the throne from birth? Do you think your son's replacement only needed to look somewhat like him? Rohan is my brother. If

I am a monster, then he is my match. Death surrounds him. You've seen it yourself."

Rohan did have a gentler soul than he did, but Jafar had seen the dead duckling in Rohan's hands. He'd seen the way Baba emerged in Rohan's actions at times. He didn't know what his brother was truly capable of doing.

Jafar was the one who had given the Sultana what she had needed. *Jafar* had been the one to pass her test. Barely a day later, this was his reward.

"I'm queen," the Sultana said. "I don't waver in my decisions. I will say again that you are welcome to remain here as the prince's companion and even continue your studies in the House of Wisdom. Or leave."

It didn't matter, he told himself. If the Sultana wanted to dig herself and her kingdom a grave, that was her choice. Perhaps Rohan *could* be taught. He was young and willing to learn.

Jafar looked to Iago to see if he'd found the rubies, but the parrot only shook his head. At the question in Jafar's furrowed brow, Iago gestured to her other pocket with a wing.

The Sultana heard the rustle of his feathers. She started to turn around. "Wh—"

"F-fine," Jafar half shouted.

She lifted her eyebrows at him. "What did you say?"

"I said fine. Yes. I accept your offer."

For you, Mama. For the oath he'd made to her long ago.

The Sultana smiled and clasped her hands. "I would not be half the queen that I am without my vizier, and I know for certain the same will apply to you and your brother one day."

Jafar returned her smile, but he had no intention of remaining long enough to find out, not when Iago was grinning ear to ear from the edge of the Sultana's throne, something shiny gripped in his talons.

He owed the Sultana nothing. It was she who should be thanking him for delivering her a replacement on a gilded tray. Iago returned to his shoulder, and the pair of them turned to leave.

He would be there for Rohan's banquet, the moment where he'd officially assume duties as prince. A betrothed prince with an entire court of people to guide him, at which point he would no longer need Jafar.

Still, Jafar would be there for his brother, because he carried an oath.

And then they would be done.

32

ROHAN

In the dressmaker's quarters, Rohan stood on a pedestal where he was spun around and poked and prodded. He had come to Maghriz to atone for—and rectify—killing his baba, not to be rewarded with luxury. He had come to Maghriz for a genie in a lamp, not a crown. He had come to Maghriz for his brother, not a courtship.

A life of grandeur. A crown. A courtship. A *wife*. Somehow that was more nerve-racking than inheriting a kingdom. He was only seventeen. He wasn't ready to entrust his life to another and have her life entrusted to him.

After taking measurements, the dressmaker shooed him away and rushed to work, ignoring Rohan's profuse thanks.

He was then sent to another room, though "room" was putting it lightly.

If only you could see your penniless boys now, Baba, Rohan thought: the lush bed, the wide windows with a view of the gardens more colorful than the dressmaker's textiles. The marble on the floor gleamed with polish, and the threads on the rug beneath his feet were so tightly woven, the piece would have taken weeks to complete.

It was exquisite. It was overwhelming.

He wasn't a visitor running his fingers over the lacquered dresser. His clothes would soon sit in its drawers. He owned the dresser, the rug, the bed, and the gossamer curtains fluttering at the windows.

He would soon own this kingdom.

Rohan felt very sick, and very, very alone.

"You fit right in."

The Sultana stepped through the door, regal in her obsidian gown. The fine lines across her brow deepened with her smile, though he could see the sorrow that was more pronounced now. As if she had given herself permission to grieve in his presence. Or because someone was swiftly taking the place of her son.

"What if neither of us looked like him?" Rohan asked. "What if you couldn't find a replacement, and the king of Hulum needed to be told the truth?"

"I would have found a replacement regardless," the Sultana said. She reached into her pocket and gave the slightest pause. "I was in the House of Wisdom the day I found you and your brother, preparing to buy myself more time. The king of Hulum last saw my son when he was three years of age." She tilted her head. "What is this about?"

Coincidence never worked out well, did it? If one coincidence could be made in a matter of days, so could another. If she could so easily replace her son with a random stranger, how easy would it be to replace Rohan with someone else?

The Sultana seemed to guess his thoughts. "Do not mistake circumstance for coincidence. And do not devalue a gift simply because it was given to you and not someone else. You crossed the sands for a better life, and I was here to provide it to you."

"I went from an orphan to a prince as if I'd called upon a genie," Rohan said. It was too much too soon.

She smiled. "Being a prince isn't as glamorous as one would assume. You may need more wishes than you think."

Rohan found himself waiting for Jafar's quip, waiting for him to answer her or scoff under his breath and whisper a response for Rohan alone, but he wasn't here.

"He will come around," the Sultana said.

Rohan looked away. "I wasn't thinking about him."

"Of course," she replied with a look that made him feel

like a little boy. "But worry not. He will be by your side at all times. I would not lead as well as I do without my vizier, and my hope is that Jafar will be that for you."

Rohan did not see that happening, but he smiled nonetheless.

"Now come, your clothes will be ready shortly, but a boy needs more than fancy clothes to be a prince," the Sultana said. "I need you to know the basics, at least, of Maghrizi history, and some etiquette. Like how to walk like you own a kingdom and not merely the baubles in your pocket."

Rohan followed her away, knowing that no matter how much he learned, he would never be fit for a crown. Unlike Jafar.

33

JAFAR

Jafar found himself on the rooftop terrace again. Below, the reflecting pool shimmered under the early light. A black cat lapped at the turquoise waters, darting into the bushes when a pair of attendants walked past.

Beneath his burning anger, Jafar felt a deep and aching loneliness in the pit of his stomach, the rest of his emotions a blistering storm around it.

"I thought you'd be a lot happier to have those in hand," Iago said.

He spoke of the rubies.

Jafar rolled them over in his palm. Over a decade since he'd heard the story from Mama, since he'd snuck into her room and read all that he could about them, and they were finally his. He'd never seen anything like them, and Baba had owned a fair share of jewels. These were brilliant, clear crimson, faceted in a way that mesmerized and pulled him closer. *Possessed* him, almost.

"Can they really control someone?"

"Indeed," Jafar said, closing his fist around them. He had what he wanted now: the ability to control those around him, after years of having every inch of his life controlled by another.

But it was also a feat he could have easily accomplished as prince. A thought that quickly diminished the value of the rubies he'd traversed all this way to retrieve.

"You know, if you really want that crown, you could use them to get the Sultana to change her mind," Iago suggested.

Jafar laughed sadly. "Why are you always trying to help me?"

No one else ever did—Rohan would at times, yes, but there was always a limit with him. Help was never offered so adamantly, so selflessly.

"You got me the answers I wanted," Iago said.

"You've been helping me longer," Jafar countered.

Iago tilted his head, considering his reply. "I want you to succeed, I suppose. I know I didn't live with you all that long, but the time I spent on that pedestal in your baba's room was long enough. I know what it's like to have your worth trashed, to have no control over your life. I've eaten a lot of crackers, you know."

"I promise you'll never have to eat crackers," Jafar said, and then pursed his lips. "Unless it's for a cause."

"What kind of cause requires eating crackers?" Iago asked, squinting an eye at him.

"You never know," Jafar replied.

Iago *hmm*ed. "We'll revisit that one. Oh, heads up. Oh, *wow*."

Jafar felt her presence before he saw her. Moon girl. Boisterous girl. He'd never seen her outside, under the sky. Even the sun brightened, its rays grasping for her bronzed skin. She was dressed in pure white, and when she tilted her head, he saw a dusting of freckles over her nose.

"Do we know her?" Iago asked, voice hushed.

"Yes and no," Jafar replied.

Iago muttered something under his breath.

"Every time I see you, you're a little sadder," the girl said in that voice of silk. He wanted to close the distance between them, to shut his eyes and let her voice take him away.

"Play another round with me," Jafar said. He sounded desperate, even to his own ears.

She considered him with a tilt of her head so like Iago, he almost laughed.

"Always," she said, softening.

He contemplated his words. "I—I'm sometimes called Jafar."

Her lips curved in a one-sided smile, but it looked sad. "I'm sometimes called Yara."

"Pleasure to make your acquaintance, Yara," Jafar said, dipping his head in respect. He flicked his gaze up, crashing dangerously into hers like flint.

"You shouldn't look me in the eye like that," she whispered.

Her gaze was on his mouth; her breathing was a little louder than it had been seconds before. If he listened closely, he could hear her heartbeat beneath the hum of the city, quickening with his own.

"Oh?" he asked in the same whisper. "Am I in the presence of a princess?"

Her breath caught, and Jafar had a horrible, horrible thought. He did not allow himself to think it.

"Well?" he asked. "Why not?"

"Because," she replied, stepping closer with a boldness he was not expecting. "It makes me want to do catastrophic things."

"Nothing is stopping you," Jafar said. There was a rasp in his voice and something abrading in his chest that threatened to claw out of him. He saw the same war in her, the same *need*.

"Everything is," she said with a humorless laugh.

She sounded terribly, tragically sad, and Jafar wanted to know why.

A horse protested in the stables beyond the gardens, drawing their attention. Sand stirred clouds of gold everywhere Jafar looked.

Yara turned to him, eyes wide with an idea. "We should go to the bazaar. Just the two of us, and your beautiful bird." Jafar started to object. "*Now*, before someone notices that we're missing."

Jafar didn't have the heart to tell her no one would.

34

ROHAN

The Sultana gestured to the map for the thousand and first time, and Rohan restrained a sigh. The map spanned the entirety of the floor in this fortified room, tucked in an almost invisible corridor. The Maghrizi palace had a good number of guests on any given day, and the Sultana's generosity allowed them to wander as they pleased.

And so the palace also held many well-kept secrets.

"Agrabah," Rohan said, pointing. Then he pointed to the west. "Hulum."

He recited the rest of the kingdoms and cities, remembering a time not too long before when he had pored over a much smaller map, his and his brother's heads pressed together as they charted out their new lives.

"Ah," the Sultana scolded. "Chin up. Spine straight."

He remembered Jafar telling him that, too, while he studied the upper-class men and women in the bazaar and the way they strutted about.

Rohan rearranged his posture, feeling like a peacock.

The Sultana nodded. "Better. Do you know how to fight?"

"I—" Rohan stopped. *I can kill.* What was he supposed to say, that he'd never held a blade in his life? Neither he nor Jafar had. Most of the boys in their village knew how to wield a sword and parry one another, but Baba had never thought it important to let his boys learn.

It would have required too much effort on his part.

"I see," the Sultana replied, and then pinched her lips tight. "We'll have to get you a wooden blade soon, then." She turned to the royal vizier. "Fetch Sharif and tell him to prepare his training swords."

Rohan said nothing. He wanted to say he was sorry for learning too slowly, for lacking the skills of a prince. Sorry her son was dead and that he was the only option.

But he hadn't asked to be a prince. She'd insisted.

She pulled out another book, and Rohan's eyes threatened to fall shut. She thunked it down in front of him. "Read. Until we get you in front of Sharif."

35

JAFAR

The bazaar was alive with wonder, mostly because Jafar was holding Yara's hand. He didn't know when that had happened. They were like moons orbiting the same planet, gravitating round and around until they'd collided, sparks rupturing the peace he had attempted to cultivate in his soul.

She twined her fingers between his, locking him in place. Yara. It was a lovely name for a lovely girl. Jafar had never considered himself to be like one of those lovelorn fools from Mama's tales, but it felt *nice* to hold her hand. It felt right. He liked to think of himself as a man of many words. He was versed in history and language and, if he was vaunting, the arcane.

Yet Yara continued to make him speechless.

"I seem to be trapped," Jafar managed.

Yara looked down and swiped her thumb along the back of his, making his breath catch. As if that weren't enough, she swung their clasped hands between them, letting the backs of his fingers graze the warm curve of her thigh. He savored the gasp that shuddered out of her.

On his shoulder, Iago was just as starstruck.

In this moment, Jafar could forget that Rohan had taken credit for his work and won the Sultana's secret competition. The world could crash and burn and he wouldn't care, for he was happily, gloriously, blissfully drowning in the marvel that was Yara.

She leaned into him, as close as she could without touching him with her body. "That you are, ink boy."

This was torture.

"Shall we?" she asked, gesturing ahead as if she wasn't at all affected.

Jafar led them deeper into the bazaar. Men, women, children—even the desert came to play, dust stirring in excitement, sand glittering like diamonds. There were rolls of fabric in every hue, spices in just as many shades, mounds fragrant and rich. People bartered with good-natured merchants, surprising him. None of them wore a permanent frown as his father had. None of them snapped and shooed customers away when they asked too many questions.

Yara bounced in her shoes as they meandered the stalls, and pulled him along with her, five fingerprints of fire sending shock up his veins. "Where do you want to go first?"

"Anywhere," Jafar said. *Everywhere.*

They passed a man selling oils in every scent, some deep and enigmatic as the night, others bright and flowery as the girl by Jafar's side. The man indulged her questions, and just before they left, he dabbed one of the oils on her neck. It took everything in Jafar to not press his nose to her dusky skin.

He took her to a merchant selling baubles and jewelry, watching as her eyes shone even more at the sight of the glittering trinkets.

"You like what shines," the merchant-woman said.

"Don't we all?" Yara asked.

The woman tilted her head. "We like what gives us power, and to shine is to be powerful, no?"

She directed the question at Jafar, as if she could see his thoughts. He didn't know if what she said was true, but a jewel did make one stand out from the crowd. Like the rubies in his pocket.

"Let's get moving," Iago said, shivering.

Jafar agreed.

"My mama loved shiny things," Yara said with a laugh as Jafar led her away.

"Were you close with your mother?" Jafar asked.

She laughed. "Kill my mama and I'll weep. Hurt my baba and it's as if you've hurt me."

Jafar couldn't imagine anyone feeling that way about their baba. He tugged Yara over to the next stall, and then the next, drinking in her reactions and her laughter. Her awe and her excitement.

He bought her a flower from a vendor who had traveled from a far-off isle, the bud matching the pure white of her gown. He bought her a pastry filled with almonds and drenched in honey, topped with crushed rose petals the same hue as her pretty lips, and she bought him knafeh, warmed and gooey from the heat.

He told her of the alchemical findings he had just unearthed during one of his many excursions through the House of Wisdom. He told her of how he had survived a fire that took down the empire of a merchant. When she pushed and prodded with her questions, he even told her he had saved a boy close to his age before the flames could claim him.

But as he and Yara continued through the twisting paths of the bazaar, he remembered that all things came to an end. He still didn't know who she was, and really, he didn't know who *he* was, either, in the grand scheme of the Sultana's plans now that Rohan was the prince.

Yara froze. "Oh, camel humps, no."

Jafar followed her line of sight to a riot of sound. A

caravan had paused by one of the stalls on the outer edge of the bazaar, closest to the road.

This was no normal caravan, either; it dripped elegance, with steeds draped in jewel-toned cloth and wheels glinting in the sun. The burly driver looked as though he doubled as a bodyguard, and Yara seemed to recognize him.

"They're here," she whispered. "We have to get back to the palace."

36

ROHAN

Rohan had just finished memorizing far too many details he wished he didn't need to know about the deceased Maghrizi prince when the door flew open. It wasn't Sharif with wooden swords, but the dressmaker and a servant boy, both red-faced and white-robed. The dressmaker dropped a pile of clothes on the large table in the center of the room.

"What is the meaning of this?" the royal vizier asked.

"You could have called us to your quarters," the Sultana agreed, eyeing the intruders.

"The Hulumi king has been sighted. His arrival is imminent," the dressmaker said, gesturing for Rohan to rise. The king of Hulum was here. *Here.* "Arms spread. Basim, disrobe him."

"I had hoped he would have time to bathe and dress more comfortably," the Sultana said, closing the doors. Rohan held back a sigh of relief when she turned away.

Why were they all panicking? He was the only one allowed to panic. If *they* panicked, his panic would amplify tenfold.

The servant boy stripped him to his underclothes, and the dressmaker looked like he wanted to set them on fire.

"Dress the boy," the royal vizier snapped, and the dressmaker and his servant leaped to attention, dragging a washcloth along his body first before dressing him in layer after layer. When they took a step back, Rohan wriggled his shoulders and straightened the cuffs. The threads were immaculate, the linen spun so finely that the almost white, barely there green of his shirt had a sheen the deeper green of his robes wanted to swallow whole.

The dressmaker had worked quickly, and well. They wrapped and secured a headdress in bright white with a plume of green that matched his robes. His entire ensemble was astounding, and he wished Jafar were here to approve of it. He wished this moment didn't feel as though he were preparing for his beheading.

"Perfect," the Sultana said with approval just as the door flew open again.

A messenger darted inside this time, panting. "The Hulumi, Your Highness. The king is here."

Rohan's heart leaped to his throat. It felt like an army was at their door, rather than a peaceful convoy.

The Sultana squared her shoulders, relieving the messenger and the others before she and Harun turned back to Rohan.

"Remember, these people are the enemy," Harun said. "You're—"

"I'm marrying the enemy," Rohan said, a flustered laugh breaking out of him. He no longer felt like he'd been promoted from pauper to prince. He felt like a free man suddenly caged. His future was suddenly controlled by a woman he barely knew but would now call Mother.

"Yes and no," the Sultana said. "In this particular situation, neither of us is at war yet—this will be no different from your interrogating the Maghrizi prisoner."

Rohan snapped his head up to look at her. *She knows.* She winked and led him out of the room and through several halls. He didn't want this. He could barely breathe. He wanted Jafar. He needed Jafar.

But Rohan was the prince now. He would one day lead an entire kingdom of people. He trailed after her. The emerald cloak over her gown undulated in the light, mocking him, almost. *What* are *you doing here?* it seemed to ask.

He didn't know.

What if the princess was rude? What if she saw straight through his ruse and knew he was nothing but a villager? Rohan paused as another thought suddenly rose from the chaos of his mind: *What if she's ugly?*

The Sultana laughed, and he realized he had asked the question out loud. He chewed his lip. Vain was the last thing he wanted to be seen as.

"That is always a concern, isn't it?" the Sultana asked. "We royalty have power over much, but the freedom to choose upon looks isn't one of them."

That was infinitely unhelpful, and it must have been clear on his face, for she pondered him for a moment.

She gestured to the archway leading to the meeting hall up ahead. "Worry not, you'll be meeting her father first."

His heart sank to his knees, and before he could formulate a response, they turned the corner and Rohan saw the king for himself.

The king of Hulum stood by the window overlooking the courtyard. He was tall and built as though he could crush Rohan's skull between his palms without breaking a sweat. A black cloak edged in gold shrouded his robes. His beard was thick and dark as the pits of his eyes, which scrutinized Rohan as he entered the room with the Sultana.

Make sure you walk beside me, not behind me, she had said.

He couldn't read people like Jafar could, but he knew immediately that the king of Hulum disliked him. Contempt tightened his mouth as he swept a look down Rohan and turned away. The dismissal was worse than his distaste.

He had failed as a prince already.

"Marhaba, Qadir," the Sultana said, inclining her head. "Please, be seated."

He was an older man, with streaks of white in his dark hair and fine lines drawn across his austere features.

"It has been long," the king said to her, smiling like it pained him to do so. His gaze was cold and shrewd. "The years have treated you well."

The comment made Rohan uncomfortable, and it wasn't even directed at him.

"As they have you," the Sultana said with a smile that told Rohan she didn't actually think so.

Rohan knew that the king of Hulum was searching for a reason to nullify their agreement. What kind of king would be on the lookout for war? It promised death not only for the Maghrizi, but the Hulumi as well.

Rohan thought of the duckling that he was still uncertain if he or Jafar had killed, or if it had simply been a runt on its last days. Still, there was something powerful in knowing he could control what might be something's last breath. And sometimes, he'd felt powerful knowing he'd caused Baba's death; someone with that much status in their village was gone because of him. Was that how it felt when one was king?

"I take it your journey here was uneventful?" the Sultana asked.

"Only the usual suspects," the king said. His eyes tracked her as she sat down and patted the spot beside her for Rohan. "Bandits hiding in the dunes, ruffians underestimating a modest caravan."

"A boon, then, that you sent your daughter ahead of time," the Sultana said, her voice hard. It seemed as though his daughter wasn't a welcome guest. *But wait*—that meant the princess was here in the palace. *Had* been in the palace, likely before Rohan and Jafar had even arrived. It was a wonder Rohan hadn't already met her.

"Your tone suggests I sent her here with ulterior motives," the king said. "Are you implying that she is a spy?"

"Do not mistake a sore throat for an insinuating tone, Qadir," the Sultana said. "I allowed her free rein of the palace while heeding your wishes. I did not allow my son to meet her without your being present."

Rohan was going to need lessons on how to speak to royalty by severing heads with words. This back-and-forth was brutal.

The Sultana smiled. "And now my son looks forward to being reacquainted with her at tonight's banquet."

Rohan had to remind himself that the son in question was him. *Tonight?* Disappointment flooded through him. He hadn't realized he had been hoping to see her now. *Listen to yourself. Already an entitled brat.*

Jafar's voice in his head was very loud.

The king continued to scrutinize Rohan, his gaze frigid and relentless as a servant appeared in the room, gripping the antique gold handles of a tray with white-knuckled fingers. Everyone was strung tight.

She set the tray on the ottoman and stepped back.

"Please," the Sultana said to the king. "There is nothing finer than Maghrizi tea."

King Qadir all but sneered. "Only because the rest of us have acquired the taste for qahwa."

It was a slight, Rohan realized, a subtle attack on the Sultana that she took like a slap to the face. Red bloomed in her cheeks. The royal vizier looked ready to summon the guards. Rohan's fingers closed into fists, anxiety coiling them tight.

"I'll have a cup, please," he said, breaking the tension in one clear cut. The Sultana smiled, relief in her eyes. King Qadir worked his jaw. "Not all of us can stomach qahwa, unfortunately."

"I can attest to that," the Sultana said with a hearty laugh.

Rohan moved to pour himself a cup before the Sultana held him back with a subtle squeeze on his elbow. A servant moved to serve him. Right. He had completely forgotten.

And he was the only one with a cup of tea now. He wished he could retract his words along with this wretched crown. He sipped, and it took everything in him not to spit the mouthful right back out. It was beyond scalding.

"Will that be all, then?" the king asked. The Sultana looked taken aback. "Until tonight."

"I was under the impression you wanted to meet with me and my son," she said.

He stared at Rohan. "I am tired. I only wanted to meet now because I'd heard rumors of your son's demise, and after a week of traveling in the desert sun, I was beginning to believe them. I see now that they were unfounded."

It seemed he was done being subtle.

"Indeed they were," the Sultana said with a brittle laugh. She patted Rohan's hand. "Here he is."

The king of Hulum did not smile or laugh or say a word, only stared at Rohan as if he could see every lie.

37

JAFAR

Jafar and Yara returned to the palace in record time and stumbled into a flurry of movement: servants marching to and fro, some hefting furniture, others carrying oil for lanterns and chandeliers. Iago hopped off his shoulder and disappeared with a grumble, leaving Jafar alone with Yara at last. The two of them ducked into a corridor away from the ruckus, and Yara turned to him with her signature wicked grin. She had a way of making him feel like the only person in the world.

He wanted to know why fear had crossed her face when she'd seen that caravan, and why she was in such a rush.

"One last trade?" she asked.

Last? Was she leaving after the banquet? Jafar wanted to ask her, but that wasn't how the rules of their game worked.

He was willing to give her anything. He nodded.

She ducked her head, her smile turning shy. "Me first?"

Jafar nodded. The evening breeze slipped through the windows, tousling her hair and painting it gold in the fading sunlight.

"I wasn't supposed to fall in love with you."

Her voice was a deep, dark lullaby. Her words were a thousand and one scrolls unfurling inside of him, filling him to near bursting with their secrets.

Why not?

"To love is to live a life of exhaustion," he said.

She ran her tongue along her lips. "So melancholy. Exhaust me then, ink boy."

"Oh, is it my turn?" he asked, his throat hoarse with a knot, something heavy coursing through his limbs. It was weakness and power wrapped in one, an ache and a yearning.

And he couldn't ask the questions he wanted to ask.

Instead, he closed the distance between them. She looked up with a gasp, exposing the smooth column of her neck. He wanted to bury his face there, nibble at the unblemished skin, make her gasp again.

Jafar didn't need to be a prince. He would be a thief forever, stealing her breath over and over.

He was being selfish.

Her eyes darkened to a fathomless black, and when he opened his mouth to apologize, she rose on the tips of her toes with a strangled, impatient growl and pressed her lips to his. Her hands slipped over his chest, fisting his robes and pulling him into her. He gripped her waist to keep from tumbling into a chasm from which he might never return.

She was soft, warm, and enchanting, everything Jafar was not. Their bodies fit together like pages bound in a book. A mewl of a sound escaped her mouth, her fingers trembling and ceding control as they kissed. It was gentle, hard, rough, sweet, wicked.

Jafar had never felt so powerful.

She pulled back, gasping for air, gripping the wall to steady herself.

He wanted more. He wanted that power in his pocket, that control at his fingertips.

He had ruined her hair even more than the wind. He had altered the color of her eyes. It was delicious alchemy, and she was his beautiful destruction.

She touched her lips and took a step back. "That was . . ."

"Catastrophic," he agreed.

Her answering laugh was breathless. It almost sounded like half a sob. "I—we should go."

His mouth curled. "Or else?"

"Or things might turn indecent," she whispered, and then

she paused, her expression turning serious. "Jafar, there's something you should—"

He pressed a finger to her lips. It was all he could do to stop from pulling her to him again. "Don't. Don't ruin this moment."

And then he let her go.

Jafar sent the pair of attendants away from his rooms so he could dress himself, thinking about her the entire time. Yara. Their kiss. Their catastrophe. Jafar wasn't even ashamed of how giddy he felt, how *happy*. With her, like Iago, he didn't have to worry about his work being stolen. He didn't have to worry about lying.

There was no reason to concern himself with being second best. She was falling in love with him as he was with her, in a way that rivaled his love for knowledge. Her soul spoke to his much as the scrolls on alchemy had.

"Iago?" Jafar called into the emptiness. "Where are you, wretched bird?"

"Hiding so I don't have to see your stupid lovesick face," Iago called from somewhere under the bed.

Jafar felt his smile widen. He felt nothing but bliss, which made it easier to pretend he wasn't getting ready for his brother-turned-prince's betrothal feast. He hadn't seen

Rohan since the Sultana had chosen him, but then again, Rohan hadn't tried seeking him out, either.

Not that he'd been here in the palace *to* seek out.

Perhaps Jafar might have use for a genie after all. He would rewind time back to before their journey to Maghriz—no, that would mean never meeting Yara. Jafar sighed. He'd figure it out; he always did.

He pulled his dwindling handful of dinars from his robes, along with the pair of rubies Iago had swiped from the Sultana's pockets.

They were luminescent, facets carving them into the shape of a crown. They were hypnotizing, drawing him closer, commanding him. The more he stared at them, the less control he had over his own thoughts.

Could he use them as Iago had suggested? To claim the crown for himself? As Jafar layered his robes over a fresh linen shirt, he thought again of the royal vizier, and how much more power the man held over the kingdom, over the crown itself.

And a plan began to take shape.

38

ROHAN

In the rooms that had once belonged to the real Prince Aman of Maghriz, Rohan smoothed out his robes and straightened the green plume in his headdress. The silken, featherlight fabric felt heavy over his head, like he already bore the weight of the kingdom.

The emotions churning through him were more fitted for an appointment at the gallows than an engagement banquet. It was all happening far too fast. He knew next to nothing about the prince he was posing as, and now he was expected to behave exactly like him while being betrothed to a princess.

The Sultana's kind words and sure smiles extended as far as his obedience. The king of Hulum, his soon-to-be father-in-law, despised his very existence. If the princess was anything like her father, Rohan was in for a real treat.

And yet, despite it all, he was most anxious about seeing Jafar. Rohan splashed water on his face and stared at his reflection in the looking glass, aware of the empty space beside him. He didn't want this. He wanted to go back to being at Jafar's side. He wanted to curl up in Jafar's shadow, where everything was safe.

Why had he ever wanted to leave? Was Jafar's list of lies and questionable actions really so terrible if he'd done it all to help both of them? Maybe Jafar would be at the banquet tonight. Maybe Rohan could speak to him and mend things between them.

He thought of the Sultana and her vizier, and how Rohan could give Jafar that same power, that same control that Baba never allowed him to have.

And then his escort was knocking on the door, reminding him that dreams were often a sweet, sweet torment.

Rohan paused by the Sultana's side as the doors swung open and a caller announced their names, and he reminded himself not to ogle the lavish furnishings or inhale the aroma of the food.

He was the prince now. Delectable dishes were nothing

but a snap of his fingers away. He didn't have to count dinars when he was hungry, nor did he have to wait until his father was hungry for food to be brought from the kitchens.

The banquet hall was beautifully built, with a pitched ceiling from which a large chandelier hung between a pair of smaller matching ones, all three set with a multitude of candles flickering in hypnotizing harmony.

The Sultana nudged him, and Rohan tore his gaze from the tiled ceiling. An older man with a gold-trimmed cloak and the thickest beard Rohan had ever seen was watching him expectantly. A small yellow parakeet sat on his shoulder, so unlike Iago that it was disappointing.

The man looked as though he was waiting for an answer, and Rohan wished someone would repeat what was said, but neither the Sultana nor the man cared to waste their breath.

Smile, Jafar would say to him. *Make them feel good.*

"Architecture!" Rohan said in amazement. "No reason to have your head in the clouds anymore when there's so much to see inside, no?"

The man gave a stilted laugh. "Such is the danger of modern life, my prince. You are just as I remember you. Wit and hilarity abound."

"You are too kind," Rohan said.

Beside him, the Sultana was tense enough to snap.

"Shall we, Aman?" she asked, gesturing to the end of the low tables where the fanciest of cushions were laid out for them in hues of gold and cream that matched the rest of the hall's decor.

Rohan gave the man one last smile and followed her to his seat, ignoring her glare.

"I don't know who that was. I don't know who any of these people are," he said.

"Every person here was announced as we were," the Sultana said. "If only you were paying attention, *Aman*. No— do not sit before the king's arrival, you lout."

Rohan froze. Jafar would never allow anyone to insult him in such a way. The Sultana didn't look the least bit apologetic, and Rohan bit his tongue.

The caller's next announcement cut her words short. "King Qadir of Hulum, and his daughter, the illustrious princess!"

Rohan looked past the sea of people and tables to the double doors as the king stepped through, as sour and dour as at their prior meeting, even dressed in finery.

But the princess—Rohan's breath latched tight in his chest. Once, he had strongly believed there was nothing in existence more beautiful than the full moon. Until her.

Her skin was like amber, her hair like the depths of the forests he'd only read about in stories, the brown so dark it could almost be black, threaded with silver chains that shimmered like stars in the night. Her lips were lush, the same vermillion as Iago's feathers.

Rohan was, to put it simply, infatuated.

But the princess of Hulum did not seem happy to see him. And not because she didn't like how he looked. No, she seemed . . . *sad*.

She barely looked at him, her gaze downcast as she walked beside King Qadir.

The doors opened again, this time without an announcement attached. Several servants and attendants stepped through, amongst them a familiar figure.

Jafar. He paused, taking in the beauty of the space, the parade of people, and then his shrewd gaze reached Rohan and the Sultana, then King Qadir and the princess, who was looking at him, lips parted in breathless anguish.

And Rohan watched as the color bled from Jafar's face.

39

JAFAR

Jafar remembered, acutely, the pain he'd felt when Mama died. He had thought his heart would split in two, that his soul would separate from his body. That pain did not compare to what he felt now.

It couldn't be true. The princess of Hulum could not be his moon girl, his boisterous girl. It couldn't be Yara, the woman he had fallen in love with. How could this be? How could she have allowed that?

Jafar had stomached his brother taking credit for his work. He had stomached his brother being crowned prince of a kingdom unlike any other. He would not be able to handle this.

She lowered her chin. She had been expecting him and

had worn her best for him, a wondrous, sweeping dress in a shade of scarlet as wicked as her grins and lightning-fast raillery. She was a work of art, her gown an illustrious frame worthy of holding her.

Jafar's heart ached.

Say no, he begged of her. *Refuse him.* He wanted her to throw out her hands and proclaim her love for him, a boy who was nothing and no one with barely a handful of dinars and a pair of rubies to his name. But he knew that she wouldn't.

She was here for her kingdom, for marriage. She had love for her father, even if she'd said she was falling in love with Jafar. He remembered, then, the sorrow that had crossed her features, the regret, the reluctance to get close.

He watched, heart sinking, falling, breaking, as she did and said nothing.

I've been known to give in too easily.

Royal weddings to fulfill treaties happened regularly. Love didn't need to exist between the two parties. If her father wanted her wed to an imposter prince who wasn't Jafar, his moon girl would accept. He was sure of it.

There were scores of people in the room, yet in that moment, it was only the three of them: clueless Rohan; obedient Yara; and then Jafar, numb and cold and hurting.

A burst of red rushed through the doors and landed on his shoulder.

"There you are," Iago panted. "I thought I couldn't come

in here, but some of these bozos have pets, and I was coming to tell you that—*oh*. You already know."

Yara had arrived days before Jafar and Rohan had set foot in Maghriz. She had known all along that nothing between them could work out. She'd *told* him as much: *There's something thrilling about meeting a person wholly unaware of who you are, no?*

He didn't know why he hadn't made the connection sooner. She moved with practiced grace and a sense of innate pride. She exuded riches and splendor. Every inch of her had screamed royalty, and he had ignored every hint.

And so, Jafar came to a horrifying conclusion: she had used him.

Their tryst was as catastrophic as she'd promised it would be.

Jafar could not stand to see her, or his brother, or the Sultana and her dinner party. He fled the room, slamming into more than one servant in his rush. Iago said nothing, just hopped off his shoulder and kept pace beside him.

Jafar sat on the edge of his bed, the night nipping chilled teeth along his skin. The room was dark, but he didn't bother with the lanterns, and the moon didn't offer anything more than the thinnest of smiles.

The rubies looked sinister in his palm.

"Whatever you're thinking, slow it down," Iago warned. "Don't be hasty."

Jafar turned the stones over and likened each facet to a different part of his life:

There was Baba, who had locked him in the broom closet on that fateful day, forcing him to befriend his demons and listen to their whispers. And when Jafar learned of what Baba had done to his scholarship and his dreams, he'd snapped. He had listened with a keen ear as his father screamed, gasped, and begged his way to death.

He turned the rubies again.

Then there was his brother, who looked up to him like he was more than a boy who couldn't stop opening his mouth, even when his words earned him a slap. At first, Rohan was a nuisance, but then he became the only one who appreciated Jafar's ideas, valued and respected his opinions. Jafar had sought his brother's adoration because it meant someone was giving him the recognition he deserved—until he lost it. No, until his brother *stopped*, because he'd discovered the fortitude to step out from Jafar's shadow.

Rohan's bravery would have been admirable, if it hadn't come at Jafar's expense.

Jafar turned the rubies over again.

Yara. Sweet, sweet Yara. She had loved him for a flicker of smoke. No, he reminded himself. She had used him.

Jafar rose and pulled his headdress back over his head. He clutched the rubies tight, the sharp edges digging into his skin.

"Jafar, what are you doing?" Iago asked shakily.

"We're going to show every last one of them who truly holds power here," Jafar replied.

An important oath.

For what? Jafar thought. He had tried helping his father, he had done everything for his brother, he had obeyed his mother.

What had any of that done for him? He was beginning to hate the person he was, though he was all he had. It was time to choose himself, thoroughly and wholly. He could have had the rubies the day they'd arrived in Maghriz, but he'd chosen to protect Rohan. He could have used the rubies the moment Iago had dropped them in his hand, but he'd chosen to entertain Yara.

He had trusted Yara; he had trusted Rohan.

Now he was through—with choosing others, with trusting others, with allowing anyone to think they were his equal.

Power could not be shared.

40

ROHAN

Dread and confusion had a way of filling one up quite well, for Rohan wasn't the slightest bit hungry anymore. He didn't know why his brother had fled or the princess looked so miserable.

"Eat," the Sultana commanded. "Stop being so sullen."

But the image of Jafar's face was seared behind his eyelids, and the myriad of dishes the servants had spread before them faded to dust.

"She's beautiful, and you know it," the Sultana said, seething. "Sit up before you ruin this for me."

For me. She was always concerned with herself before

anyone and anything else. She had made Rohan a prince and done worse to Jafar—she had stripped him of purpose and abandoned him.

The princess appeared beside him.

The Sultana looked surprised. "Is something the matter, princess?"

"I only wished to introduce myself to Prince Aman," the princess said, and then added, "if I may."

"Of course," the Sultana said with far more enthusiasm than was warranted, and the princess glared until the Sultana finally turned to the emir on her other side.

Rohan immediately liked her, and he could only stare as she sat down beside him, the warm folds of her gown brushing his side. Rohan had never been the focus of someone so beautiful before.

Watch yourself, he chided. Here and now, he was the prince. The Sultana's son.

"You are doleful," he said to her.

Doleful? Ridiculous. Rohan saw that her eyes were much like her father's: astute. She missed nothing. She had seen him spot and recognize Jafar. She knew the two were acquainted.

But how did *she* know *his brother*?

She looked away, her reflection distorted in the empty silver platter in front of her.

"You must think me horribly rude," she said, and Rohan

was amazed at how these royals could shuffle between expressions and emotions like they were nothing. "My name is Yara."

Rohan, he wanted to say, but could not.

He couldn't even give her his name. Something as small and simple and mundane as his name. His name—the one and only thing he had left of his childhood, of his life in Ghurub.

And he was to be *married* to her? To spend the rest of his life beside her?

What was the point in being able to speak if he could not do so freely? What was the point in wearing a crown and having every dish imaginable if he had to take the history of himself, his most precious possession, and lock it away for good? What was the point in appeasing a woman who meant nothing to him and losing the best brother in the world?

Rohan shot to his feet, teetering from the abrupt movement and his thoughts alike. The entire banquet hall fell silent. Every eye turned to him and his bright robes and fancy adornments as if he were some sort of peacock.

He wanted to laugh at it all. Or possibly cry.

But what he needed was to find Jafar and make things right. Rohan, like his brother, wasn't good at apologizing, but it was never too late to start. Every important emir in the kingdom had seen him, which meant he would never be able to right his wrongs and cede the crown to Jafar.

But they could run.

The two of them could go anywhere and be anything, so long as they were together.

"Aman?" the Sultana asked, and he heard the warning in her voice. He had seen the condition of her dungeons, seen how quickly she could turn a smile lethal.

Rohan paused, aware that there was no turning back from this moment. He would either be Aman for the rest of his life, or die as Rohan.

He glared down at her. "Don't call me that."

And then he fled.

Rohan's footsteps echoed dully through the halls, growing louder as he left the roar of the banquet hall farther and farther behind him until the palace spat him out into the cold night. Wispy clouds shrouded the moon, ominous and haunting. He lowered his gaze to the sprawling building across from the palace.

He knew where he would find Jafar.

But as much as his brother loved the House of Wisdom's library, when he was upset, he preferred to busy his hands more than his mind. As he could in the laboratory.

Rohan took off down the dusty path, stumbling to a

halt in the open space between the palace and the House of Wisdom. He was alone. Nothing but him and the expanse of the night, stars twinkling above, the future just out of reach.

He could run on his own, leave the palace and the House of Wisdom and everything else behind. He wouldn't be Aman or Baba's son or Jafar's brother.

He would be his own person. *Rohan*. He would claim his name for his own.

Not without making amends.

The House of Wisdom was deathly silent, not a guard or scholar in sight. Rohan had not expected the crimson cloud crowding the dark ceiling, strange and eerie. Heart in his throat, he navigated the blood-drenched shelves, avoiding the glinting shadows and beckoning darkness.

For a moment he was back in the dungeons, in front of those dank cells, desolation creeping up his arms and power thrumming in the air. Rohan followed flashes of red to the back of the library and an archway that he assumed led to the laboratory. He paused and looked up the short rise of steps to the platform ahead, but he had no reason to be afraid. This was his brother, and they were going to make things right between them.

Something sharp cracked across the floor, as jarring as a clap of thunder. A pair of eyes flashed in the gloom, vividly red. Rohan flinched, freezing in place as a figure emerged from the haze.

He could only muster a whisper. "Jafar?"

The shadows accentuated his height, stretching him like the plume in his headdress. His robes undulated in the breeze from the wide windows behind him. His long fingers curled around a dark gold staff with brilliant ruby eyes that Rohan could not look away from. Iago sat on his shoulder, equally imposing. Standing in front of them, Rohan felt small and droll.

"Oh, it's a serpent," Rohan ventured, trying for a laugh.

Jafar glided down the steps to face him, his eyes hard. It was how he'd looked at Baba, how he had begun to look at the Sultana.

Rohan took a small step back, and the words blabbered out of him. "This was doomed from the start, Jafar. I came to apologize. I—I tried speaking to the princess, and I know it's all a big mess, but—"

Jafar didn't let him finish.

"What do you want, *Aman*?" He spoke in that bitter cold tone he reserved for those he loathed.

He might as well have struck Rohan across the face with his shiny new staff.

"That was uncalled for," Rohan managed to whisper. "I know I made some poor decisions, and I regret everything. I want us to be *us* again, Jafar. We can make the Sultana pay for everything she's done. Easily, too. If we leave now, she'll be princeless, and the Hulumi will have everything they've ever wanted: a reason to go to war with her, while we go anywhere else. Agrabah, maybe."

"Uncalled for?" Jafar asked, rubbing the head of the serpent almost lovingly and ignoring everything else Rohan had just said. "Did you hear that, Iago? We were only trying to be more accepting of the new you, brother. I mean, *my liege*."

Iago snickered. "That's right."

Rohan drew a slow and measured breath, and it loosened the lid he had latched tight since he'd put on the ridiculous robes of the Sultana's son. Anger thrashed its way free.

"I didn't ask for any of this," he snapped. "Not to be a prince, not to be engaged to a girl I know next to nothing about, not even to be brought to this place."

Jafar's eyes flashed like the rubies set into the serpent's head. "You never *ask*, Rohan. You only ever take, and I only ever allowed you to."

Rohan couldn't stop the dark laugh that tore out of him. "Then you have no one to blame but yourself, do you?"

"As you do, for Baba's death?" Jafar asked. He scoffed at Rohan's shock. "You came all this way for him. All this way to find the two halves of the scarab beetle, to find the genie lamp and waste your wishes on that boor, but you couldn't even do that, could you? You went and got yourself a crown instead."

"I told you, I'm cursed—"

Jafar laughed, sharp and dangerous. "Don't give yourself too much credit. I killed him. I was tired of him hitting me, and holding me back, and spinning you around in whichever direction he pleased, so I got rid of him."

Rohan stumbled back, nearly falling off the steps to the laboratory. "Then—that means you started the fire."

"And then I made sure he stayed in it."

Jafar did it. He killed Baba, and their servants and their maids, and yet Rohan could barely focus on the horror of it—he was too overjoyed by the fact that he wasn't cursed. Too upended by the realization that people didn't die when he made desperate wishes.

It had never been real.

"See what I do to my enemies, brother?" Jafar continued. "They were *our* enemies, up until you decided I was not enough for you."

"The Sultana promised us that we'd be equals."

Jafar rapped the staff on the tiles. "She lies, and you know it. I'd rather be in control of my own fate than be a puppet to a prince whose shoes you will never fit."

"A prince will one day be king," Rohan snarled. "You will always be second best."

That was the wrong thing to say.

"Is that why you told Baba to tear up my scholarship?" Jafar asked, deathly quiet. "Were you afraid you couldn't keep up?"

A chill dragged down Rohan's spine.

"I didn't," he whispered. "He asked long before your scholarship arrived, and you know I—I have—*had* a hard time opposing him. I didn't know he'd tear it."

"Oh, it wasn't hard to oppose him, Rohan," Jafar said. "You simply didn't care enough to do it. I've come to learn that your backbone works whenever you want it to."

That wasn't true. Still, Rohan had known about it, and he should have apologized, but the pride he'd inherited from his father would allow no such thing. Jafar drew closer, and Rohan shrank back from his brother's dead, flat stare. The stare of a boy who was wholly capable of murder.

"I didn't want this any more than you did," Rohan said, voice taut. "I thought . . . I was tired of being in your shadow. I thought taking credit for the papermaking secret would make me feel better about myself. It didn't, and I was wrong. I should have listened, Jafar. I should have done exactly as you said."

Jafar's lips curled into a smile Rohan would remember for the rest of his days. "I can help you with that."

Rohan had the sinking feeling that this was the end. His end. Jafar was past the point of accepting apologies, of caring. Jafar flourished his scepter. The ruby-red eyes set in its face flashed, drowning Rohan in crimson, scarlet, blood, *fear*—and then he lost all feeling and remembered very little after that.

41

JAFAR

Jafar didn't think it would be smart to divulge this to Iago, but he had fully intended to test the rubies' efficacy on the parrot before Rohan had come strutting in. And they were perfect. His brother fought for barely a moment before he relinquished control. Jafar refused to look at him, instead lifting up his staff and admiring his handiwork once again. The serpent gleamed in the dim light, fanged mouth bared for a strike, red eyes brilliant. It was beautiful, worth all the tinkering he'd done in the laboratory since they'd arrived in Maghriz.

The rubies had never been treated so well.

Jafar strode for the archway leading back to the House of

Wisdom, his robes rippling with the shadows. "Now come, let us see how our new toy works."

And the palace banquet hall was the best place to play. The Sultana had made sure of it, albeit unknowingly, by changing out the guards and the staff.

"N-no," Rohan protested. He sounded sluggish, as if he was fighting to articulate his words while half-asleep. "I'm—not—coming."

"Jafar?" Iago warned. "I don't think it's working."

Commit to it, Jafar told himself. Alchemy relied on the one who cast it. But it was hard seeing his brother struggle and knowing he was the cause of it. His brother, whom Jafar had protected since he could walk, whom Jafar would do anything for because Rohan had been the only one to ever love him back. To look out for him. To visit him in the unlit broom closet.

Rohan had also betrayed him. Jafar swiped the angry blur from his eyes.

He had swayed Baba's hand with the scholarship.

He had taken credit for the papermaking secret, after the prisoner took a piece of Jafar's humanity.

He had stolen Jafar's crown, and thus, his princess. *Yara, Yara, Yara.*

Jafar faced his brother and rapped his staff on the floor. Rohan fell to his knees.

"That's better," Jafar whispered. "I'm doing this for us, brother. The Sultana must answer for her crimes."

Rohan said nothing, just stared blankly. Jafar wasn't certain he liked that.

"You did it, boss!" Iago exclaimed. "Excellent work."

But he had Iago, and the sight of Rohan on the floor because Jafar had commanded it truly *was* excellent. This was the prince of Maghriz, the greatest kingdom in the desert.

Under Jafar's control.

"We did," Jafar said. He had never felt more free. "And this is only the beginning."

42

YARA

Yara had known since she'd first met Jafar that anything between them would be impossible. She was betrothed to the prince of Maghriz, whom she thought was quite handsome if she could look past the boyishness of his features and personality.

She'd known all her life that she could only marry royalty. That a princess like her could never marry a House of Wisdom apprentice. And yet she'd gone and fallen in love with one.

When she'd seen Jafar in the library, sighing with a book in his hand, she hadn't been able to resist. It was meant to be some harmless fun, a little bit of a thrill before she secured her life to another's forever. But one word became another, then a laugh became a shy glance, and then she'd held his hand, and in the dark corridor of the palace, he'd kissed her soul into submission.

Oh, how she'd wished she could pull him into a room and memorize every inch of his skin.

Her face burned with the thought, her mind shielding her from reality with the impossible fantasy. The banquet hall was a cacophony, but Yara was secluded in the lush chambers of her mind, where she didn't have to hear people eating and discussing her betrothal, conversing about the long-uncertain future of a united Maghriz and Hulum.

That should not have been Yara's burden to bear, but it was one she was prepared to endure for her baba. Even if she wished she could walk through an endless bazaar beside Jafar, holding his hand and learning his secrets.

She hadn't expected Prince Aman to be his friend. Close friend, judging by how quickly the prince had snapped at the Sultana and run to comfort him. Yara didn't know what sort of leader that would make him, but she wasn't too concerned. She was the daughter of King Qadir of Hulum; she knew how to wield both blade and power enough for two mighty kingdoms. It was her birthright.

At last, the doors at the end of the hall swung open again, and Prince Aman returned. He seemed . . . different, less like a passionate boy and more like an emotionless rag doll.

As she watched, he straightened, his spine sharpening and chin rising as if he'd been told to do just that. Jafar strode in behind him, dressed in black and crimson robes that would match her gown perfectly, and her heart lurched in excitement, but he didn't even look at her. He didn't appear upset or heartbroken in the slightest anymore. A veil she could only describe as sinister rested over his face, twisting his beautiful mouth into a wretched smile. Even his parrot looked a little vile.

The Sultana rose to her feet and rushed toward them. "Aman, my heart! You've returned!"

"Sit down," said the prince.

She recoiled as if he'd slapped her. The hall fell silent at the striking command.

Prince Aman kept walking. His gaze flitted from the Sultana to her royal vizier, then drifted to Yara and her father and the guards surrounding the room. He appeared to be analyzing more than looking, like a hawk assessing its prey.

Behind him, Jafar was saying something only Aman could hear. Yara tried to catch his eye, but he wouldn't look at her. It felt deliberate, somehow, as if he was angry at her now. As if he wanted to punish her.

Aman stopped at the front of the room, on the dais near the banquet throne, and every eye turned toward him. He lifted his chin a little higher and spoke, his voice crisp and clear, but empty. "My mother, the Sultana, who has prepared this grand feast for us"—he paused with a dry laugh—"did not intend for me to be here. She sent me on a voyage across the seas in the hopes that I might never return."

Yara had not spoken to Aman much at all, but she'd thought him timid and soft-spoken, certainly not *this*.

Gasps rippled through the banquet crowd. They'd all heard of the voyage. Even Yara had known—this betrothal had been delayed several months because of it. But his insinuation was clear. Had the Sultana truly intended to kill off her son?

She and her royal vizier looked stricken.

"But here I am," Prince Aman called. "Returned from the dead, safe and sound. King Qadir, you must know that she would rather go to war with you than see me married to your daughter."

No. A cold sweat broke out along Yara's brow. That was the wrong thing to say. Everything about it was wrong, as if it had been designed to vex Baba in the worst possible manner. Her father had been waiting for any excuse to end the treaty they'd agreed upon a decade ago.

He shot to his feet now, wrenching Yara up beside him. The Sultana looked pale.

"You think your armies are capable of defeating Hulum," he snarled, his next words an oath. "I will send this kingdom back to the sands from whence it rose."

The Sultana struggled to rise. "I—"

"There, there," Aman continued, speaking over her. "No need to be so hasty, Qadir." Yara flinched at the disrespect in his bold tone, but her father quieted and listened. He respected those who challenged him. "When I'm sultan, I'm certain we can work out a new treaty."

The Sultana gasped. "You will do no such thing."

"Then you will deny me my right, *Mother*," Aman countered. The way he spat the word *mother* made Yara flinch. The way he held the Sultana's gaze with steel made her pity the woman. The Sultana regarded Aman like she could not believe his words and actions were his own, her gaze flitting between Aman and Jafar as if trying to work out a puzzle.

Yara understood one thing: power was shifting. Yielding. Aman drew closer to the front, Jafar behind him. He held a staff in one hand. It was beautiful, a wicked serpent with vibrant eyes of red that seemed to reflect in Aman's.

"Guards!" Aman shouted. Spears snapped to attention. "Put my mother in a cell and put her royal vizier in another. Far apart—I don't want them plotting against me again."

The Sultana began to laugh. "They will not obey."

But Yara had been here long enough to notice that the guards were new, and Aman's words were moving—*had* the Sultana attempted to kill him? Still, the guards appeared torn, at first. Then one by one, like puppets slowly being brought to life, they moved. Several stormed toward the Sultana, and another group moved against the royal vizier, who put up more of a fight than she did. The guards were merciless as they restrained them both.

"How is all of this happening?" Yara whispered.

"A divided family can ruin the world, my daughter," Qadir said, his hand a comfort on her shoulder. "Here we are witness, and we must leave."

He turned to his own retinue while Yara watched as the Sultana and royal vizier were taken away. Prince Aman walked the remaining steps to her throne—*his* throne now—and sat down, Jafar just behind him with his parrot on his shoulder and staff in hand.

Aman's eyes still glowed the same red as the rubies in Jafar's staff, almost . . . Almost as though the two of them were connected by an invisible thread.

She drew her gaze to Jafar's cold and angry one.

He was watching her. Reading her. That was what was wrong with Aman: he was acting like Jafar. She'd seen Jafar glued to the section on alchemy in the House of Wisdom, learning, studying. Was he controlling Aman? If he was controlling the prince, why had the Sultana looked so stricken by Aman's claims, as if they were true? Why had the guards listened to him without hesitation?

Yara did not know, but she did know with a sickening feeling what was coming next: punishment.

"Guards!" she shouted, but they were slow to move. Something whizzed past her ear, flying into her father's neck.

She didn't know what it was or where it had come from, but did it matter? It was the Maghrizi removing a threat in the most cowardly of ways.

Hurt my baba, and it's as if you've hurt me.

The king of Hulum was sinking to his knees. Blood gurgled from his neck. He was fading fast. Unnaturally fast. *No, no, no.* People were yelling now, some of them trying to leave, others rushing to her aid.

"Baba, no. Don't—"

"Hush, my honeybee," Baba whispered, blood trickling from his mouth. "Rule well. Destroy admirably."

She had to stay strong.

"I will, Baba," she said softly, holding him tight as his blood darkened her crimson gown. Gripping him against her as the last of his life left his body.

She carefully set Baba on the stained cushions and rose to her feet, turning to face Aman and the real threat: Jafar.

And that is the cost of hurting me, he seemed to say. Was he . . . blaming Baba because they couldn't be together? He was a fool, a monster.

And Yara would end this now.

She ran toward him, her vision burning the same red as the eyes on his staff, the same red as the plume in his headdress, as his blood begging to be spilled.

He curled a hand, and an invisible wall rose between them. He hadn't even flinched from the effort.

"Tsk, tsk, princess," his parrot snarked. *It talked.* "You've been a bad girl."

Chaos had erupted throughout the banquet hall, but here, by the throne, it was just the four of them.

"You killed my father," Yara breathed. She'd kissed him, held him, bared her soul to him.

"He said he'd kill us," Jafar said, cavalier and uncaring. "I didn't want to be second best."

Yara's heart shook. "I will end you, Jafar. I will destroy this kingdom, and then you."

"Do as you wish," Jafar drawled. "I'm getting tired of playing here. When I'm done, you can even have the prince. He's not the real Aman, anyway. He's my brother."

Yara froze, staring at the boy on the throne. That was why the Sultana had said nothing. Why the betrothal feast had been delayed so many times. The real prince truly had died, and she'd hired an imposter to take his place. Yara looked at the mayhem around her, officials and diplomats from throughout the kingdom and beyond. She wanted to tell them the truth, but what could she say that the Sultana hadn't thought of saying herself?

"Do you need help, moon girl?" Jafar asked, and Yara was surprised by the way the words stung. He rapped his staff on the dais. He looked handsome, powerful, *horrible*. "It seems the results were as catastrophic as we feared."

"Guards!" the fake Prince Aman called. "Put her in a cell, too. This one just threatened to kill me."

"Don't worry," Jafar said quietly. "I won't keep you here long. I know how politics work, and you'll soon be on your merry way back to Hulum, where you can plot my demise."

He tightened his fingers, retracting the wall between them seconds before the guards grabbed her.

She seethed. "This is not over, Jafar."

Epilogue

Jafar did not have to wait long for Yara to return. His moon girl, his catastrophe, carrying a sword with an army behind her. She was dressed like a warrior queen, vengeance as bright in her eyes as the rubies set in his staff.

He'd always known she was magnificent.

The rubies only worked within range of their victim, and Jafar controlled Rohan and the kingdom of Maghriz until her arrival and through the war. As he ruled the kingdom from the shadows, she had searched for him with the zeal and determination she really should have put toward finding a way to be with him, but it was too late for that now. Jafar wanted nothing to do with her anymore. He'd found a new love: power.

The war lasted four months, but Jafar had never touched a sword in his life. He was versed in trade routes and treaties, not battle strategies, and he could only command Rohan-turned-Aman so much before the Maghrizi generals were overcome without proper direction, but by the time Yara and her platoon breached the palace, Jafar was long gone. He had paused only to rap his staff one last time in the halls of Maghriz, to watch the red fade from Rohan's eyes, to watch his brother regain his senses and search the room, frantic and alone.

Calling his name.

That was many nights ago. Now, Jafar closed his eyes against that echo of an ache and tipped his head to the skies. In a tea shop on the side of the road between kingdoms, he sat on a cushion with his legs crossed and a parrot on his shoulder, his ears open to the discussions of the other patrons around them. The sun was lazy, dappling through the cluster of date palms where a man served tea with a kind smile that came from honest work in a small village.

"The Hulumi-Maghrizi war is finally over," an older man said to one of his companions.

"Don't get me started," another man said, taking a long sip of his tea and drumming his fingers on the low table. "We're not Maghrizi. Why do we care?"

A third man straightened, excited to dive in. "They found the Sultana and her vizier in the dungeons and beheaded them both. Brutal, yes, but it serves them right for lying about the prince."

"I don't know. One would hope they'd exercise some leniency," said a fourth.

"After the Sultana killed the Hulumi king in cold blood? Not even her guards wanted anything to do with her. They're the ones that *put* her in the cell. I hear the Hulumi queen took the prince as prisoner, though."

Jafar couldn't tamp down a smile.

"She's not Hulumi anymore. Or Maghrizi," the first man said. "I forget what they decided to rename the combined kingdoms."

The drummer sighed. "Everyone gets what they deserve."

They sipped their tea and exchanged solemn nods.

Jafar watched them sitting around their cups of tea with dusty clothes and the opinions of kings. He had seen every side of life: from the perspective of a thief to that of a middle-class merchant's son, from a House of Wisdom apprentice to nearly a prince, *better* than a prince.

People were always the same. Opinionated as royalty, petty as thieves.

Jafar set down his empty tea glass, rattling the cardamom pod that remained at the bottom of it. The sun would set soon; the air was already turning cool. It was Rohan's favorite time of day.

Despite what the men said, Jafar knew Queen Yara hadn't taken Rohan prisoner. Iago had watched her reach for Rohan's hand and pull him close, letting him walk beside her as his equal. They had much to bond over, after all. No one but Yara knew who Rohan truly was, and Jafar was a large part of both their lives, even if the time he'd spent with Yara had been short.

An oath is an oath, Jafar thought. In the end, he'd taken care of his brother well, and now he was done with him.

Something told Jafar Yara would not be attempting another royal marriage anytime soon. Understandable, for her hands were full with two kingdoms now—and a budding new love.

Jafar licked the crumbs of a honey cake from his fingers and rose from the table, leaving a handful of dinars behind. "That was good cake."

"It really was," Iago said, his beak sticky. Iago loved any food that wasn't crackers.

Jafar rolled his eyes and saddled his camel, checking to make sure his water was full and his bags had not been touched. They were all he had, though that made it sound like there weren't enough coins in those bags to make him richer than his baba had ever been.

"Where to now?" Iago asked as they headed in the direction of the setting sun, leaving the small village behind.

"I was thinking," Jafar began, as Iago perched on his shoulder. "I can't go back to life outside a palace. There's just too much I miss."

"Like squabbling with your brother and kissing princesses in dark corridors?" Iago asked.

Jafar cut him a look.

Iago squawked. "Too soon, too soon. I hear you, though. I do miss those soft sheets and good food."

"Precisely, my pet," Jafar said, as the sands ahead burned orange with the sunset. Dunes spread out as far as he could see, like piles of gold.

"I don't know, though. Shouldn't we lie low in case Yara comes looking? Especially now that she and Rohan are best pals?" Iago asked.

"We'll just have to be more powerful." He tucked his staff against his side and held up some of the scrolls he'd taken from the House of Wisdom. This camel was laden with them, and would be until Jafar found a place safe enough to store them. "The chance of finding another queen in need of a replacement for her son is fairly low, but I've been told a genie might help our cause."

"Thought we didn't like genies," Iago commented.

Jafar looked down at his staff, where the rubies glinted

in greeting. "I think I'm clever enough to figure out a way to control one, don't you?"

Iago unfurled one of the scrolls, where Jafar had marked the location of half of a scarab beetle. "Oooh, I was told Agrabah is mighty exciting this time of year."

"Mmm," Jafar said, lips curling. "I love the way your foul little mind works."

Acknowledgments

To play in someone else's sandbox is both exhilarating and daunting. *Aladdin* is a movie I first watched as a young girl, and I distinctly recall finding Jafar as enthralling as our protagonist. But it wasn't until the incredible Elana Cohen reached out to me, asking if I had any interest in writing an origin story for a Disney villain that I realized I actually *did* have interest.

Little did I know, writing such a story would be a lot harder than anticipated, but I didn't have to go about it alone. My first thank you goes to Elana, of course. If not for her kind and generous words, this project would not have come to fruition. You were missed! Still, her editorial shoes were quickly filled by powerhouses Hali Baumstein and Flannery Wiest, whose notes were in-depth, resourceful, and oh so thorough. I enjoyed working with you both, and appreciate your patience with me more than you know. A great big thank you to the rest of the Disney team for bringing this book to life, and to Corey Brickley for the stunning cover art.

There were other hurdles involved in bringing *The Wishless Ones* to life. It was written in between deadlines of another project, in the midst of getting married and while moving across the country, and I owe immense gratitude to those who've been in my corner throughout it all: my agent, Josh Adams, always a quick text, email, and phone call away. To my sisters, Asma and Azraa, for knowing exactly what my stories need and for keeping me afloat throughout many a dark time. To my husband, Cayce, roohi. Thank you for uplifting me and pushing me to stay true to myself. For keeping me sane and always lending an ear when I need it— which I did for this book. A lot.

And last but never least, my gratitude goes to you, dearest reader, for picking up yet another story of mine and joining me on yet another literary journey. Thank you.